MW01536932

the Yellow Cart

a love story

Cart

T.L. CLEES

32 of 100

© 2022 T.L. Clees All rights reserved. This book or any portion thereof may not be reproduced or used in any manner whatsoever without the express written permission of the publisher except for the use of brief quotations in a book review.

ISBN 978-1-66787-338-1 eBook 978-1-66787-339-8

To my children who had to grow up never really knowing what to believe. Long live popsicle trees, the James Bond package on the van, and the washing machine that teleported our clothes to China to be washed!

One

May 16, 107 Days Out, 210 pounds

And so it began. The alarm went off at 3:30 am and Don Ream rolled over and pushed the "STOP" icon on his phone. He paused for a moment asking himself if he really wanted to do this. Did he really want to wake up at this ungodly hour every day, clear skies or rain, for the next fifteen weeks and walk the streets of Flint, Michigan for an hour? He further asked himself did he really want to make one last run at getting his bodybuilding pro card at the age where most men would get sore just by bouncing their grandchildren on their knee. The resounding answer to both questions was absolutely. He was absolutely determined to do whatever it took to know that he left no stone unturned in his quest for bodybuilding's elusive gold standard. The judges might not find his physique worthy but he was going all in. And when it was said and done he would rest comfortably in knowing that no one will have outworked him. No one would be more disciplined and determined. No one will have given more than Donald Faust Ream had given.

He stumbled to the kitchen, making a pit stop in the bathroom. His new house was small compared to the family sized home he recently sold in Grand Blanc. He wanted the smallness—the simplicity of a smaller home. He didn't want to waste time doing hours of yard maintenance. He outfitted the little home with all new appliances so that he didn't have to worry about them breaking down during prep. He wanted the peace of mind that he wasn't going to come home to spoiled food in a failed refrigerator. He also wanted the financial freedom that came from downsizing. Money was not going to be a stressor for him for the first time in all of his twelve previous contest preps. He was also single and planned on staying that way to avoid relationship stress and distraction.

Don wasn't good at relationships anyway, even he admitted that. He was great at making women fall in love with him, but because he himself never felt "in love" he couldn't sustain the relationship. His most current ex-girlfriend had made him realize that even though he thought nothing of breaking up it destroyed the women that he had romanced. That made him sad. He wasn't an evil person and most everyone who knew him, except the three ex-wives and countless ex-girlfriends would say he was a great guy. And it wasn't like he didn't crave that feeling—he just couldn't experience it. He wanted more than anything to have a fairy tale type romance that a bard could write wonderful songs about. His current therapist told him it was because he had experienced such a large amount of grief at an early age that he had closed off his heart. He felt like walking out of her office when after he asked how he should go about opening it she replied with "Well that is something we're going to have to work on." He translated that as "I don't know Cash Cow but we will just stumble along blindly and maybe we will come to an answer on the journey." He wanted a simple answer. A turning of the key. An equation to punch numbers into and get an answer.

He grabbed his favorite gray and black blender bottle off the counter and filled it with two different powders that equaled fifty grams of protein and sixty grams of carbs. One was a vanilla ice cream flavor and the other was an orange flavor so when mixed together it tasted like an orange cream-sicle. He had researched multiple studies arguing the veracity of whether or not he should do his "cardio" on an empty stomach or not. As with all things fitness and bodybuilding related you could find any study to support your idea if you looked hard enough. There was even arguments and studies trying to determine if indeed his low impact steady state cardio (brisk walk) was even cardio or not. However at 56 years old and with forty years of weightlifting wear and tear on his body it was as close to cardio as he was going to come to.

The shake went down easy and was one of the better tasting things on his diet. Pound the carbs and protein first thing upon waking an old friend had told him and he had stuck to it over the years with great results. The house was quiet. He missed owning a dog. It had been over a year since he had to put down Beowulf, the pitbull puppy that he had rescued twelve years ago. He considered getting an older rescue dog to walk with him and be his companion but he was trying to simplify his life not complicate it. Maybe after the contest he would rescue another dog. There was that cute blonde that volunteered at the animal shelter that he talked to on occasion. He felt they had a connection. Perhaps she could help him find a dog and more. Do you really want to fuck up her life, he thought as he put on his ultra-comfortable artic grey No Bull runners.

The May air was warmer than he expected. He would regret wearing a hoodie because he was going to be too hot; not to mention wearing a hoodie at that time and walking around the streets of Flint might just be a poor decision. He hoped if he was going to get shot it happened early on in the prep. He imagined how awful it would be to suffer for 12-15 weeks and then get shot and not seeing the fruits of all that labor pan out on stage. His workout partner, Jack Penny, asked him why he didn't just go to

Planet Fitness and walk on a treadmill. Don had just glared at him because he knew how much he liked treadmills and Planet Fitness for that matter.

Don walked through his subdivision and exited onto the main road across from the General Motors plant where Jack worked. Don thought he would go crazy if he ever had to work on an assembly line. He didn't feel he was wired for that type of repetitiveness at work even though he found comfort in the repetitive nature of contest prep. Don loved what he did. He worked for a nonprofit organization, Love Through Literature, that took literature into places where it might not be so readily available. He had written several journal articles about the importance of literature in care for those who felt lonely. He won an award for his article, "Alleviating Loneliness through Literature". The article detailed, through studies he had conducted, that people who read or are read to have a substantial decrease in feelings of loneliness. The critics countered with they felt less lonely because someone was taking them books and someone was taking the time to read to them. He responded the difference was almost the same in people who read books on their own and other studies had shown people who read rarely considered themselves lonely. He sighed and thought there are always going to be critics.

Don liked the research, studies and writing. He enjoyed being sequestered in his office pouring over data and writing out conclusions. But he also liked the action of taking books to lonely people. He went into orphanages and senior assisted living homes and met the residents. He would discern what he thought they might like to read and then he would bring it to them. Often times he would read to them. It wasn't exactly where he thought his literature degree with a focus on ancient British literature would take him, but it was work he loved.

There was a faint hint of skunk in the air that ushered him to the present reality. No, it was weed. Since Michigan legalized recreational marijuana, it seemed to be the smell most associated with Flint. You couldn't escape it. People reeked of it at the store, at the gym, at the barbershop—everywhere. Don turned down a side street away from the glowing lights of the plant. The street was littered with trash. A new smell assaulted his olfactory nerve—decay or rot. Don hated the smell of weed, but it was preferable over the smell one likened to death. Don involuntarily wrinkled up his nose and picked up the pace. A car bouncing with the loud bass blasting from its speakers slowly rolled by him. He imagined the driver had a nine millimeter in his lap and was high on crack. He wondered how closely he came to getting shot on that his very first day of morning walks.

Wondering was something you did when you walked. Don didn't like wearing headphones. He didn't wear them in the gym and he didn't wear them on walks. It wasn't that he didn't like music or podcasts, but he liked the ambient sound around him. In the gym it was clashing of weights, grunts of fellow lifters, banter back and forth among friends, encouragement and razzing from training partners and the whispers of lifters past whose spirits had never quite left the place they longed to be. On a walk, it was the crickets, the wind, birds, nature in general. It was also for safety. Don wanted to be aware if someone was walking behind him or rustling in the shadows. He didn't want to be taken by complete surprise.

His heart skipped a beat when a raccoon ran out from behind a tree across the road in front of him. He initially thought it was a skunk and feared his first day of contest prep was about to be completely ruined. So many things could derail a prep and so many things had to go precisely as planned to achieve maximum success. An injury in the last weeks was the thing he feared most. You could work around minor setbacks and still present a great package on stage, but a late injury would likely cause you to have to withdraw.

Don peered into the darkness of a driveway. He took a deep breath. The smell reminded him of his childhood where his neighbor had a burn barrel and seemed to burn something nearly every day. It was, however,

5

more foul than that everyday burn. There was an underlying smell of burnt rubber. He took a step into the driveway and saw the darkened wood and shadows of the burned out house. He wondered how long ago it burned down. He wondered how long the smell would linger. The charred wood and soot covered brick against the night sky made it look like a black and white world. It was as if the fire had sucked the color out. However, in stark contrast to the darkness there was a yellow shopping cart near the porch. It looked to have come from the Dollar General on the corner.

Don saw a shadow pass by one of the glassless windows. He squinted hard as if he could force his eyes to see into the darkness like he could force a weight off his chest. There was no more discernable movement. Don thought it had probably just been a flicker of light from a street light-bulb that was fighting to stay alive. He had an uneasy feeling. His stomach felt queasy. He reasoned it was from the morning shake, but he knew that wasn't the case. He didn't like admitting a place gave him the creeps. He felt anxiety gripping him as he thought of all the evils that could take place in a burned out abandoned building or worse the evils that could have taken place before it burned or even the evils that were a catalyst to it burning. He was letting his imagination fuel the uneasiness. Geoffrey Chaucer, the old English poet whom he had studied feverishly in college, reminded him people could die of mere imagination and he shook the thoughts from his head.

He made a very concentrated effort to pull away and just when he thought whatever strange connection there was between him and the house was going to snap he became aware that someone was watching him. Don didn't see any eyes or a face, but in his heart he was absolutely sure there was someone inside that burned out mess leering at him. He felt it in his soul. He wanted to go in and find the source of that feeling. He wanted to see who was watching him. Yet, he knew that his walk needed to be steady and not filled with starts and stops. Besides being near the house was making him feel worse with every passing second. Slowly he backed away, turned and hurried up the street. He made a mental note not to go in this direction on his walk ever again.

Two

May 19, 104 Days Out, 208 pounds

Don walked into the gym after parking his gunship gray Lincoln MKZ and the first thing he heard was JT's booming voice asking him if he was sick of chicken and rice yet. In any other setting, he would have probably despised JT but in the gym, Don liked him. JT was loud and brutishly obnoxious—a throwback to the glory days of the gym when people talked back and forth and not everyone had headphones on or ear buds in. JT was also big and strong. Don admired how hard he trained and how he had done it over the course of many years. He was not a flash in the pan all juiced up for a few months.

"First of all," Don hollered back, "I'm only three days into the cut so no I'm not sick of anything. Secondly I don't eat chicken or rice." What Don said was mostly true. He would have a chicken breast occasionally and he did have rice cakes scheduled in for the duration of the cut. But it wasn't the chicken and rice or fish and rice diet that so many coaches put their bodybuilding clients on. Don was a big believer in "calories in, calories out" and "if it fits your macros" style of dieting. He ate foods he liked as long as his protein, carbs and fats were where he wanted them and his calorie intake was spot on according to his plan.

"You should fire your coach," JT yelled and then laughed a deep belly laugh.

Don was his own coach and of course JT knew that. Don loved doing the research and coming up with his own plan for contest prep. He loved playing with the numbers and getting things exactly right. He also loved bucking the system that said everyone needed a coach. Had he placed lower in some contests because he didn't have a coach. Absolutely, but not for the reasons you might think. Most judges were also coaches and they scratched each other's backs. Don couldn't count on one hand how many times he had questionably lost to someone only to see that person's coach glad handing with the judges. The politics of it all shouldn't have been surprising. Don's introduction to the sport was the 1981 Mr. Olympia where Arnold's best friend, Franco Columbo, won with gyno and very little leg development.

"I fire him daily, but he just won't stay away," Don offered back and slapped JT on the back as he made his way to the locker room. The first thing he saw when he entered the locker room was the poster on the wall. The words on the poster he had once posted on social media about the gym. A friend of his had turned it into a poster and the gym owner gladly hung it up in the locker room as a daily reminder for all those who entered. It read:

When you walk through the door everything changes
You Change
Your heart races, your head itches, your teeth clench
Mother fucker is no longer an obscenity
But a term of endearment
Torn calluses and deep bruises are won

Like badges of honor

A nose bleed a silver star

A subconjunctival hemorrhage

A distinguished service cross

Passing out or peeing yourself

Not from drunkenness

But from max effort garners applause

Blood, sweat and tears isn't a motivational cliché

But a workout lived

Going through the motions is heresy

Punishable by weakness

Strength cannot be faked, effort cannot be overlooked

And when you've given your all

And stagger out the doors

You look forward to coming back

And doing it all again

Except the next time going even harder

Don smiled every time he saw it. It meant as much to him as the banner on the main gym wall that proclaimed him "2018 Great Lakes Ironman Bodybuilding Champion". He sat on a bench and took out a small shaker bottle. With fumbling fingers he scooped two scoops of his high stim preworkout into it. He then added just enough water for the powder to dissolve and drank it down. It didn't taste good but he didn't care as long as it did the job. After his early morning walk and a long day at work he needed the stimulants to get through the grueling workout. He tossed the empty bottle into his bag and then tossed the bag into an empty cubby before hitting the gym floor to warm up.

Donald took great care in warming up. At 56 he often spent as much time warming up the muscle to be worked as he did actually working the muscle. He credited his careful warming up protocol for the fact that after many years in the gym he had never had a significant injury. Oh, he had a few shoulder issues, a couple of knee issues and even some elbow pain, but nothing that required surgery or even caused him to miss a workout. He was careful, meticulous and would not be rushed through his warm up.

When Jack finally arrived Don yelled across the gym floor. "You're late!"

Jack shot back, "Your old decrepit ass needed the extra time to warm up!" Jack then hurried to the locker room and emerged a short time later covered in yellow sweat pants and a black and yellow sweatshirt. It was his favorite apparel to do calves and abs in. When Don was in prep he worked out every day bucking the traditional need for multiple rest days during the week. Jack did whatever his training partner did and was undoubtedly a perfect workout partner.

Their workouts always started off slow and light hearted. They talked about work, families, sporting events, but when it came down to the balls to the wall working sets it was all intensity and assault on the muscles. The talking ceased and the intensity increased until it looked like a violent dance between two men trading leads. They had been workout partners for so long that they didn't need to say a word to communicate—that was done with a series of looks and grunts that called for strip sets, drop sets, forced reps or some other sort of amplifier.

Once they got into the actual working sets, the workouts went fast and they finished with some volume work. When asked about his training style being heavy duty or high volume Don always responded "yes". He called its SAS. Stimulate, annihilate, and stimulate some more until every muscle fiber worked was exhausted. By the time they finished they were both sweaty and ready for the workout to be done. They almost always plopped down in the lobby on an old couch and watched ESPN while they finished their postworkout shakes. For Don it was the exact same shake he drank before he left for his morning walk. Pound the carbs and protein upon waking and right after working out for that mythical anabolic window.

They walked around plotting their course of action. "I really feel like I need to bring my chest up a bit this contest so let's plan on really crushing it tomorrow and the weeks to come." Don said dictating the plan.

"Right on," Jack agreed. "Your shoulder good? Can we press heavy or do we have to get a little creative."

"It's good enough. Let's go heavy on it as long as we can."

"How is the diet? I know you have a great plan, but anything you foresee having to change?'

"I might have to go with some solid food first thing in the morning as we draw closer, but right now the shake is easy to make and easy to drink so we will stay with that."

"How is the walking going?" Jack asked with a smirk.

Don rolled his eyes. "It's easy and I like walking. It gives me a sense of peace and being one with nature."

Jack laughed. "You mean the peace of being surrounded by drug dealers and prostitutes? Those are the only people up and about in your neighborhood. I'm sure you already seen some weird shit."

Don thought about mentioning the burned out building and yellow cart. He couldn't shake the uneasy feeling it had given him. He couldn't forget the smell or how it felt like he was being watched. He wanted to tell Jack all that but really the only thing strange about the place was the feeling it gave him. There was really nothing to tell or describe. "I did have a car roll by pretty slow with the bass popping at four o'clock in the morning."

"They were probably trying to figure you out. Just remember when you get a cap in your ass it was your buddy Jack who said you should be doing your walk in the safe confines of a Planet Fitness. Seriously though man, what we do in here day in and day out is pure dedication and determination, but for your crazy ass to get up that early and do cardio…that is a whole different level"

"Thanks, but I hardly call it cardio."

A couple of people stopped by to say hi to Don. He was a popular figure in the gym which stemmed from his willingness to be nice to others and help out any time he could."

"All right, Arnold, you ready to get busy?"

Jack referencing Arnold's popularity from when he walked into the gym in the documentary "Pumping Iron" made Don smile. It was what most would consider an easy day, but Don took training his calves and abdominals very seriously. He trained every muscle group with the same focus and energy. It was a trait he hoped would pay off if the judges ever decided to reward proportion again.

Jack and Don attacked the weights with an intensity unrivaled in the gym. They may have goofed around a bit before the workout started but once they got rolling they had a laser focus and a single mindedness that was unmatched. Don's gray tank top that read "The Wrecking Crew" above a tribal pitbull head and "#WorkHarder" below it was soaked in sweat in no time. They fed off each other's effort and knew exactly what buttons to push to make the other get the most out of every set. They moved silently from piece of equipment to piece of equipment as if they were completely in tune with each other's thoughts.

Finally, the grinding effort came to a halt and Don looked at Jack and asked, "Good enough?"

"That will do the trick," Jack responded and walked towards the locker room on calves that didn't want to respond—that wanted to cramp up. Don felt it too. The pump was insane. He thought they had actually worked their abs harder, but the calf pump was crazy insane. A couple of guys, sensing he was done training, came by to ask him how it was going. Word had spread that he was competing at the North America Bodybuilding Championships. Don replied like he always did: "just trying to get better every day, man."

Jack looked at Don, cautiously looked around to make sure no one was listening and asked, "What's your gear intake like?"

Don grinned at the secretive nature of Jack's question. He never tried to hide the fact that he took performance enhancing drugs and if someone were to ask him he would tell them exactly what he was taking and why. "Just Test E right now. I'll be adding compounds as we go along and won't lie that it will be pretty intense about four weeks out. No stones unturned!"

"Cool, you know what you're doing. And…well just keep me informed and let me know if…um…there is anything I can do to help."

Don thought about making some smart-ass comment, but his energy was low and he simply smiled and said thank you.

"I mean, I'll put a dart in your ass if you need me to," Jack added, slapped Don on the shoulder and laughed. Before Don could reply, JT walked in.

"What are you two homos laughing about!" JT was the poster child for politically incorrect comments. He had no filter and said pretty much whatever came to mind. He was very much The Miller in The Canterbury Tales right down to his red hair. Although, Don didn't see him as a cheat and as far as he knew JT was an honest guy. Loud, bawdy, foul mouthed… yes. Cheat…don't think so.

"I was just telling Don how you sell your sweaty underwear on your onlyfans page and that there is a niche of gay men who like your scent." Jack never backed away from giving it to JT just as much as he liked to give it.

JT played right along, "Those gay guys are going to put my kids through college. You want a sample of what gets them all excited?"

"No thanks! I can smell you from here and it ain't good!"

Don once again thought about adding to the conversation but he simply withheld comment. When the barter seemed to have died he added, "I left my post workout shake in the car. Besides I have meal prep to do. See you guys tomorrow."

"Don't overcook your chicken!" he heard JT yell at his backside as he walked out. A few new faces smiled at him and said hi as he walked the length of the gym to the exit.

"You got this, man!" Dave, who worked the counter, said and pumped a fist in Don's direction.

"Thanks!" Don replied back and was thankful to be out of the gym. Don liked the attention and the gym was really that one place where he was very social, but truth be told he was a die-hard introvert. It wasn't just the physical exhaustion of the gym that he needed to recover from; he also needed to recover from the social interaction. He had begun calling his new home the Fortress of Solitude. In it he was surrounded by silence, simplicity and solitude. It was the perfect place for him to recover and prepare for the trials that awaited him.

Three

May 27, 96 Days Out, 200 pounds

Don sat on the edge of his lazy boy and put on his shoes. Almost two weeks into prep and everything was clicking along as smooth as could be. The diet was good, the training was animalistic and the walks were nondescript even though he thought about the burned out house the entire time he was on his walk. That feeling it had given him and the way the yellow cart almost seemed to glow against the darkened backdrop was something he couldn't let go of.

He put the bow in his shoes just like he had for the last 53 odd years. It struck him how that basic skill he learned before entering kindergarten had stood the test of time and was used daily. Oh sure, Velcro came along and even now some slip on shoes were popular, but for the most part you tied your shoes the same way you had since you were a little kid. There was not a little kid version and an adult version—they were the same. In Don's mind he was ready to pontificate the merits of such a simple skill when a movement outside by the road caught his eye.

There were two people standing around his trashcans. It looked like a man and a woman. Both seemed to be relatively young. Don guessed they were in their late 20s but it was hard to tell in the darkness. He made himself small in the recliner; he didn't have any lights on so he hoped they couldn't see him watching them. Don was fascinated. He found it odd he was spying on people outside his own home as if they somehow belonged and he didn't.

The couple didn't just tear through his garbage and leave a mess in their wake. They were careful and meticulous to untie the bags instead of ripping them open. Don's mind rolled back through the previous week trying to visualize what they might find in his trash. It was mostly empty cardboard boxes. Don shopped almost exclusively online. He gasped when he saw the man pull out an old hoodie and hold it up like it was the Holy Grail. Don had fought with himself about whether to keep it or throw it out. Simplicity Don said throw it away you never wear it anymore. Nostalgic Don reminded him that he got it at Quad's Gym in Chicago and he wore it while working out there for a few days. Simplicity Don had won out in the end and now Don felt himself feeling jealous over the man who had claimed Don's refuse as his own personal treasure.

Don watched as they made quick work of his trash and moved next door where they had a mountain of garbage. They went through each bag and he found it interesting that they seemed to be pulling out mostly items of clothing and blankets. It was almost June and the days were already warm. He wondered where they drew the line on food items. Did it have to be sealed or would a half-eaten candy bar tempt their taste buds? Were a few untouched slices of pizza in the cardboard box a honey hole or unedible? They retied the bags and walked across the street with their new belongings. It was under the low hanging branches that their other worldly possessions waited.

They added to their bags the items just claimed and began to pick up to change locations. Don let out a muffled "oh my god" to himself when he saw the man use an old weed whacker as a bindle to carry several bags on. He looked like a bum from the old television shows. He rested it on his shoulder and he and his female companion silently walked off into the night. Don froze as the man stopped and looked right at him. He held his breath for what seemed like minutes as the man gazed towards his house and into the window. In real time, it might have been three seconds. The man's expression never changed. He simply turned his head and walked along.

Don wasn't sure how long he watched them. He did know it was long enough that he now felt behind in his day. He had plenty of time, but in prep every minute seemed to be magnified exponentially. He walked out the door almost forgetting his keys in his haste. He reached back to grab him and felt a sharp pain rip through his trapezoid muscle. You've got to be kidding me he thought. I tore a muscle reaching for keys? The pain subsided as quickly as it came and Don had dodged another bullet targeting his contest prep.

He stepped out into the street and the voice in his head reminded him to steer clear of the burned out house. He snapped at himself: "be more specific, there are lots of burned down houses." He could sense the inner demon laughing as if to say "ok, you want to be a smart ass." But it was true, there were lots of burned and abandoned houses on his morning walks, However, there was only one that gave him anxiety and left him feeling as if he had just lost his best friend.

Maybe, Don thought to himself, it was just the first walk jitters mixed with drinking a protein shake that early for the first time. Maybe that feeling had nothing at all to do with the house. He thought about walking to the house to test his hypothesis.

"Good morning!"

Don nearly jumped out of his skin and pissed himself. When his senses rebooted he saw the garbage pickers lying on a pile of clothes a few yards off the road. The man was lounging back against the bags and the woman was leaning back into him. He was picking things out of her ratted blonde hair. It reminded him of a picture of monkeys he had seen long ago in National Geographic. "Good morning," Don offered back.

"We see you out walking almost every morning," the man stated. The woman with him added, "you trying to get your steps in?" Don noticed in better light that they may even be younger than he originally thought. Their white skin poked through holes where mud and filth had rubbed off. He couldn't tell if their teeth were a broken and a chipped mess or if like the rest of them they were covered in muck. He was shocked they didn't smell worse than they did. He guessed if he had moved closer he might not be thinking that.

"Something like that," Don answered the girl asking about his steps. He was about to get moving again when the man asked him for a smoke. Don launched a myriad of obscenities in his head at what he thought was an absurd question, but the only thing that escaped through his lips was "no". He was expecting them to ask for cash next and wasn't disappointed. "Sorry, I never carry cash anymore." He was mad at himself for apologizing. Why should he be sorry? And what did they mean they noticed him out walking almost every day? Was he being watched? Were they casing his house and one of these mornings he would walk in to the back door kicked in and his few valuables gone?

"Well if you can scrounge up a twenty she gives an amazing blow job. She swallows and everything."

Don was taken aback but it didn't stop him from wondering what "and everything" meant. What was there besides sucking and swallowing. Did she have some crazy finish that he was unaware even existed? Had he been missing out on something his whole life?

19

"I see you're thinking about it. If you get that twenty we live back there," the man said and motioned to a small brush covered wooded area behind the apartment complex. "Just holler for Micki and we will come out."

Don was indeed an introvert but he also had a nervous tic that caused him to speak whenever there was an awkward silence around people he didn't know. "You guys need one of those yellow carts to put stuff in."

The man's look changed from hopeful to terrified from a simple phrase. "What?" he screeched. "We don't know anything about that. We know nothing. You know what forget about the blow job and just leave us alone." With having said that they grabbed their loot and scurried off until they were no longer visible.

Don shrugged his shoulders and started back to walking. He contemplated what caused such a reaction and drummed it up to them having either a serious drug problem or a serious mental health problem, more than likely both. He chuckled to himself and wondered how many people had been offered the "and everything". He then wondered how many had taken the offer and now knew that "and everything" probably meant "that's all folks!" He increased his pace as the feeling of being behind dragged its nails across his loins making him shiver.

He was thinking just how much someone would have to pay him to stick his dick in that girl's black hole of a mouth when he took notice of the smell. It was the smell of a frayed power steering belt that warned you tragedy was around the corner. He looked up and realized in his increased pace he had taken a wrong turn and was back in front of the house he was trying to avoid. The smell made his stomach clench. He instantly wanted to run and thought how weird that his fight or flight would kick in so fast. He took a deep breath in through his mouth and could taste the blackened char. It tasted like the toast his mom had burned when he was a kid but made him eat it anyway because times were tough.

A droplet of rain fell on his forehead. He wished he had his Quad's Gym hoodie to put on. A few more drops smacked his face and a distant rumble seemed to reverberate through the scorched pine planks. His time of flight had passed. Don now felt like his feet weighed a thousand pounds. He heard a hiss...no...it was a sizzle. The rain hitting the torched house sizzled and evaporated into the night's sky. Not possible, Don mused and wished his alarm had failed him this morning.

Lightning flashed and Don caught sight of a disembodied head on the porch railings. His body that was so disciplined was failing him. For all those years he taught and coached muscle memory and now when he needed his legs to walk away on auto pilot they only served to keep him upright. Lightning flashed again and through the falling rain he realized the head was that of an old porcelain doll. The body was in the yellow cart by the garage. Yellow cart! That had not been there a few moments earlier. How did it get there and why? *Son, you're driving with the emergency brake on—can't you smell it?*

A dog growled and a raven squawked its displeasure. The dog broke large branches as it moved around the house unseen. Chains rattled. Don thought Barghest, the goblin dog, was surely present and death was present with him.

The third lightning strike hit the television antenna that had been mounted on a triangular post bolted to the house fifty years ago. There was a sound of a mosquito dying an electric death followed by the roar of ground shaking thunder. There was a flash of green in the upstairs window. Two orbs...two eyes maybe...two old Christmas lights resurrected like a key wired to a kite. The rain increased and seemed to dissolve the shackles that kept Don bolted to the ground. He was freed and high stepped away from the house at a pace his feet hadn't seen in years.

Don was out of breath and his calves ached. He took a moment to look back and saw the moon shimmering above the house. It looked every bit like the haunted house in every child's nightmares. Clouds raced in front of the moon and then passed creating a drama of dancing shadows around the house. The storm had passed through Flint but for Don the storm was just getting started.

Four

May 31, 92 Days Out, 199 pounds

Don had made it through the holiday weekend unscathed. He had a built in cheat meal where he ate a hotdog and some chips along with an ice cold Pepsi. It tasted amazing. He had completely stuck to his plan. Weekends were hard, holiday weekends were harder. Not only is everyone out and about doing things, but your regimented routine is turned upside down. Don still tried to stay on schedule eating and training at the same times as if it was a normal weekday. But even for someone as regimented as he was it was difficult and he found himself turning into a clock watcher anticipating when he could eat again.

He walked into Whiskey's Aged to Perfection Assisted Living Apartments glad to be at work and in the thick of routine. Right away, he noticed an aide struggling with some boxes and ran over to provide assistance. "Let me help you with that Amanda." He said taking several boxes from her. She smiled and said thanks. Don told her how nice she looked—a radiant glow was his how he described it. She blushed and smiled again. He helped her put the boxes away and inquired about her weekend. She told him money was tight so she didn't do a whole lot but did enjoy having the day off.

Don felt like he was performing whenever he walked into a facility. He knew the importance of having a good relationship with the different places he visited. He wanted to be welcomed back and he wanted the staff to take literature seriously as a means of care. He wasn't being fake and if anything maybe this was more real than the brooding hermit he turned into when he was in other social situations. He was helpful, complimentary and a great listener.

Don walked into the common room and noticed Sally Murphy sitting all alone. Sally was 79 and had been the victim of an unfortunate incident several months ago. She was sitting in the same spot on the couch and an elderly man next to her had reached out and taken her hand. She seemed ok with it and for a few moments they sat next to each other holding hands. Then unexpectedly the man took her hand to his mouth and promptly bit her index finger off. She pulled her hand away. He sat there and chewed her finger up and swallowed it. She kept her hand in her lap where it bled all over her pants. They both sat in silence like nothing at all had happened. The only way anyone knew what happened was after she was discovered with a bloody stump they looked at the footage from the security camera that had captured the whole event.

Don, being a likable soul, was allowed to view the footage by several different staff members. He was utterly shocked every time he watched it how nonchalant they both acted. She expressed no pain and he expressed no regrets that he bit off and ate her finger. A lawsuit was avoided thanks to the footage and the fact that the gentleman was relocated to another facility.

"Sally, did you send all the suitors home?" Don graciously said and swept his arm around the facility. Sally barely acknowledged his existence and slightly turned her head towards him. He sat down near her, but not next to her, just in case there was some post traumatic stress disorder lingering about from the finger incident. He told her how much he loved seeing her and how he looked forward to coming by the facility just because she was going to be there.

One of the staff members, a pretty woman in her thirties named DeLisa, walked by and winked at Don. He gave her a sly grin and then winked back. He knew she had inquired about his relationship availability from another staff member. Since that time, they casually flirted and talked when the opportunities presented themselves. Truth be told he stopped by the facility more often than was needed for that very reason. He also knew she was waiting for him to ask her out and he would probably do so after the contest was over.

"Well Sally, I need to go deliver this wonderful piece of literature to Ruth or else I would stay and chat the day away," Don said and held up a copy of The Omen by David Seltzer. He wanted to hug her, but the biting incident caused him to keep his distance, Not to mention COVID had made him worried that some people no longer desired physical contact. In the past a hug was almost assumed at places like Whiskey's; now he always made a point to ask if they wanted a hug. It was a little awkward but not as awkward as going in for the hug and being stiff-armed.

Don walked from the common area down the corridor to his right. The hallway, the carpet, even the doors reminded him of Kubrick's version of the Overlook Hotel. He was thankful there was no room 237 or if you prefer the book, room 217. A staff member opened a door and rushed out just as he was approaching. He ended up catching her in his arms as opposed to knocking her to the ground. She apologized profusely to which Don replied, "there was no need to apologize, it was just a case of two ships passing in the night." He was very unsatisfied with the use of that metaphor. He might have held her a moment too long, she certainly didn't try to move away. He thought in a different setting he would kiss her. He made sure she was stable on her feet and released her. "How is Ruth this morning?"

She, Samantha, was still flustered and blurted out, "who?"

"Ruth Gates. I have a book she requested and might spend some time reading to her if she is up for it."

"Ohhh, Ruth, she was up early this morning, ate a full breakfast and is in her room complaining that the staff here doesn't vacuum her carpet enough and that she could grow potatoes on the floor it's so filthy." Samantha said in one long breath.

Don laughed and said, "She can be quite cantankerous on occasion. Hopefully the book will brighten her day and she has a story to share. Her stories are always fascinating even when you've heard them before."

Ruth Gates was quite the character. She was battling dementia so some of her stories were completely fabricated, but her sister had verified that in the 60s and 70s she had been a B-movie horror actress and even starred in Night Must Fall. She claimed to have dated Lawson Deming of Sir Graves Ghastly fame, but her sister would not confirm that. She even went so far as to say she was the reason he missed his flight out of Cleveland—a flight that crashed and killed everyone aboard.

"Have a great visit," Samantha said and excused herself to go in the next room.

Don walked in and Ruth was sitting in her wheel chair facing a blank TV screen, She reached out with her wooden cane and wacked the side of the TV. She cut loose with a string of swear words and proclaimed the piece of junk had finally died.

"Good morning Ruth!" Don said and startled her.

She turned to him with a snarl and growled "Jesus Christ! You scared the shit out of me! Who let you in?"

Don smiled at her. Her face was beat red out of anger and with her full head of white hair he thought she looked like a strawberry cupcake with vanilla frosting. "I'm sorry. I didn't mean to startle you."

"Are you the television repair man? If not you can just walk your handsome self right out of here."

"Ruth, I'm Don. The one that brings you books and sometimes I read to you," he said holding up the rare hardcover version of The Omen.

She squinted at it, seemed to acknowledge it, and said, "You know I used to be a scream queen. I dated them all. Lugosi, Lon, Boris, Vincent and even that crackpot Sir Graves."

Don thought it was interesting that she named the actors themselves but when it came to Deming she called him by his character name. He felt a tap on his leg.

"You ever date anyone famous?" Ruth asked tapping his leg a second time with her cane to make sure he was paying attention.

He made an exaggerated pantomime of thinking and replied that he didn't think so. He pulled up a chair next to her and sat down.

"You're cute enough," she said and gave him a big smile. "You know I have a daughter that is available. She runs with the circus crowd and rides one of those one wheeled bikes across a wire. All my kids were involved in the circus at one point. I don't know why they thought those unicorns were so cool, but they all rode them. Maybe it was my husband's fault. I should have spent more time with them but I was the pretty girl with the big stinking ape in the Beauty and the Beast exhibit. Oh, did I put on a show. That damn filthy ape did nothing but sit there and it got all the applause. I knew people paid to see me and if they cheered loud enough I bent over and gave my top a little tug so my nipple would pop out for just a second." Ruth clapped her leg and laughed a hearty laugh. "They stopped paying attention to King Kong after I did that!"

In reality, Ruth never married and her sister said she never had any kids. But she might have played the part of a beauty in some circus exhibit and oddly enough Don could see her popping a nipple out to get attention. He had chuckled to himself about her using the word unicorn instead of unicycle. He wondered what kind of Freudian slip that might be.

She continued, "Remember those funny fellas…Abbot and Costello?" Don nodded. "I almost made a movie with them. If they hadn't been so god damn tight with the contract I would have been their female lead. Instead, they went with Lenore Aubert to prove a point. She was no more French than a hillbilly out of West Virginia! I would have been a much better choice but those tight-wads couldn't see it. The circus paid me well. My husband was killed in Vietnam. I miss him so much."

"I'm sorry Ruth."

"Well we all die. Death and taxes right? I didn't pay taxes when I worked for the circus. But I guess my bill is coming due now. I have cancer don't I?"

"I'm not a doctor, Ruth. The only thing I know about your medical history is what you've told me."

"You can't fix a television and you can't heal me. What good are you?"

Don stood up. "Who said I can't fix the TV?" He had noticed during her lengthy discourse that the television was unplugged. He walked over, plugged it in and asked her what the magic word was.

Ruth wrinkled up her nose and questioningly said "please?"

Don laughed and said "No! Abracadabra! Now give it a try."

Ruth aimed the remote at the television and pressed the big red power button. The television flashed to life. Ruth's smile made his day. He asked "would you like me to read to you?"

"No. You can go now. I want to watch The Price is Right."

Don didn't need to ask Ruth about a hug, she always wanted one, although as her dementia progressed he might need to. He reached down and hugged her. She was already focused on the television. "I'll leave your book on the desk," Don said a bit dejected. He didn't know what was more difficult: being forgotten about by the elderly with dementia or being dumped for the next big thing by the kids in a home. He left her room and decided he had some extra time so he would visit Peggy Sue.

Peggy Sue was an elderly lady with late stage Alzheimer's that he had met while flirting with DeLisa. Peggy Sue was mostly alert although she was bed bound. She spoke only word salad if she spoke at all. Don liked stopping in to see her since DeLisa told him that she never gets any visitors. He slowly opened the door and saw her laying silently in bed. He walked in and sat in the chair next to the bed that was positioned by the ear she seemed to be able to hear out of.

"Hi Peggy Sue!" Don said softly as not to frighten her. Her eyes brightened and her weight shifted ever so slightly. "I wanted to come by and say hello and see what you've been up to." He immediately felt a twinge of guilt for asking her what she had been up to. Here Don this is what I've been up to: lying in this freaking bed staring at the far corner of the room unable to communicate my pain, discomfort or hunger. I piss and shit myself and have to wait until someone checks it before I get relief because again, I can't communicate any longer. How about you? What have you been up to?

Don offered a tight lip smile and he felt a tear roll down his cheek as he put his hand over her cold hand. "I'm sorry Peggy Sue. I wish things were different. I wish you weren't here suffering. I wish you could communicate."

"Airport. Green tea over watermelon at nine o'clock. See loud onions over the mushroom door. Wooooo, not right. Green tea. Horses, cats and lions in the bed. Green tea in the bed. Numbers. Carrots," Peggy Sue rattled on indiscriminately. Don gave her hand a gentle squeeze. "Lincoln. Red

29

paste on green tea. Yellow cart. Burnt house. Stay away. Green tea milks purple penis under an airplane."

Don felt a panic attack wash over him like never before. He could always feel them coming and take the necessary steps to diminish their intensity. This one blindsided him. He couldn't breathe, he couldn't move. He wondered for a moment if this was how Peggy Sue often felt and couldn't do anything about it. He wanted to run. He wanted to stand still and scream. Sweat streamed down the sides of his face and trickled down his back. He was sure any moment he was going to have a bowel movement. He would indeed be like Peggy Sue crapping his pants. He had to practice his techniques that he used to help stop on coming anxiety attacks. He took a short ragged breath, closed his eyes and quoted The Wanderer, an old English poem:

"Often, every daybreak, alone I must
bewail my cares. There's now no one living
to whom I dare mumble my mind's understanding.
I know as truth that it's seen suitable
for anyone to bind fast their spirit's closet,
hold onto the hoards, think whatever
"Can a weary mind weather the shitstorm?
I think not.
Can a roiling heart set itself free?
I don't think so.
So often those hustling for the win must
clamp down grim mindings in their coffer,
just as I ought fetter my inborn conceit,
often wounded, wanting where I know,
kindred pulled away, how many winters now?
I shrouded my giver in dark earth
and wended away worrisome,

weather-watching the wrapful waves,
hall-wretched, seeking a center,
far or near, where they might be found,
in some mead-hall, who knows of my kind,
willing to adopt a friendless me,
though they be joyful enough.

The panic attack almost always disappeared by this point when he recited the poem, but he was still feeling beside himself and extremely anxious. He felt something squeeze his hand. Peggy Sue had clapped her hand over his and was squeezing.

"Green tea exlir peach apple horse baby seal cardboard cardboard cardboard black burned doggie puppy clown jump." She stopped and smiled.

Don was panting and guessed this is what it felt like to have a heart attack. His lungs didn't want to fill with air. He thought how crazy it was that he could do all that stuff in the gym, but it was going to be a random phrase said in word salad that did him in. He was cold yet still sweating. He felt Peggy Sue give his hand another squeeze. He looked at her and she was crying. He wished he could read her mind. He wished he could ask her about the yellow cart or burned house. He needed to know if it was just randomness or was she trying to tell him something from some parallel universe or alternate reality. It couldn't be random—he knew that. Of all the things she could have uttered there is no way yellow cart, burnt house and stay away coincidently came out. He knew it.

He felt his breathing starting to normalize and his body temperature no longer felt hot or cold. He had apparently made it through this time. He heard the low rumbling of Peggy Sue snoring. Whatever had transpired took all of her energy. She slept peacefully. He slowly slid his hand out from under hers, stood up and composed himself. He hoped he didn't run

31

into anyone in the hall on the way out but if he did he wanted to look like a normal person and not some psycho who had just went through a mentally traumatic event.

The hall was empty, but he felt like the place wasn't going to let him go just yet—like the Overlook Hotel wouldn't let the Torrence family go. To his relief the door swung open and he lurched into the warm sunlight. He thought for a moment he had left his keys inside. It was a moment of absolute panic that he would have to go back in, but then he felt them in his side pocket and the panic vanished. He watched Whiskey's in his rear-view mirror half expecting some aberration to manifest itself above the building in his wake. Nothing happened.

Back in Peggy Sue's room her eyes jerked open and she said with crystal clear clarity: "Danger Will Robinson. Yellow Cart. Burnt house. Danger Don."

Five

June 7, 85 Days out, 197 pounds

Don woke up five minutes before the alarm went off. He felt like he was getting good sleep and his Fitbit confirmed it. He woke up a lot through the night mostly to urinate. Just as he was trying to be stress free and get adequate sleep he was also trying to stay very hydrated. He turned the alarm on his phone off and sat up. For the first time in a long time, he suddenly felt very lonely. It just washed over him. His therapist called it a grief wave. She said they were nothing to worry about as long as he didn't allow it to drag him out to sea and drown him. He was good (or very bad) at shaking off emotions.

Sitting on the edge of the bed he thought about how everything was clicking along and he was very much into a routine. He had the little stress hiccup about the house and what Peggy Sue had said, but that was over a week ago and he had not had any panic attacks or weird occurrences since then. He reasoned that he read into stupid and insignificant details; he over thought every scenario and clearly made a mountain out of a molehill. Even though he reasoned it out, it didn't stop him from thinking about it often. He understood that when he was in prep mode things were often magnified and the lack of doing social events just gave him more time to dwell on the curiosities of life.

Don went through his morning ritual without giving any thought to what he was actually doing. He was on autopilot and to him that was a good thing. He went to put his shoes on in the same place and looked out the same window that he did every morning. The difference was this morning he caught a glimpse of a person in a hoodie pushing a yellow cart. He only saw them for a moment as they were exiting off his street and going away from his house. His breath hitched and for a brief second he wanted to run after whoever it was. Then he relaxed and wondered if the little dude who had gone through his garbage had taken his advice and got a cart to put his and his lady friend's stuff in.

He walked outside and was pleased that it was a cool, crisp morning. He didn't like walking in the suffocating, humid air that was soon to be a staple of mid-Michigan mornings. Don started walking and let his mind wander down memory lane. He thought about how as the contest prep got further along his drug regimen was going to increase and his body temperature was also going to increase. He was going to be hot all the time—that was not something he was looking forward to. The normal person's response would be to not take performance enhancing drugs that made him feel like that. Don had been drug free most of his life. He had not taken any steroids until he was in his late forties. Not that he hadn't tried.

When Don had been 21 he and his training partner in Korea had tried to buy steroids from a Korean pharmacy. They had no clue the differences between steroid profiles or even what to ask for—much less the problem of not being able to speak Korean. They showed the pharmacist their muscles and made a motion like they wanted them bigger. They finally left with a bottle of pills. They didn't have any idea what they were or how many to take so they decided on one three times a day. Within a week they were broke out in what looked like the measles, but their unit medic assured them it was just an allergic reaction. They threw out the rest of the pills and gave up on the steroid idea.

However, a couple of years later Don and his new workout partner, Eddie, decided to give them a try. They were stationed at Fort Sill, Oklahoma and were not too far from the Mexican border. They decided to take a trip to Nuevo Laredo, Mexico during the upcoming four-day weekend. The plan was to make the eight hour drive on Friday. Stay Friday and Saturday nights in Mexico partying and start the return trip home on Sunday. Don's roommate at the time, Bob, whom didn't lift nor care about steroids, wanted to go along for the partying aspect. That fateful Friday morning the three young men headed out.

The trip down was completely uneventful except for Don's old Thunderbird picking up a little rattle along the way. They made it in good time and without getting a ticket for speeding. They were waved across the border with no issues and decided the first thing to do was find a pharmacy. That was not difficult. It seemed selling drugs to Americans right across the border was big business for local pharmacies. They finally decided on one and went in for a shopping spree.

Don had not learned much between his Korean steroid run and his Mexican steroid run. He knew he wanted testosterone but he had no clue about esters or how much they really should take. He also was convinced Dianabol was a good option and again wasn't quite sure about dosages. They told the pharmacist they wanted to do a cycle of steroids. The heavy set man with wire rim glasses and a white lab coat pulled out a box and made some recommendations. They were clueless and $600 later they had a box of nondescript (to them anyway) performance enhancing drugs and a bottle of valium. Don remembered being so excited. He was going to pack on some serious size from the products in the box. He was finally going to take the next step.

35

They stopped at one of the many taco carts and ate, then went to a store to purchase tequila and Mexican beer. The weekend was going great until while looking for a hotel Don was rear ended. The damage to either car was not horrible, but the police came and in some type of "screw the Americans" procedure Don was found at fault and his car was impounded until he paid the driver of the other car his asking price for repairs, that was $1000. It felt every bit the scam it sounded like to Don. But with $600 of illegal drugs in the trunk he didn't want to cause a bigger scene and get nabbed for what was in the trunk. He withdrew the money, the last he had available and got his car out of impound.

They found a hotel and even though their spirits were dampened, they decided to celebrate. They each took a small handful of valium and started drinking. Bob told them he heard that taking valium would enhance the effects of the alcohol. When they woke up almost 20 hours later they wanted to beat up whoever told Bob such nonsense. They were grumpy, somehow still tired and no longer felt like partying. They decided to just head home and take turns driving if Don got tired.

They pulled up to the American side of the border and the customs agent took one look at Eddie and Don and told them to pull over. They were busted. They were detained, strip searched interrogated, threatened with calling their commanding officer and finally held until they could pay a fine equivalent to the street value of the drugs. Don had no money left and Eddie said he had spent everything on the drugs. Bob, who didn't have anything to do with the steroids was released to go to an ATM machine while Don and Eddie were held in custody until he returned with the money.

The customs agent explained to them that most of what they purchased were veterinarian grade steroids that were out of date. He said at best they would be ineffective and at worse they would cause an infection that would require surgery. He pointed out that the redi-ject syringes had an 18 gauge needle which was fine for cattle, but would leave quite the hole in a human leg or shoulder. They learned more about steroids while they waited for their friend to return than they had previously known.

The custom agent said they were lucky they were military. He informed them that U.S. Customs rarely let anyone off with just a fine for importing illegal drugs. The border was really starting to crack down on steroids. He reiterated to them that really they were fortunate to get caught. Not only were the drugs likely to cause harm but they could cause a positive drug test which would get them busted down to private. Don didn't feel lucky, but he did swear off ever trying to purchase illegal steroids again. Eddie, not so much. He made a return trip where they hid the drugs in a spare tire that they paid a mechanic $50 to seal up. Eddie made some great gains but ended up tearing his rotator cuff, then got busted for smoking weed and was eventually discharged from the army. Don had not heard from him since.

Don stayed true to his word until he actually started competing in bodybuilding contest in his late 40s. After competing in his first bodybuilding contest "natural" and losing a lot of his hard earned muscle to obtain the condition he desired, Don considered steroids again. He went to an anti-aging clinic and found out he had the testosterone level of a 70 year old man. He was put on testosterone therapy at the clinic. The amount the clinic charged him was five times what the going internet rate was for similar drugs. Don convinced himself that he wasn't doing anything illegal or anything that should be illegal. Sometimes he was really good at justifying his actions. He purchased the drugs from an underground lab in the states and although he had no idea what he was really taking he had good results. There were rumors that underground, and overseas, labs made low doses of testosterone propionate, which was inexpensive, and sold them as everything from decca to test.

He was 20 pounds heavier at his second contest in the same condition. The drugs he had taken allowed him to get to insanely low body fat and keep as much muscle as possible. He knew that if he wanted to seriously compete in a contest that wasn't drug tested he was going to have to take drugs just like everyone else. Therefore, going natty was no longer an option.

Thinking about gear, steroids, performance enhancing drugs, whatever you want to call them occupied Don's mind for the majority of the walk. He was happy to see how much time had elapsed. He leapt over the broken piece of sidewalk with an extra bounce in his step because he was almost finished with another walk. He didn't hate them like he did cardio in other forms, but he still found it time consuming and boring.

"You!" the shrill scream pierced the dark morning. Don turned to the origin of the scream and saw a raggedy looking man emerge from the thick bushes. He half stumbled, half ran towards Don. Don braced for an attack. His legs bent and flexed into a solid base. His arms rose into a defensive posture and he watched the man's hips to see where he was going. But there was no fight in the man.

He stopped a few feet away. Don saw that he had been crying—that he was still crying. His lungs rattled from the momentary exertion, but mostly from years of smoking whatever cigarettes he could bum or find. The crying didn't help the congestion in his lungs either. He stood before Don trying to catch his breath so that he could speak his mind.

Don realized it was the man who had picked through his trash a few weeks prior. His face was more drawn, he looked more unhealthy—if that was possible, and whereas before he was upright and almost cocky, now he was clearly bent and broken. Don also realized he smelled way worse. He smelled like fresh human shit.

"It was you," he finally said after having enough breath to talk, "you're the reason she is gone. You're the reason they took her."

"Your girlfriend is gone?"

"She was going to be my wife and it's your fault they took her!"

"Who took her? Are you sure someone took her. I swear I saw her earlier this morning pushing a cart down the street."

The man drew back as if to throw a punch and then just pounded his fist into his thigh. He was clearly hurt and even seemed a little scared. "You," he mumbled and then collapsed to his knees on the ground.

Don almost reached out to console him and then withdrew because he thought the man might have some disease that would destroy his prep. "Are you sure she isn't just out trying to find some nice things for you? Maybe if you just go back to your spot," Don couldn't bring himself to call it a home, "She will show up in a little while."

"She is gone," the man sobbed and pounded his fist into the ground several times before falling to his side into a fetal position. He moaned in agony.

"I'm sorry. I'll drive around in a little while and see if I can find her."

"She's dead," he wailed, "they took her."

Don was getting frustrated. He wanted to help, but the man wasn't making any sense. He was certain the girl had simply left him for whatever reason. Maybe she was tired of the homeless life and wanted to find help. Maybe she was just tired of him and wanted to find someone else or just make a go of it on her own. He could understand that.

Don started getting an uneasy feeling that he and the man were being watched. Maybe the girl changed her mind and was watching from afar waiting for Don to leave so she could explain herself to the man. That feeling that sense was hard to explain or quantify, but that didn't make it any less real. It was almost identical to the feeling he had at the house when he thought he was being watched. He turned his head in both directions to see if maybe he could catch a glimpse of who was watching him. He had always been good at those newspaper cartoons where you had to spot the differences. He had an uncanny ability to recognize something that was just slightly out of place. There were so many shadows and so many trees that he felt someone could be almost on top of him before he recognized the break in the normal flow of things.

There was a snap of a twig followed by the low guttural warning of a canine growling. Don turned his whole body in that direction. He saw absolutely nothing. The growl came again only this time louder. He heard a rustling behind him and turned to see the man struggling to get to his feet.

"They took her and now they're coming for me," he screamed and stumbled off into the bushes disappearing from sight. Don took a slow breath, held it and listened. He could hear the cracking of the man stumbling through the brush but nothing else. He exhaled. He had no anxiety and really no fear. He was curious more than anything. The predawn hours certainly held its secrets. But the secrets hidden between the witching hour and dawn were not necessarily to be feared. Some secrets busted myths or proved them. Some secrets enlightened. Most secrets stayed secrets playing to a wake of frenzied followers curious about the unknown. He remembered reading an ancient Irish mystic who warned secrets weren't to be chased, they were best when admired because if you unraveled the secret a secret they were no more.

Don stood in the shadows of the streetlight and thought about the mystical nature of his walks. What was he learning about himself during these mostly silent walks with his wandering mind as his only companion? Did he find them transformative? Did he simply find them necessary as part of the contest prep? No, on that he was certain there was more. Something was happening in him during these walks. He hated the phrase "everything happens for a reason" but he couldn't help feel like these walks were going to be a transformative part of him growing old.

Six

June 8, 84 Days Out, 196 pounds

From MLive, Journal Flint edition: A homeless man was found dead behind the Park West Apartments. Although it cannot be confirmed, it is believed that the unidentified man hung himself from a tree branch. Foul play has not yet been ruled out, but suicide is the most likely cause of death.

Seven

June 22, 70 Days Out, 194 pounds

Ten weeks out. Time was short. Before he knew it, he would be standing on stage presenting his body to be judged. The diet was starting to tighten up, the workouts had an increased pace and sense of urgency, and the drug protocols were increasing. It had only been Testosterone Enthanate and Anavar up until this point. Now it was time to add Trenbelone Acetate and cycle in Clenbuterol and T3.

Trenbelone, or Tren for short, was a drug that bodybuilders either loved or hated. It had become popular as a drug that was injected into cattle a few weeks out from slaughter to increase lean tissue mass. It is noted for increased feed efficiency meaning one could grow on less food and increased muscle mass. However, the side effects were many including tren cough, tren sweats, high blood pressure, increased heart rate, insomnia and anxiety to name some of the more popular ones. It was said in bodybuilding circles if you could tolerate the sides from Tren than it was a must use in contest prep.

Don liked doing his injections first thing in the morning. What time of the day to do your injections was another thing that was argued constantly in bodybuilding forums. Some coaches preached to do them right before workouts, some prescribed to the theory that you should do them before bed and some argued it didn't matter as long as you consistently did them at the same time. Don mostly agreed with the latter. He liked doing them in the morning because he felt like his blood would be pumping faster and he would be moving all day which would push the compounds where they needed to go. He didn't like doing them preworkout because the post injection pain (PIP) would sometimes interfere with his workouts. He also didn't like doing them before bed because the adrenalin dump of jabbing yourself often kept him awake.

He took everything he needed out of the large make-up case he had converted into a gear box and laid it out on the table beside his bed. He took the 22 gauge, 3 ml syringe and the 18 gauge draw needle out of their sterile packages. He then used a thick alcohol pad to wipe the tops of the testosterone and tren vials. Don carefully replaced the 22 gauge needle with the 18 gauge needle and withdrew one ml of testosterone and then one ml of trenbelone. He pulled the plunger slightly back to get any of the compounds out of the needle before switching back to the 22 gauge needle and pushing the air out. Don wiped his upper thigh in a circular motion with a new alcohol pad. He fanned it dry before pulling off the cap and plunging the needle into his thigh. The one and a half inch, 22 gauge needle made a slight tearing sound as it entered deep into the muscle.

Don pushed hard on the plunger. It wasn't that the 22 gauge needle was too small for the oil to pass through, it was more the fact that he had a lot of scar tissue in that area and the oil did not want to go into that. He pulled it out slowly while still pressing the plunger until he found a sweet spot where the compound went smoothly into his muscle. Don left it in for a moment after the syringe was empty and then pulled the needle all the way out. To his astonishment, a thin stream of blood shot a good six inches out of the hole he had just created. He grabbed an alcohol pad and put pressure on it all the while feeling a metallic taste building in the back of his throat.

The next minute was complete hell. The metallic taste turned into a horrible cough that would not quit. No matter what he did he just kept coughing and coughing hard. It felt like his lungs were trying to turn themselves inside out. He grabbed short breaths in between the coughs but they weren't enough to sustain his oxygen supply. Don remembered how much he had panicked the first time he had tren cough. He had heard of it but didn't think it was going to be as bad as it was. He thought back to his younger self and wondered what would have happened if he got tren cough from the Mexican gear. He would have had no idea that tren cough was a side effect and probably tried to call 911 thinking he was dying. Before Don could finish thinking about it, the cough stopped just as fast as it came on. He had managed to somehow hold the alcohol pad with pressure over the injection site during the coughing spell. He removed it and was thankful the bleeding had stopped. He cleaned up the little bit of blood on the floor and off his thigh.

He smiled knowing this part of his day was behind him. It was arguably the worst part of the day and another reason he liked doing it in the mornings was to get it over with. He sighed as he thought about how the injections were only going to increase as the contest approached. He had previously been doing it just twice a week. Today marked the first day of every other day injections and before long would be every day. He would have to start pinning his shoulders and glutes before long—his legs were a mess of scar tissue. He stood up and felt a little knot in his thigh. It wasn't horrible. It felt like a small Charlie horse. He flexed and stretched his thigh several times hoping to work the knot out a little bit.

Don caught a glimpse of himself in the full length r.
the first time since prep started he thought he looked good.
ting leaner and more vascular yet was still full and muscular.
and thought it was going to be a good day. As he was getting dɪ ᵤₑd and
getting his shake together the skies opened up with a torrential downpour.
So much for the good day he thought. He looked outside and it was brutal.
He made the decision to get in his car, bite the bullet and just walk on the
treadmill at Planet Fitness. He could tan while he was there and kill two
birds with one stone.

He backed his car out of the driveway and started down the road. It
was raining so hard that he could barely see even with the windshield wip-
ers on high and the headlights on bright. The rain beat on his car causing
a cacophony in his normally quiet ride. He rolled through the rain slowly
avoiding the cars parked all along the road and the trash strewn about from
the wind.

A light flashed from the passenger seat. It was his phone. He picked it
up to see an alert that reminded him he was ten weeks out from the contest.
Don set his phone down and looked up just in time to see a mass of people
in the road. He didn't have to slam on his breaks because he wasn't going
very fast, but if he was he likely would have hit someone.

He watched as the multitude all dressed in similar worn and torn
clothing began to shuffle towards his car. They went around silently on
both sides. It reminded him of being in a car wash when the long strands
of cloth swished around your car scrubbing road grime from it. He started
to worry that they would scratch his car but it seemed they stayed just far
enough away not to touch it. He noticed they all looked downtrodden and
unkempt. Don wondered if he had just driven into a meeting where all of
Flint's homeless collected for a monthly soiree. He looked in his rear view
mirror with fascination as they came back together as one group after they

45

passed his car that had divided them. It eerily reminded him of a zombie horde.

He looked forward again and standing in front of his car was a solitary figure pushing a yellow shopping cart. He hadn't been aware that the rain had stopped until he realized he could make out some details of the person. The figure was wearing a Detroit Lions hoodie with the hood pulled up. Long dark hair was pulled to the front and cascaded down over the word "Detroit" in wet matted locks. He wanted to assign the figure female gender but he wasn't quite sure yet—it could be a smallish man. The figure wore cargo pants that tucked into motorcycle boots that appeared to be too big.

A dog that had been hiding behind the person and in the shadows stepped forward and sat down next to the figures leg. It was a pit bull—squat and muscular. The dog looked up at the person next to it as if awaiting instructions. It had a thick collar and Don finally noticed a rope leading from the collar up the sleeve of the old hoodie. The dog looked forward again and snarled. If it had another head or two Don would have thought it was Cerberus.

The world seemed to stop as the Mexican standoff lingered. Don began to feel uneasy. He glanced in his rearview mirror to see what the horde was doing and they were gone. He looked harder thinking maybe it was just a trick of the shadows. Nope they were nowhere to be seen. He looked out his windshield and the person with the yellow cart was also gone. He sighed. What was it all about? He nearly jumped out of his skin when he noticed the person, now clearly a female, was standing beside his car door looking in the driver side window. The cart was in front of her and the dog on the other side of her away from his car.

His instinct told him to roll down the window. Fear told him to be careful. Reason told him to slowly pull forward and drive away. He pushed the button to lower the window. He was just a few inches from being face to face with her. He tried to be calm, but he was starting to shake with excitement and fear. They just looked at each other for what seemed a very long time.

Don realized her hair wasn't dark, it was just dirty and wet. He guessed it was a shade of red. Her eyes seemed to have a natural eyeliner about them and the green discs flashed brilliantly in the darkness. Her skin was pale under the dirt. Her lips a deep red and full. He thought they were perfect, like lips you would see on an advertisement extolling the benefits of the latest lip care therapy. His nervous tic was pushing for him to say something, but nothing was coming to mind.

She slowly smiled revealing white teeth behind red lips that seemed very out of place with the rest of her homeless ensemble. The smile was the catalyst to unlocking his tongue. "Can I help you," he said in a voice that was less than confident. As soon as he said it, he thought how stupid it must have sounded. Was that the best he could come up with? And why was he acting so nervous. She didn't reply which caused him to feel very uncomfortable.

"I love your dog," was his second attempt at conversation. Her eyes seemed to twinkle and Don felt he was silently being read like a book. She was analyzing him, taking everything in from the stuff on the passenger seat to the books in the back seat. Her smile faded and she stared stoically into his soul. He wanted to reach out and touch her hair and caress her face. He felt himself being drawn to her in a way that made him feel powerless. As if she had read his mind, she reached out and briefly touched his cheek with the back of her forefinger.

It felt electric. And maybe it was because it had been sometime since a woman had touched him like that or maybe it was because of the TnT (testosterone and trenbelone) shot that morning, but he felt a stirring and a growing in his crotch. She reminded him of Lucy Westenra, the Victorian woman depicted in Francis Coppola's movie: "Bram Stoker's Dracula". Her gaze held him captive. He wanted to do so many things, but he could not open his mouth nor could he pull away from her stare. He almost felt like she was playing with him.

The dog at her side yawned and she looked down at him breaking the spell that held Don entrapped. Sensing he had an out, but not sure he wanted one, he said, "I'm sorry I pulled up on your gathering. I really need to get to the gym." He swallowed hard as she looked back at him with an intense look that bordered on ferocious. Her lips parted and he thought she was going to say something, but instead she stepped back away from his car.

"Have a good day," he said wanting nothing more than for her to tell him not to go. He thought about offering her a ride to wherever she was going. And if she didn't have the dog and the cart he probably would have. He waited so long it felt awkward. Finally he gave her a tight lipped smile, said bye and slowly pulled away. He kept watching her through the mirror. She did not come running after him. She also did not walk away. She stood in the road with her yellow cart and her dog companion. Don turned the corner and thought she was gone from his life forever. Oddly enough he missed her already.

He thought about her all the way to Planet Fitness. He thought about what had happened while he walked on a treadmill sometimes so lost in thought that he stumbled on the wide black revolving belt. Why hadn't he offered her a ride? He loved dogs and even had a blanket in the trunk the dog could have sat on. If she hadn't wanted to leave the cart he could have put it in his trunk, it was big enough. Had he been afraid of insulting her by assuming she needed a ride? Did he not want to draw attention to the fact that she probably didn't have a place to be driven to? Was he concerned about embarrassing her because she was probably going to an abandoned building where she squatted? He thought about driving around after his walk to see if he could find her.

When he convinced himself he was being silly and overly emotionally from the contest cutting process he was reminded how her touch had stirred in him a desire that he was not entirely sure he had ever felt before. It was raw and animalistic, but it was more. He imagined kissing her perfect lips and those lips parting so their tongues could dance together. He felt the stirring again and knew he better think of something else or he might become the latest gray sweat pants meme.

It occurred to him that he had not smelled her. Surely, she had body odor. Her clothes were torn and tattered. And even though she had been super close to him he did not get a hint of bad breath. Her finger touched his face. Had his sense of smell been rendered inactive in her presence? Was it all part of some hypnotic gesture she had mastered? Or was it simply because of the rain. He had so many questions, but the one weighing most heavily on his mind was is the yellow cart that she pushed the same one that he saw outside the burned building? In addition, if it was did that mean that was where she stayed? He thought if it was, his chances of seeing her again increased drastically. His heart rate quickened.

Eight

June 23, 69 Days Out, 195 pounds

Don was awake before the alarm. He didn't feel as good as he had been feeling and a check of his FitBit indicated that he had not slept well. He had trouble falling asleep and he had trouble staying asleep. He wanted good sleep to be a priority for this prep. Just taking 150 mg of trazodone before bed was likely not going to cut it anymore now that he was taking tren, clen and T3. It was time to add some Xanax or Tylenol PM to his sleep cocktail. Of course, it didn't help that he could not stop thinking of that beautiful creature as he laid in bed.

He thought of her touch on his cheek and the way she looked at him. In that moment he thought he had experienced something that had previously been foreign to him. He didn't know what to call it but whatever it was made him want to see her again so much so that he was looking forward to going to the house that had previously set his nerves on edge. He had even prayed if she wasn't there that God would somehow make their paths cross again.

Yes, he knew he was being ridiculous. When Jack had asked him why he seemed almost giddy during their workout the previous evening he lied and said it was because he started taking trenbelone. There was no way he could explain what happened nor how he felt to his workout partner. It was true that workout partners held a special bond, but Jack would think he was crazy and tell him he needed a cheat day. He didn't need a cheat day, he wasn't so calorie deficient that he was off his rocker. He simply "met" someone who fascinated him to no end. Someone who stirred long dormant emotions in his soul.

He got dressed and at the last second grabbed his keys. He realized for the first time that he was becoming forgetful. It was way too early in the contest prep to be in a prep fog. Prep fog occurred when you had been in a calorie deficit for so long and were at such a low body fat that your brain did not work as well as it once had. You became forgetful, couldn't pay attention, and the simplest of problems became difficult. He worried that he was becoming forgetful not because of any calorie deficit but simply because of his age. He wasn't a spring chicken anymore and really had not been one in quite some time.

Don stuffed his keys in the pocket of his sweats and started heading out on his morning walk. After about a hundred yards, he had to stop and adjust his keys in his pocket because they were irritatingly rubbing his leg. In Korea he had started a fifty mile march with a bayonet that was rubbing his leg in a similar fashion. By the time they took their first break the bayonet had rubbed through his pant leg and had started erasing away layers of skin. He moved the bayonet to a new spot, but the wound was already open and it promptly got infected which most wounds did in Korea. He still had a scar on the outside of his thigh from the ordeal.

He couldn't take a straight path to the house because he was unsure exactly where it was. He had a roundabout idea and would recognize the streets when he got close. He felt himself walking faster as if there was a force pulling him to the house. He was so certain that she would be there with her yellow cart. He wondered if she was the girl he had seen pushing a cart the morning his trash picker lost his mind and said his girlfriend was dead. Don thought it odd that he hadn't seen them since. It only made sense that homeless people picked up and moved often. That thought gave him a jolt. What if yesterday morning was the last time that the girl and her dog planned on being around his neighborhood? Maybe the whole horde was moving to another part of town.and he indeed would never see her again. He frowned and felt sad. He needed to see her again.

He turned onto a street and saw the old 50s Buick Roadmaster on jack stands and knew he was close. He had previously used that rusted out old car as a reference point to stay off that street—now he saw it as a beacon. He walked down the street and was struck by the smell. It was the smell of a car in serious trouble: brakes locked up, hoses and belts burning, oil dripping onto a hot exhaust and frying. And suddenly the uneasiness of being around the house came back. Don had covered all the bad mojo from being near the house up with the thought he would find the girl there who had mesmerized him the previous morning. The bad was resurfacing in a big way as he got closer.

It struck Don as odd that he didn't have any smell associated with the girl but the house challenged his olfaction with a full on assault. The smell of decay and rot made Don gag. He took a step onto the driveway and human excrement and body odor joined the dance party. He paused for a moment to give his sense of smell time to adjust and to get used to the affront. He stood in the driveway and looked for the yellow cart. It was nowhere to be seen. His spirits were plummeting and he was regretting coming back to the house. However, he had to be sure.

He took a few steps up the driveway and the nauseating smells increased. It was like all the odors were being forced into his nasal cavities. Don looked up at the porch and took the little sidewalk in that direction.

Rot, decay, shit and urine came to the forefront leaving the wrecked car behind but not forgotten. He took another step. Almost to the porch. Then he gave up his protein shake and heaved a few more times for good measure.

Fuck, Don's inner voice grunted, *now you're screwing up the contest prep. What the hell are you doing? What are you chasing and why? Have you become so desperate that the touch from a homeless woman has you putting contest prep in jeopardy? Hell, she is probably a prostitute. A filthy $20 whore! Get the hell away from the house!* He wretched again. He momentarily wondered if any of this was even real or was it some made up scenario to keep him from the girl and make him focus on contest prep.

"What the fuck man?" A kid, no more than a teenager came out of the house and onto the porch to question why Don was puking so close to his home. He was tall and life had not been kind to him, but Don still was able to recognize his youth.

"I thought I heard someone yelling for help inside," he lied. "The smells just overwhelmed me."

"You need to get out of here. This is no place for you."

"Have you seen a girl with a dog? She was pushing a yellow cart." Don said still fighting the nausea.

The kid tilted his head back as if what Don said had surprised him. He collected himself and said, "Ain't no girls here. We come here and do smack and get out of the weather."

"I saw a yellow cart here a couple of times. Then I saw a girl pushing the yellow cart. I have something of hers that I would like to give her," lying was getting easier. Probably because he was pretty sure he was being lied to.

"Listen man. I don't know what you're talking about." He shook his head and started to turn around to go back inside.

"Maybe I could just have a look inside," Don said his voice cracking, completely unsure of himself. He felt his fingers trembling and his insides spasm. He was normally confident and tough in almost any situation. The smells were acting like his Kryptonite. *Why the hell do you want to go inside a burned out crack house. Have you truly lost your mind?*

An older black man joined the kid on the porch. "Get out of here. Unless you got $20. If you do, I'll bend you over this rail and call you cracker faggot while I pound your ass with my big black cock."

Don was feeling sicker by the moment. If they decided to attack him he would be done for. He didn't think he could defend himself. They would take his keys and phone, find his house, rob him blind and probably steal his car. Maybe even rape him. He muttered ok and backed his way to the street. They watched him go, staring at him curiously. The house had beaten him again. It was house three, Don zero. He had gotten closer to it this time. Next time he would unlock its secrets. *No, there isn't going to be a next time. You have a pro card to win and this foolishness isn't worth giving that up for. Have some basic common sense unless you really want to be that black guy's bitch. Is that what you want? Is that what it has come down to? Are you so afraid you're not going to do well that you are trying to self sabotage the prep?*

I need to find the girl he thought and she is somehow connected with that house. *You're a freaking moron.* He was far enough away that he felt comfortable turning his back on the house and walking quickly away. He instantly felt better when he could breathe in deeply without gagging. He thought how he was stressing himself out when one of his goals for this prep was no stress. He was inviting stress, he was pursuing stress and for absolutely no good reason. No, you don't need to find the girl he told himself. *If you did you would probably find that she isn't anything like you remembered. She would be no different than any of the other homeless crack whores begging for dollars and cigs outside the convenience stores at night. Be content with the fond memory and let it go. It's for the best.* And Don finally agreed with himself.

He looked at his Fitbit and was behind in time and steps. He picked up his pace as he came to Broome Park. He would walk around the baseball field and then head home. The field was a genuine diamond in the rough. A well-manicured and cared for baseball field in the midst of a dying neighborhood. He knew teams traveled many miles to play at Broome Park, but he was certain they kept their doors locked upon arriving and leaving.

He thought nothing of the barking dog in the distance. There were many dogs in Flint that spent their lives at the end of a chain and never enjoyed the comforts of being in a home. The blonde girl he liked who volunteered at the animal shelter had told him horrible stories about the way animals were treated in Flint. He marveled at her willingness to care and nurse dogs back to health. She took in and loved many foster dogs as well as going around the city making sure dogs had food, water and some shelter from the weather. He thought she had a heart of gold and was good looking to boot. She was much more, and real, then the homeless girl pushing a shopping cart in Flint.

This time the dogs bark was closer, substantially closer. He turned toward the sound and coming from the woods behind the ballpark was a pit bull. No, not any pit bull. The girl's pit bull. He recognized its shorter legs and thickly muscled torso from a distance. It was carrying something in its mouth. Not once did it cross Don's mind that the charging dog might be coming to attack him. He dropped to one knee as it got closer. The dog dropped whatever it was holding in its mouth, barked and ran off from where it came.

Don yelled after the dog: "Come here, boy. Good boy, come here." He whistled a few times but the dog was not coming and disappeared out of sight. Don was riding a roller coaster of emotions that peaked at hopeful and dove to the depths of despair and back and forth again several times.

He thought the dog was a sure sign that he would see her again. It ran off with his hopes back into the woods. He thought about trying to follow it and he realized that would have been futile. He walked up to see what it had been holding in its mouth. It looked like some rag or torn piece of clothing. He was about to dismiss it as randomness but there was something purposeful about the way the dog approached him, dropped it and barked before running off.

Don picked up the rag between his thumb and forefinger. He rotated it a couple of times. It didn't appear to be anything but an old soiled white t-shirt that was wet from the dog's slobber. Then he noticed it had writing on it. Written neatly with a black sharpie were the words: "I'll see you in two weeks--Alless".

Nine

July 3, 59 Days Out, 195 pounds

For ten days, since the dog left him the message in a bottle in the form of a tattered t-shirt, Don had questioned over and over every aspect of this girl who called herself Alless. How was she going to meet him in two weeks? When and where was she going to meet him? Was there more information on the t-shirt that he had over looked? Why hadn't he kept the t-shirt? Why did they have to wait two weeks to meet? Was she checking into some quick detox clinic? Was she getting her shit together? Was she leaving a past life behind and needed time to readjust? Was she really wanting to meet him or was this just a ploy to keep him from looking for her for a couple of weeks so she could get out of dodge?

The deeper questions were about himself. Why was he infatuated with a girl who was likely homeless? Why couldn't he stop thinking about her? Was she really as he remembered her? Was it the rain and the darkness that made her alluring? Would he be highly disappointed if he did see her again? Was she worth putting his prep in jeopardy? Was he having some kind of Pretty Woman fantasy? Had her touch really felt electric or was it just some static discharge from the weather? With all the girls he knew and had put on hold for this prep why was someone who had never even spoken to him captivating his every thought?

There were so many questions and so very few answers. However, even though Alless was always on his mind, Don had a renewed focus and intensity towards his prep. His walks had been more purposeful and not filled with distractions. His diet was spot on and he had one last cheat meal scheduled for the Fourth of July. What had benefitted the most was his training. He had a pent up energy that exploded during his workouts. It could have been the trenbelone but Don thought it was more likely because of Alless and the fact that he had to wait so long to see her again. It was foreign to him. It was the day and age of instant contact. You texted someone and got a reply right away. Having no contact for two weeks was an aberration! But there was nothing he could do about it except focus on his prep. And he had, but time seemed to be dragging.

Don sat in the empty gym. It had closed early to the public for the holiday, but the owner had given Don a key so he could continue to train at the same time every day. Don took two scoops of his favorite preworkout, Cracked Gold by Dark Labs, and swallowed it with a minimal amount of water. Cracked Gold was intense and gave him great focus, unreal energy and an unusual sense of euphoria. The euphoria was very much the same feeling that Alless' touch had given him. He shook his head and laughed aloud. *Everything comes back to a girl you encountered once on a dark street in the very early morning hours. You're ridiculous!*

Jack's 2022 black and blue Camaro pulled into the empty lot. Don went and let him in the gym making sure the door was locked behind him. He didn't want someone to wander in and then he would have to tell them the gym was closed. To which they would give Don a dirty look and wonder why he was there.

Jack and Don made minimal small talk and then got right to it. They set up a hack squat machine with bands. The bands made the load lighter as it descended downward. Don loved banded hack squats because he felt they attacked his legs through the whole range of motion. Without the bands the weight was either too heavy on the bottom portion of the movement or too light at the top of the movement. They started with two forty-five pound plates per side and did three reps. After each set they added another forty-five pound plate per side keeping the reps at three until eventually they had nine plates per side. They both stretched between sets and did unweighted sissy squats. Finally, it was time for their working set.

"Does ten seem reasonable," Don asked Jack.

"No, three seemed reasonable, but let's fucking go!" Jack said and smacked the row of 45 pound plates with the palm of his hand. Don pulled out his iPhone and set it on the bench. He found Guns N Roses "Welcome to the Jungle" in his iTunes and turned it up as loud as it would go. He got into the hack squat machine and yelled "mother fucker" at the top of his lungs before raising the weight off the supports and moving them out of the way. The first three reps were hard, but not so hard that Don didn't think he couldn't get ten. He did two more before pausing at the top with his legs ever so slightly bent. He sucked in a large gulp of air and on shaky legs got two more reps before pausing again.

"C'mon! Three more," Jack screamed and positioned himself to the side where he could assist in raising the weight if necessary.

Don's lungs were burning and it felt like his heart was pounding out of his chest. His legs were pumped and full of blood under his red sweat pants. He took a couple of quick breaths and dropped down. With everything he had he drove the weight back up. "That's it," he hissed and started to rerack the load.

"Fuck that!" Jack screamed. "You have a fucking contest to win! You have a pro card to earn. Now quit being a bitch and earn it. Two more! I haven't even helped yet."

Don tried to take a couple of more deep breaths but his lungs weren't exactly cooperating. He threw his head back and lowered the weight. He yelled out as he slowly pushed the weight back up with Jack's assistance. He lowered himself again and again pushed the weight up with increasing help from Jack.

"Great job!" Jack exclaimed.

"Fuck that! One more. Work harder!" Don yelled his face red and visible veins crisscrossing his forehead. Had he been looking at Jack he might have second guessed the decision to do eleven because Jack's face told of a man who was entirely unsure whether or not he could give enough assistance for Don to get one more rep. Don sucked in as much air as his lungs would allow before lowering the carriage all the way to the bottom supports. He tried to explode upwards. Jack was screaming something Don couldn't understand. Don pushed until he thought his eyeballs were going to explode out of his head. He knew the weight was moving upwards. He could feel it. And finally after what seemed an eternity he made it to the top. He racked the weight and collapsed on the platform.

Don's lungs gasped for air. His heart thumped quickly and loudly in his ears. His legs ached and burned and no matter where he rolled to or where he put them he couldn't get comfortable. He staggered to his feet, a pool of sweat on the platform in his wake, and stumbled, holding on to various machines along the way, to the big industrial sized fan. He turned it on and stood in front of it. He was not only trying to cool his overheated body; he was also trying to force air into his lungs. He looked down at the sweat dripping off his face and saw that it was tinted with red. He reached up to discover that his nose was bleeding.

Once he was able to breathe again without great difficulty he found some paper towels and pinched his nose closed. It didn't take long to stop the bleeding. He cleaned up the bloody puddle and peeled off his sweat pants. He stood by the counter in a red t-shirt and black and red shorty-shorts. He couldn't wear those shorts without thinking about Larry the Cable Guy and his bit on short shorts. Despite everything it made him grin.

"You ok?" he heard Jack ask. Ok? Maybe. At least he finally felt comfortable enough to assure himself that he wasn't going to die. He stood up tall and flexed his quadriceps. They looked massive and a multitude of thick veins ran throughout the entire surface of his leg. Jack looked at them in astonishment before pronouncing Don the Quadfather.

"Your legs look the best I've ever seen them. They're pumped to the max and you still have deep separation," Jack said pointing to the separation that defined each of the four muscles in the quadriceps. "And the vascularity is out of this world. You're going to have the best legs on that stage!"

Don was very happy with the way his legs were looking. He flexed and posed them for a couple of minutes before returning to the hack squat to help Jack with his set. Jack did six and tapped out. They proceeded to do leg extensions, hip abductors, lying and seated leg curls for a couple of drop sets on each. They were both sweating profusely when Don declared that he had enough. Jack concurred and they sat on the bench with their postworkout shakes.

"That set of hacks nearly killed me," Don professed.

"It was mostly all you. There just isn't anywhere to grab and help when we have nine plates on each side. I was worried you were going to bottom out and not get back up."

"It was stupid to do that last one. That is how people get hurt in prep."

Jack rubbed his chin and asked, "Is it how people get hurt or how people win championships?"

Don took a long drink of his shake, stopping just before brain freeze would occur. He swallowed and said, "I don't know. There is a fine line between going hard as fuck and getting injured. You think of the guys who trained insane, Platz, Yates and Warren and they had a lot of serious injuries. But the guys who believed in stimulate not annihilate seemed to have relatively injury free careers. Maybe there is something to the thought of work smarter not harder."

"Says the guy with hashtag work harder on all his shirts."

"I just don't want to get to a show and wonder if I could have worked harder or wonder if someone out worked me."

"Hey buddy," Jack said seriously, "I don't think there is anyone who out works you. I'm with you day in and day out and I'm always amazed at the effort you give. For fuck sakes some of your warm up sets are harder than most people are willing to go on their all out sets."

Don smiled. He did take pride in how hard he worked—he always had. He never felt he was a gifted athlete, but felt he could make up for it by practicing more and practicing harder. "Thanks Jack. And the reason you're my workout partner is because I know you'll go hard right alongside of me and you're not even training for a contest."

"All right well let's not start sucking each other's dicks and getting all emotional," Jack said and finished his shake.

"I love you man," Don said reaching out for him.

"You sir, don't even know what love is. To quote Carla from Vision Quest 'Love is more than a hard cock.'"

"That's not what she said!" Don said while laughing.

"Close enough, Pal! I gotta get home. See you tomorrow?"

"Yes, same bat time same bat channel! I'm going to stay and do some posing practice," Don said knowing he had to really ramp up his posing practice.

"Since when did posing become a euphemism for jerking off?"

"Ha! Jerking off only takes a few minutes. I'll be posing for an hour!"

Jack laughed and walked out. He yelled "the doors unlocked" as he made his way through the doors.

Don waved. His legs ached and were tired. He wasn't ready to move. He thought about what Jack had said "you don't even know what love is". While he certainly thought that way sometimes he didn't like it that others thought that of him. He remembered reading somewhere that psychopaths were almost completely incapable of love even though they often craved love from others. That had bothered him for a long time. He didn't want to think of himself as a psychopath or even a narcissist. He really and truly wanted to experience love that would manifest itself in a long and lasting relationship.

A thought waifed across his consciousness: maybe this odd feeling you feel towards Alless is love. And his thoughts began to wrestle with themselves.

What? No. Certainly not. How would you fall in love with someone who you've only seen once? What about love at first sight? Poppycock! It happens. I don't believe in it. People fall in love who have never met each other in person. That's nonsense. Is it? Explain why she is all I've thought about? Because it was an odd occurrence and I'm curious. I think you're scared. Scared! Scared of what? Scared that the woman you have finally fallen in love with is a homeless prostitute. If she is a prostitute I will not love her, have you not read Walpole: "It is sinful to cherish those whom heaven has doomed to destruction." Now my turn to say poppycock!

Don buried his face in his hands. This was agonizing. He wondered if other people had outrageous debates warring in their own minds. For him it was a common occurrence and it seemed he always chose the path to misery. He remembered reading a quote from Viktor Rote once about making poor decisions. The quote read:

"I stumbled into my choices like a drunk down the steps of a bar. With the same clarity I made decision after decision. I didn't worry about making bad decisions because I was certain that each decision I made was the worst possible one. I blamed insomnia, I blamed depression, hell I even pointed the finger at God quite often. But in the end I realized the poor decisions stemmed from a lack of creativity to be someone different than who everyone thought I should be."

Right away, his mind jumped to another Viktor Rote quote where the man tried ending his agony by killing himself only to realize he was already dead. He thought hard and pulled the quote from the many files tucked in the deep recesses of his mind:

"Xavier Bonaparte walked through his garden and noticed two beautiful flowers fighting over the same fertile ground. He realized that if he left them alone they would choke each other out and both would die. He retrieved his garden shears because he knew he had to cut one of them down. He agonized over which one to cut down; after all, he had planted and cultivated both of them. After several hours of being indecisive, Xavier plunged the garden shears deep into his own heart. He was shocked that it didn't kill him, and then he realized he had already been dead."

Sometimes he thought death would be an easy option. Then remembered Twilight Zone episodes, Alice Cooper songs, countless movies and basic theology that made him reconsider and think an afterlife quickened because you killed yourself might not be all that great.

Enough! He forced himself to stand and went and locked the door. He had to focus on posing practice and retreated to the room of mirrors at the back of the gym. For the next hour he practiced without pause exorcising any other thoughts from his mind. His lean muscular body glistened with sweat as he posed only in his shorty-shorts. He would make himself too tired to think. However, when he was done he did think: In a few days I will get to see her.

Ten

July 7, 55 Days Out, 194 pounds

Christmas in July they say. Last night certainly felt like Christmas Eve to Don as he tossed and turned awaiting the morning Alless had said she would see him. His new sleep cocktail of Trazodone and Tylenol PM wasn't even enough to put him out and contain the excitement of seeing her in the morning. Well, really, she hadn't said morning but he assumed he would run into her during his morning walk. He had determined that he would skirt as close to the burnt house as possible without actually going down that street. He wanted to make himself easy to find. He wore black and orange NPC sweat pants and his black and orange hoodie with the tribal pit bull head and the phrase #WorkHarder. He might have even went out of his way to make himself smell better. *Is this a walk for contest prep or a date for some irresponsible fantasy?*

He walked with his head on a swivel. He didn't want to miss her. Don hadn't been this excited in a long time—a fact that made him think his life must be pretty dull. He tried to think positively but there was that annoying voice that warned him the likelihood of her actually finding him or him finding her was minimal. There was a good chance she was in another town or even the morgue. He absolutely didn't want to think that way.

Don tried to redirect his mind and thought how he needed to call and set up his tanning appointment for the contest. Tanning was a necessary and expensive evil. If you weren't expertly tanned you were going to wash out under the stage lights. He thought it was money well spent and he would let the experts take care of it. Over his years of competing, Don had seen guys still trying to do their tan themselves. Most of them looked like they were painted at best and a streaky runny mess at worst.

Getting tanned by a professional was a unique experience. It was something to stand in a small tent, naked in a room full of other small tents and get cold spray tan applied to you by a professional who was usually a female. Every time Don got spray tanned, he heard in a George Costanza voice, "she knows about shrinkage, right?" The second time he got tanned was the worst. The woman doing the tanning wanted him to cover his penis with a sock. He laughed and said, "isn't being naked humiliating enough?" She wasn't amused and grabbed him a sock from what he hoped was a box of clean socks in the middle of the room. It was so cold and he was so depleted that the sock just would not stay on. Finally, after it fell off for the third time the girl simply said, "Leave it off, you don't need it." It was quite the humiliating experience.

It was always humiliating when they told him to face the rear of the tent and do the bikini pose with his glutes, Something touched his hand. Don felt himself jump and looked to see Alless had come along side of him and taken his hand in hers. In the other hand was the rope that led to her ever-faithful companion.

"You scared me," he said. She didn't reply and for the first time he wondered if she couldn't talk. She was a mute and that was why she was homeless. She had fallen through the system and didn't get any help from social services. For all he knew she was also deaf! She had looked at the dog when it yawned but maybe that was because she caught his head movement out of the corner of her eye. People lacking certain senses were supposed to have super senses in the other areas. He thought all of this while he was thoroughly enjoying how her hand felt in his. Her hand was small and surprisingly soft. He couldn't quite describe the feeling of happiness that simply holding her hand was giving him. It was completely unexpected. It was as if he had waited his whole life to hold a hand like hers. As much as he thought about her and seeing her again he never really thought about what would happen when he did actually see her. Alless taking his hand seemed a natural way for them to avoid the awkwardness of really meeting for the first time. They walked in silence.

When they reached a point between streetlights and under the cover of darkness she stopped walking. His momentum with her holding his hand pulled him around so that he ended up facing her. She looked even more exotic, more beautiful, than he had remembered. The hood on her hoodie was still up but her hair seemed fuller and less stringy poking out around the hoodie. Her eyes still seemed perpetually lined which was unusual for someone with such fair skin and light colored hair and eyes. Her lips were a deep cherry red and shaped in what magazines called rounded Cupid's Bow lips. Yes, he had googled "perfect lips" several times since he had last seen her.

They stared into each other's eyes. His icy blue eyes and her dazzling green eyes locked together silently conversing a language that only they could understand. Don felt butterflies in his stomach and he had a strange melting sensation in his heart. It melted away from him and became hers to hold and protect. He didn't know how long they stood there and looked at each other; time seemed irrelevant to him. He was aware of nothing else in the world other than her gaze and the feelings gently flowing through his body and mind. He could have stayed like that forever. Don could feel himself start to breath harder as his heart beat was strong enough that he was sure Alless could feel and hear it.

Slowly, very slowly the corners of her lips started to turn up. He watched enraptured by the way her beautiful full lips parted and became a smile. He thought she was pretty, but when she was smiling, she was absolutely stunning. The smile gave her a plus two. So if she was a seven when not smiling she was a 9 when she did. And then she spoke. She spoke with a voice that was light and sweet and something he instantly knew he could never grow tired of hearing. "Don't be nervous, Don."

Pulled in by the symphony of her vocal chords Don was unable to wonder how she knew he was nervous or how she knew his name. He wanted her to speak again. He wanted to hear that voice as they laid on a blanket under a clear starry night away from the rest of the world. Under the hypnotic melody that Don called her voice was his inner being screaming: *She is siren pull away before she leads you to destruction.*

Alless reached down and took his other hand. They stood facing each other as if they were ready for a forbidden nighttime ceremony where they would be wed despite the outcries of society. Don couldn't look away from her gaze and even though she had only said a few short words they echoed over and over in his mind. She shook both his hands in an effort to snap him out of the trance that held his every sense. And it was every sense. This time he could smell her and she smelled of heliotrope. He could almost see the beautiful purple flowers in the cherry and vanilla scent that passed through his nose and lead directly to his heart. The inner voice screamed, *it's probably aconite!* He ignored the voice and knew at once when he finally touched her lips with his she would taste of cherry pie.

He wanted to scream out that he loved her. He wanted the world to know. He wanted her to know that she was his forevermore.

"Don," she said and squeezed his hands gently. The dreamlike state he had fallen into lifted and he found his faculties working again.

"I'm sorry," he said, "but I've never met anyone as captivating as you." In the darkness and through the dirt on her cheeks he could see a slight blush building.

"Hug me," she said and moved toward him. He pulled her close. She was light and frail in his arms. She squeezed him and held him tightly. He realized she was what society would consider short, but he too was on the shorter side and her height was perfect for him. She buried her face into his chest and shoulder. He thought for a moment that she was crying, but she was just nuzzling him—trying to get as close as she could. He would hold her as long as she desired.

Alless pulled her head back and he lowered his face towards hers. There was nothing agonizing in the slow manner in which their lips approached. The anticipation grew and grew. It was something Don wanted more than anything, but also something he could wait forever for. He felt her sweet breath on his face. He wondered how such a beautiful creature could roam the city and be cursed as a filthy vagabond and be lumped in with the dregs of society. Their lips touched together perfectly and with no sense of awkwardness. It was as if they were used to kissing each other and had never kissed another.

A raven passed overhead and landed on an electric pole. It ominously turned its head from side to side. The wet croak of the raven came from deep down in its throat and filled the early morning sky. The dog followed with a low growl that transitioned into a high-pitched bark. Alless pulled away from Don. "I'm sorry! I have to go," she said and her beautiful voice now hinted at danger.

"What's wrong? Let me help you!" Don pleaded.

"I will see you again. I promise." She looked down at the dog and in a voice more harsh said, "Come Omega, let's go".

"Wait," he cried after her and almost blurted out I love you. He watched her go. He wanted to chase after her. He wanted to know what caused her to suddenly run off. He had hoped their meeting that morning would answer some of the questions he had, but instead the questions only increased. She moved quickly and silently into the blackness and out of his range of vision. He thought he must be dreaming or having a nightmare.

Don took a deep breath. She said she would see him again, but this time he had no date to hang his hat on. He stood in that spot for a long time replaying that kiss. First kisses were something you remembered. Almost everyone could recall where and when they first kissed someone who was important to them. He had kissed quite a few girls, although, probably fewer than most people would have guessed, and he could say with certainty that Alless' kiss was the greatest he ever experienced. Often the first kiss was kind of awkward and surprising. His kiss with Alless was nothing of the sort. And the way they slowly moved into each other was amazing.

Don's thoughts on the rest of his walk were a cornucopia of what ifs and what could be. Pleasing thoughts about a romance that might be, a relationship that could be, and finally a love that he hoped would be. Oh, it was quite ridiculous to say love in conjunction with someone he knew absolutely nothing about. Don didn't know how else to describe what he was feeling. It was something he had never felt before and something he wanted to feel over and over again.

Don sat in his lazy boy upon returning home. He wanted to take a moment and decompress before showering and getting ready for the day. It was then that the dark clouds swept in front of his bright sunny outlook and cast a gray pall over his roses and rainbows.

You still know nothing at all about this girl! For fuck's sake you're not even sure how to pronounce her first name which is the only name you have for her. You might be completely wrong and Alless might be her last name or even a made up name. And how do you feel about a girl that would hug you and kiss you like that and doesn't know anything about you? Sure, you're trying to live out some repressed fantasy—is that what she is trying to do as well. Or maybe she senses a free ride and before you know it you'll have a drug addict with three times your mental issues living with you. And guess what? You won't be able to get rid of her—she will milk you dry physically, emotionally, spiritually and financially! Here's one bud, what if she isn't a girl at all, but a crossdresser or transgender? Are you going to be ok with that? What will all your gym friends think of you being with a queer? Hell, what will all your gym friends think about you being in love with some homeless floozy that again you know nothing about?

Don tried to derail his train of thought by muttering aloud that he wasn't sure he loved her to which his train of thought jumped all over.

You're not sure, sport? Here is a clue, you should be sure you don't love her. You have nothing to base that emotion on other than a stiffening cock just like Jack said! What is her motivation? You're not exactly attractive. Your best feature is your body and she hasn't even seen that yet. Unless…unless she has been spying on you. She did know your name and you sure as heck never told her it. Maybe she has been casing you like a thief studies a jewelry store. She knows all the right buttons to your emotional safe so she can get exactly what she wants. She is going to play you for all you're worth and then cast you aside like trash to be picked through by homeless people like her!

Don's voice in his head was sounding like Sam Kinison's voice had when he was alive and did a rant bit about how messed up society was.

Four months ago you were bitching about homeless people begging for a dollar or stinking up the public library. Now you claim a great emotional catharsis in the arms of the very same kind you had cursed? Did it occur to you that none of this is as it seems. Maybe someone is playing a Shallow Hal mind fuck on you and you're the only one that doesn't think she is some nasty street skank. You're not a princess and she isn't a frog. And even if it were true you've already kissed her and guess what? No change, bub. She is still what she is although you may be a little more defiled. God knows if you've caught some disease or bugs. You might want to throw those clothes out.

"Jesus!" Don slammed his hand on the armrest of his lazy boy and stood up. The inner voice disappeared and its demons skittered off with it. "Why is everything so hard for me?" Don muttered. "Everyone else gets to experience love, why not me?" He looked at his Fitbit. It was time to eat meal number two. Eating and training were the only effective means of keeping his mind off of her and the many emotions and questions that swirled and twisted around in his cerebral cortex.

Eleven

July 12, 50 Days Out, 194 pounds

How did I lose my keys, Don thought as he rummaged through his tiny office at the Flint Campus for Transformation. It was a non-profit home for teenage boys who were likely headed for a life of crime if left to their own devices. The Campus for Transformation hoped to intervene and set up these youth for successful adulthood. They welcomed in court appointed students on a first come first serve basis. The campus was home to a maximum of one hundred students. Don's employer was brought on board to not only alleviate loneliness but to do so through educational literature. It was one thing to find a book that he thought a teenager might like to read. It was on a whole different level to find one that was also what the campus might find educational.

Don was under the impression that every book was educational. If you were reading you were increasing your intelligence no matter what the content of the book was. The heads of education at the Campus didn't want the kids reading scary, violent or racist novels. Don didn't waste his time informing them that this would cross off most of the classics and the

Holy Bible from the reading list. He had learned long ago that arguing with people with advanced pedagogy degrees was fruitless and did nothing but soil their opinion of you. He simply said ok and gave the students books he thought they would read. He would pay the piper if a student ever did anything wrong and pointed to one of the books handed out by Mr. Ream as a reason for their indiscretion. It was a risk he was willing to take.

"Mr. Ream, Mr. Ream," Justin Willard yelled running down the hall to his office. Justin was at the Campus for multiple petty thefts that the justice department was sure were going to turn into future hardcore crimes. Don didn't have any formal training in social behaviors but his opinion of Justin was one of a lonely kid acting out to get attention. Now that didn't mean he wouldn't someday commit a violent crime, but Don thought sticking him in a place with violent kids his age was probably not going to help the situation.

"Not so loud, Justin."

"I was worried I missed you. You're not around here as much as you used to be," the fourteen year old African American boy said and smiled. It was true. Since he started contest prep he had dialed back his visits at facilities. Before prep he thought nothing of 50-60 hour work weeks, but now he was trying to manage a forty hour work week. "Well did you get it," Justin pleaded excitedly.

Don went to his desk which seemed to be a leftover from a bygone era when steel and wood ruled the day. He opened the top drawer and felt like he was doing an underhand row with the effort it took as rusted steel rubbed on rusted steel. He pulled out a tattered paperback and handed it to Justin. "Here you go! Now remember the deal. Don't flaunt it in front of everyone and use the prison parts as motivation to keep you out of prison."

Justin turned the forty-five year old paper back in his hands. The edges of the paper were yellowed and the cover had several scuff marks on it. He had wanted to read this book since Mr. Ream told him about it. He slowly read the words: "One in a Million: The Ron LeFlore Story". Ron LeFlore had been a troubled youth on the streets of Detroit and ended up being sentenced to prison for armed robbery. He played on the prison baseball team where he was discovered by one of the all-time great managers, Billy Martin. Martin had worked with the prison to get LeFlore paroled and signed him to a minor league contract. A few years later Leflore was playing in Major League Baseball's All-Star game.

"Two things I want you to remember about that book," Don said waving a finger at Justin. "One, LeFlore didn't let the mistakes he made in his youth keep him from becoming a success as an adult. And two, when you are having success don't forget your responsibilities. Now, it doesn't mention it in the book but LeFlore had a very embarrassing arrest at the closing ceremonies at Tiger Stadium and then later at an autograph signing for not paying child support. Take your responsibilities very seriously whether you are extremely successful or not. Got it?"

"Yes, sir," Justin said with a big smile on his face.

"Keep practicing. Keep your nose clean. There are millions and millions of people. LeFlore was one in a million, but you can be too."

"Thanks. I'll see you later." And with that Justin was off and running. He ran fast just like the man in the book he held once had. Don smiled to himself. Justin wasn't going to read Paradise Lost or anything like that, but Don was sure Justin would read One in a Million from cover to cover.

Now where are my keys, Don thought. As the contest prep progressed Don was finding himself becoming annoyingly forgetful. Most things he did on autopilot and that was ok, but if he varied from the norm, he often seemed lost. He moved around a bunch of different books on his desk to see if the keys somehow made it under them. In the pile were some of his favorites: The Strange Case of Dr. Jekyll and Mr. Hyde, Frankenstein,

Call of the Wild, Slaughterhouse Five, and Catcher in the Rye to name a few. With each book he had written a paper on why that book would be useful to a troubled and lonely teen.

Don thought about books and he wondered if Alless read much, if at all. He thought being homeless would be ideal for having time to read. There were several places in Flint that gave away free books. One of the parks had a neat little set up called the Free Library. It was a little enclosed stand where people could drop off or pick up books any time they wanted. He imagined he was wrong about the homeless having a lot of time to read; they probably spent most of their waking hours looking for or begging for resources.

The not so quiet voice saw an opportunity to chime in. *You know, you don't even know she is homeless. She could be married and living in a house down the street from you. You literally know nothing about her. Yet, she occupies most of your thought. You should be watching videos on peak week and deciding how you're going dial yourself in and instead you're replaying a kiss over and over in your mind. How many girls have you kissed? Why is this one so different? And don't you dare start spouting off about love and maybe this is the one or any of that nonsense that has been running through your mind as of late.*

Why couldn't she be the one, Don countered. There is obviously a connection between us that transcends what most people who have spent their whole lives together have. We are assuredly captivated by one another. And you're right we may not have had long discourses about meaningful things, but what is silently communicated between us when we are together is deeper than a bunch of mindless chit-chat.

You know if you two are so in love why haven't you told anyone about her. You have an appointment with your therapist coming up, tell her. Let her hear how you've fallen head over heels in love with a homeless crack whore who follows around a bunch of other crackheads looking for a way to get more crack.

She hardly looks like a crack whore.

She has had on the same clothes both times you've seen her. Did you hear what I said? Both times you've seen her. You've only seen her twice!

I wear the same clothes a lot. It doesn't make me a crack whore.

Get a grip man! I wish you could listen to yourself.

Ummmm...you know you are me and I do listen to myself. Did you ever consider that I want to experience something magical, something out of a fairy tale, something extraordinary so badly that I will chase a stranger all over the streets of Flint looking for it? Is it wrong that I want to feel the way that these old widowed men in facilities felt about their wives? I want the love that everyone but me seems to experience. I want the love even if it ends in a Shakespearian tragedy. It is true that it is better to have loved and lost than having never loved at all. I want to miss someone the minute I walk away. And as crazy as it might sound I fucking miss Alless!

The inner voice skittered back into the shadows of Don's mind. He took a deep breath and saw his keys behind his chair against the wall. He felt old and tired. Arguing with himself was more exhausting than arguing with another person. Yes, the voice made many good points, but he knew what he was longing for at this stage in his life. He didn't want another relationship of convenience or complacency. He wanted something special—something that would change his life.

He got out to his Lincoln and cranked the AC. It was time to get to the gym. Tuesday was triceps day—a body part he loved working. He felt like an old blacksmith pounding out horseshoes in the forge when he trained triceps. He was also at the point in his prep where he noticed changes almost daily. There seemed to be more definition, a new vein sticking out, or deeper separation every time he looked in the mirror. He was progressing nicely, but there were some concerns.

His resting heart rate was steadily increasing. When he started the prep it was at sixty-seven. Now he found it to be in triple digits and trending upwards. He was also dealing with a lot of shoulder and elbow pain on his right side. The list of chest and shoulder exercises he could do pain free were dwindling. He would hate to be this far into prep and have an injury or illness take him out.

Don pulled into the gym parking lot and recognized most of the cars. People tended to come at the same time of the day when they worked out and you started seeing the same cars and same people every day. Don sat in his seat and it took a monumental effort for him to get out of the car, grab his gym bag and head into the gym. The prep was really starting to wear on him. He was tired of eating according to a schedule. He was tired of eating the same things. He was tired of being tired and wanted to slam a few shots of Fireball cinnamon whiskey and sleep for twelve hours. It was the dog days of prep: deeply into it, but not so far along that you could see a light at the end of the tunnel.

He wondered what Alless' body looked like under the hoodie. She didn't feel heavy and he easily got his arms around her. He imagined she had really nice perky breast. He also entertained that she had three breast like the prostitute from the first Total Recall movie. He laughed at himself. He did thoroughly enjoy thinking about her and all the mystery surrounding her. He hoped when they talked more frequently that there would still be an aura of mystery about her. Just not as much mystery as there was now.

Don was greeted by the usual suspects upon entering the gym. It was the same comments: you look great, I don't know how you do it, I could never diet like that because I like food too much, looking skinny (which was not a compliment to him even though he was dieting). Don smiled and offered thanks or countered with "you're looking great too". He quickly did his preworkout ritual and hit the gym floor.

Don's phone buzzed. It was a text from Jack saying that his daughter was sick and he was sorry but he was going to have to miss the workout. Don texted him back that it was ok and he should be there for his daughter. And he meant it. Jack rarely missed a workout and was just about as dependable a workout partner as there was. Don could never thank him another for his help during prep. He was more than just a workout partner. He was another set of eyes. He was someone to bounce ideas off of. He was someone to give valuable input about supplements and drugs and evaluating whether or not they were working as they had predicted. Don was extremely grateful for him as a friend as well. Some friend! He doesn't even know about the love of your life. Don rolled his eyes and started warming up.

If there was a good day to not have a workout partner, it was triceps day. Don felt like less rest in-between sets caused his triceps to get a better pump. He also didn't go too heavy and therefore rarely required a spot. He would just do drop sets for maximum stimulation. He pounded out pushdowns, overhead extensions with a rope, cross body extensions and finished with kickbacks. He flexed in the mirror between sets and marveled at how big and chiseled his triceps looked. They weren't exactly horseshoes but that was genetics and nothing he could do would drastically change the shape of the muscle. He squeezed down and watched the veins fill with blood all over the inner head of his triceps.

"When is the contest," someone asked.

"I'm a little over seven weeks out."

"Shit you look ready now!"

Don smiled and said thanks as he left the gym. But he did not look ready now. The average gym person had no idea the level of conditioning it took to look good on stage. There were many guys who looked great in the gym all pumped up. They looked huge and full and even lean, but not stage lean. There was a reason that there were so few competitive bodybuilders. It took an insane commitment to look great on stage. He didn't want to minimize the work that people like JT put in—those people who looked great compared to 98% of the population. However, it was a distant effort compared to those who actually prepped for 12-16 weeks and took it seriously.

He wondered if Alless had ever been with a bodybuilder. He wondered if she even liked guys with that kind of body. He wondered when he was going to see her again. Every morning he set out on his walks with the hope he would feel her hand in his. He didn't care if they did anything else he was content to hold her hand and know that she was next to him. He wished he wasn't doing the contest. Then he could look for her at night and not have to worry about how much sleep he was getting. He could go and explore the house and not care that it might mess up his prep. But that was one thing the voice was right about—this contest needed to be his priority. He had planned and prepared for this one last shot at his pro card and he needed to be at his very best when he stepped on stage.

How cool would it be, he thought, if Alless was sitting in the audience watching him compete. He could come off stage and hug her. He could celebrate with her. She would be proud of him. He pulled into his driveway and got his gym bag, lunch bag and giant water bottle out of his car. He walked to the door fumbling with his keys so he could unlock it without putting anything down. He pulled the screen door open and a piece of paper went fluttering to the ground. It was wrinkled and stained notebook paper. On it read: Hi Don. I hope you're having a great day. I can't wait to see you again. It will happen soon. I know you have many questions and I promise someday they will all be answered. See you soon. Love, Alless

He was so excited about the note that he left his keys in the lock and didn't realize it until the next morning when he thought he was losing his mind because he couldn't find his keys.

Twelve

July 14, 48 Days Out, 193 pounds

Don must have read that letter a thousand times. Maybe more. He analyzed it, looked for hidden meanings, tried to decode it, and even held it up to the light to see if there might be a secret message etched into the paper. There wasn't. He looked for a cipher; it was too short. It was simply a fine point black marker written on scratch notebook paper seemingly in haste. It was as if she randomly passed Don's house, remembered she needed to see him and wrote a note with the materials available in that spur of the moment. No, he reassured himself the letter was intentional and meaningful. Once he subdued the inner voice of doubt he felt really good about the letter. The marker, paper and content may not have held any hidden meaning for Don, but what he believed to be the obvious meaning spoke volumes. He broke it down like he was analyzing poetry for a class he was teaching.

"Hi Don, I hope you're having a great day." She cared about him. She earnestly hoped his day was going greatly. Not a good day, but a great day. That meant she cared about him. She wanted him to be happy. She wanted his day filled with peace and not stress and anxiety. Most importantly she had spelled "You're" correctly. She was educated and smart. Not some dumb crack whore who would have written "UR", but someone with intelligence. She was also someone with hopes and dreams. She "hoped" and didn't just take life as it came but saw something to gaze towards the horizon for. She hadn't given up on life.

"I can't wait to see you again." She looked forward to seeing him. She wanted badly to see him. She longed for him. The time they had spent together was meaningful to her. She wanted to do it again. She wanted to hold his hand again. She wanted to kiss him again.

"It will happen soon." She was in charge of when they would see each other, that much was clear. She didn't give him a date but said it would be soon. Soon meant before you know it. Soon meant get ready it was about to happen. Soon meant your wait is almost over.

"I know you have many questions and I promise someday they will all be answered." Whoa! This sentence knocked his socks off. With this single sentence, she pronounced relationship and a long-term future. She again expressed how much she cared for him in that she recognized how many questions he must have. And instead of leaving him in limbo she promised that they would all be answered in time. Promise. That was a huge word. People didn't use "promise" unless they had something meaningful—something heartfelt to do or say. I won't just do it, I am putting a guarantee on it by saying "promise". In time meant that she couldn't possibly answer all his questions in one sitting, but over the course of weeks and months of seeing each other she would answer all his questions. She planned on seeing him often over a long period of time.

"See you soon." She is reiterating that she will see him and the wait is almost over. She can't say enough about how badly she wants to see him and how soon she wants it to happen. She is injecting hope into his soul in case he missed it the first time.

"Love Alless." He wouldn't go so far as proclaiming she loved him. But she was educated and could have used a dozen other words than love to close with. She might not be in love with him yet but she was open to the idea of loving him. She used a lot of romantic language with "can't wait," "promise," and "love." You didn't have to be a professor of literature to know that this wasn't a letter to a simple acquaintance or even friend. This was a letter to someone who she hoped to have a long relationship with. Someone to who with love was certainly on the table.

Please, just stop, the depressing inner voice wailed. *You're dissecting a hastily written note like it's a line from "Elene" by Cynewulf. She scribbled some words on a piece of trash and you're once again smitten to the moon. Did you ask yourself why she wrote the note instead of actually seeing you? Did she have an important sales meeting to attend to or could she not wait around because the stock market was about to close and she had to make some pressing transactions? I can't sit back and watch you blather on about some woman because of what she scribbled on a piece of trash. And does it concern you at all that she knows where you live? How does that happen? That should be what is running through your thoughts. You do realize I want what is best for you, well best for us? This contest was supposed to be your sole focus. You even sold your house so that you can focus completely on contest prep. Don't get pulled down a rabbit hole that you will later regret. Remember if you're so gaga over her tell your therapist and see what she thinks. It's time for you to get in there by the way.*

Don had been feeling pretty darn good. That was his life though. Any time he started feeling good about himself or his *sitz im Leben* he found a reason to knock himself off his pedestal. That inner voice of doubt had been with Don his whole life. Maybe that was something he should tell his therapist about. He walked into her office and she was waiting for him. It was a rarity that someone had to wait on Donald Ream.

After some very brief and uneventful small talk, Sue Edleson wanted to get down to business. She wore a conservative dress suit and her chestnut hair was pinned up in a bun. Don guessed she was his age and he did find her attractive. She was that librarian fantasy—the hot older woman that shushed you when you were grunting from having sex with her in a row of books.

They sat in a pair of Herman Miller lounge chairs that were extremely comfortable but not so comfortable you wanted to curl up and go to sleep. The office was very nondescript in a charming sort of way. It didn't demand to be looked at and analyzed. It was simply there but not so simply that you felt you were in a sterile environment. A lot of thought had gone into making the office a place where someone felt comfortable and at ease.

"Don, I'd like for us to start with a little exercise," she said looking down at some notes.

Don hated these things. He felt like data was being collected and he was being put in some type of paradigm as if he belonged in some type of group. Little did he realize that Sue didn't care at all about the exercise itself. She used them as a prompt to get Don talking. It was a way to distract him from being defensive about what she really wanted to accomplish.

"I want you to take a moment and tell me what you think your theme song would be. You know what song would you pick to tell your story. Take a few..."

"Behind Blue Eyes by The Who" he said cutting her off. He didn't need to think about it. Whenever he heard the song he couldn't help but feeling it deeply in his soul. Jumbo, the villain Townshend imagined singing it when he wrote the song, felt he was forced into the position of being a villain but thought himself to be a good guy.

"That was fast," Sue said looking at him intently, "Why do you think that?"

"I feel like in most of my relationships with women I'm put into the position of being the jerk. I think they don't think I have feelings too. Like when we break up I don't hurt too. Or they think I'm hurting them on purpose."

"I want to come back to this, but isn't it interesting that when I asked you to come up with a song that defines who you are you went right to a song that you think defines your relationships. Do you feel that your relationships define who you are as a person?"

Don didn't have a quick answer to this question. He shifted in his chair uncomfortably. "I mean it's what people think about you. You can be a great person but if everyone thinks you are a jerk what does it matter what you think. In everyone's eyes you're a jerk."

"This brings us right back to an issue we've talked about in the past. You should not put so much weight on what everyone else thinks. You certainly should not let it define who you are as a person." Sue crossed her legs and put her clasped hands on her knee. Her well-manicured pink nails were very much in tune with the look she wanted to portray.

"But I do. You can tell me I shouldn't and I can agree with you but it doesn't stop me from thinking that way. And another thing, maybe if everyone thinks you're a jerk and you think you're a great guy you're delusional and are a jerk!" Don felt he should follow that up with something more profound and Sue waited for him to do so, but he could only slowly shake his head.

"Don," Sue said compassionately, "not everyone is going to like you. I know you're a people pleaser and I know the decisions you make trying to please everyone often puts you in a position where you do the opposite and hurt everyone instead, including yourself."

Don waited for Sue to ask another question and when she didn't he felt he should say something and added, "You know, I just want to be happy."

"What makes you happy," Sue said rolling in whatever direction Don seemed to want to go. This was the way her sessions with Don often went. If she tried to steer the conversation at all he almost shut down and was very guarded. However, when she let him speak and followed him conversationally he opened up and they were able to root out some of the things that were troubling him.

"I don't even know anymore." Walking beside Alless. Holding Alless' hand. Kissing Alless. Those make me freaking happy.

Sue sensed Don was holding back and gave him space to let his thoughts come out.

"Ok. I met someone who makes me happy. I know we talked about how I should wait until I learn to deal with my guilt over the last relationship. And I was trying. I was not looking for someone at all when I met this girl. But just being with her makes me happy," Don said and twisted his face in a way that projected he was not at all happy he had shared that. He hoped she didn't ask him for details about it. If she did he was going to have to lie. Don's old psych professor in college had told him that when he did counseling he assumed that patients were lying and didn't put much stock into what they said. He said the more important thing was the stories they built. Don wondered if Sue was listening to his story.

"If you think I am going to chastise you or say to stop seeing this woman you would be highly incorrect. I think the fact that you met someone when you were not looking who makes you happy is a wonderful thing. You probably do not feel forced and are letting things happen naturally which based on what you have told me about your other relationships is a foreign concept for you. I do encourage you to really think about your last relationship and how things went so wrong and got turned upside down—not to feed your guilt, but so that you can avoid the same mistakes this time.

"Don, I know you want me to fix you. I also know you find it irritating when I tell you that you have to do the work to fix yourself. If I were to ask you what you were good at you would bang out a list of ten things without even thinking. If I asked you what you were not good at you would say 'relationships' and be done. Yet, when I asked about a song that defines you, you went right to something you are not good at and ignored all the things you are good at. Why do you think that is?

Don fidgeted in his chair and Sue worried she had said too much and lost him. As they sat in silence she was resisting the urge to lead him forward with a follow up question. He was an INTJ and she knew that he often took time processing questions. She also knew that around her he felt awkward sitting in silence. He told her once that he felt like they were wasting their time sitting in silence and he should either be telling her his troubles or she should be "fixing" him.

"I might seem like I have a lot of confidence, but I really don't. I am very self-conscious and don't think very highly of myself. I think that makes it easier for me to identify my faults."

She nodded her head to acknowledge that she was still listening. "I don't know. This contest prep was supposed to be easy. I worked extremely hard to set up everything so I was one hundred percent prepared to knock this contest prep out of the park. And I feel it is blah. I thought it would be more rewarding and maybe that is why I'm not happy." He looked at his Fitbit hoping his time with her was almost up. It was not. He was trying to think of something to say that would make the time go by faster.

"Do you feel misunderstood," Sue asked after Don looked at his watch a second time.

"Jesus!" Don blurted out. "Of course I do. You don't know how much I would love it if someone else could just experience my thoughts and feelings for just a few moments. People have no idea what I think. Everyone wants me to be in control, to be a leader. I don't want to have the answers to everything. I want other people to make decisions. Maybe I come off as arrogant or when someone else does make a decision I make them feel like an idiot for the decision they made. I know I'm not really a good person, but it doesn't mean that I'm not misunderstood."

Sue wanted to jump on him saying he wasn't a good person but she thought it more beneficial to continue down the road of him being misunderstood. "What are you doing to help others understand you? Are you expressing your thoughts and feelings to those closest to you? Does this new woman in your life know anything about you or have you begun this relationship by hiding behind the great wall of defense?"

Don almost laughed out loud. That was rich: does she know anything about him!? He knew nothing about her. And then he had an interesting thought. What if I am falling for this girl because I don't know anything about her? And when I start learning about her I will find her irritating and unlovable? Is that really what I always do? I hate that I always do the same thing. "How do you bring about change? You know, how do you stop from going back to the same old patterns and cycles?"

Sue loved the line of thinking Don was doing about himself. "You have to be intentional to break it. It will never happen on its own. You know how you prepare for a bodybuilding contest and do not leave anything to chance. That is being intentional. That is what you have to do to break old habits and get out of the same old ruts."

Don rubbed his chin. How could he be intentional about cultivating this relationship instead of sabotaging it? He was going to have to give this some serious thought. "I really have some things I want to think about so is it ok if we end a little early?"

Sue smiled. He wasn't aware at all of how much of a people pleaser he really was and how much he wanted people to like him. He could have just said this meeting is over, but he felt the need to tell her why he wanted to end it and to make sure it was ok with her. "Of course," she said. "I know your contest is coming up," she got out her newer model iPad and pulled up her schedule maker. "I have August 15th open for your next appointment. That is not too close to your contest is it? We can do nine in the morning."

"That's perfect," he said without giving it any thought. "Just send me a text reminder so that I don't forget. Thank you," he said and walked out.

Don's mind was racing. If he wanted something completely different out of a relationship than he had to treat the relationship differently. He was going to have to treat the woman differently. If he went about business as usual his relationship with Alless would likely end up the same as all of his failed relationships. He didn't want that. He could not absent-mindedly think he was doing the right things. He had to be intentional. He thought all of this on his way to the car. He got in and started the engine with a push of a button. It didn't take him long to find Behind Blue Eyes on his iTunes. He turned up the volume as the song started.

Then Don sobbed. Tears ran down his cheeks. He wanted someone to think of him as the good guy. He didn't want to be the bad guy. He didn't want to put himself in a situation where he felt the need to lie to save someone's feelings because that never worked anyway. He wanted someone to see beyond his blue eyes. To see his dreams and how badly he wanted that once in a lifetime, amazing love. He felt that he had almost had it one time and thrown it away. But when he reflected on that relationship he was appalled at how he had acted and thought, I couldn't do that to someone I loved. His nose began to run as the tears flowed freely. I want someone to feel my pain and woe and when I start back into those bad relationship habits I want someone there who will help me break them and comfort me. I so very badly want Alless to be all of that.

The song ended and so did the waterworks. Don found a napkin in his center console and blew his nose. He had to be intentional he kept

91

reminding himself. He had to break the vicious circle. Self-doubt creeped in and told him he thought the same thing before every relationship. He cranked up Billy Joel's Captain Jack to drown out the self-doubt, but it crept into the melodies like a bad infection and ruined the song for him. Don turned it off and drove in silence where the inner demons badgered him all the way home. He pulled out her note, it comforted him and he cried again.

Thirteen

July 18, 44 Days Out, 193 pounds

Don was finishing entering a few notes into his computer when his boss came into the office and asked if they could talk. Don said sure. He and his boss, Kenneth Palm, were more like partners. Ken had started the non-profit and was the president but it was Don's ideas and theories that were implemented under the non-profit organization. Ken was the quintessential business man and salesman. His appearance was super neat and even when he dressed casual his clothes were sharp. In some ways he was almost the exact opposite of Don.

"I just got a call from the Campus for Transformation. Apparently, a book you gave one of the kids to read had sodomy in it and he was telling other kids about it. They were very unhappy that you would provide a book to a child with sexual content, especially homosexual content."

Damn it, Don thought, I told him not to tell anyone. Well at least I know he was reading. "I'm sorry Ken, but hey, at least we know he read it," Don said light heartedly.

"Don the board is already talking about pulling funding. I was given an ultimatum. Either I replace you with a tech in their facility or they will no longer require our services. I guess you know what I told them."

"And that's why you're the businessman," Don said with no emotion in his voice.

"Don, if we don't have funding, none of us gets paid. We both have pretty comfortable salaries, but those salaries don't magically appear out of thin air."

And you have a much more comfortable salary than I do, Don thought. No, that wasn't fair. Ken did all the hard work and deserved whatever salary he was getting. I get to go out in the field and have fun as well as collect research information for future papers. Ken's right. "I know. I agree. I just don't agree with some of the stuffed shirts who think they have all the answers and want to put parameters on a subject they know almost nothing about. They want the kids to read. They want the kids to not feel lonely. They want to reduce stress and anxiety, but they won't listen to the experts. It's just frustrating and I'm sorry for putting you in a difficult position. I'll assign one of the techs to that facility and give them my notes."

"Thanks. Trust me I know these are your ideas and that this whole thing is your baby. I just want to see it come into fruition and be part of it being a success."

Don replied, "I know, thanks." He did really like Ken even when he had to play the president or CEO or whatever title he liked to claim. Truth was without Don, Ken would be working middle management somewhere. However, on the other hand without Ken, Don would be teaching classes and wondering if his ideas would ever be implemented. They needed each other. But the whole situation still pissed him off. Why didn't someone call him instead of going right to the top. In addition, why couldn't they be happy that a kid was reading a book rather than committing a crime?

Not any book! A book that was a great example of how someone had over-come an early life of crime to become a success. That book should have been required reading not banned because of a few sentences about sex in prison.

Don got into his car in a bad mood. He wasn't mad at Ken. He was mad at the situation. It didn't help that he had been in a foul mood before talking to Ken. He and Alless had their first disagreement. Apparently, they did not agree on the meaning of the word "soon". To Don soon meant coming right up. He had no idea what it meant to her because it had been almost a week since she said she would see him soon. He had not heard a peep. He had not received another note. No sign of the dog. Nothing. He wasn't mad or angry, but he was a little bit frustrated. He wanted to see her in the worst way, but had no control at all over when that would happen. He also worried about her. He had read some dire statistics on being a homeless female. Very rarely was there a good outcome. He hated to think of the girl who might be the one who stole his heart laid up in a hospital or worse. He thought about calling around to some of the hospitals to see if they admitted a homeless girl named Alless, but he figured they would not be able to give him any information. He was seriously thinking about heading to the burned out house again. Maybe he could go there while it was still light outside.

To add to his already sour mood the gym was quite crowded. A lot of kids were home from college and a new promotion had membership up thrity-three percent. Don looked around as he walked to the locker room. He was checking to see what most people were doing and trying to pre-plan his workout. However with this new crowd they seemed to just jump all over the place so predictability was quite difficult. He got to the locker room and JT was in there.

"Hey man! What's up?

"Another day grinding," Don said. And both of them bitched about how crowded the gym was. JT took the opportunity to refer to the new people as "dumb asses who didn't know what the fuck they were doing." Don wrinkled up his nose as the smell of weed was really bad in the locker room.

"Right," JT said. "It smells like a dope factory in here! All these new people and kids coming in here high as fuck!"

"I don't get it," Don replied, "Doesn't weed make you mellow and just want to chill. It seems like the last thing you would want to do before working out." Don had taken a lot of drugs but smoking pot never appealed to him. He hated the smell and he just flat out hated the idea of smoking anything. He had some relatives and friends that got high a lot and they had absolutely no motivation when they were high.

"They don't work out hard anyway. They just want to take selfies." JT said and slammed his locker shut.

Jack walked in and the first thing he said was, "Who burned one?"

"Right, we were just talking about that. I guess it's this generation's preworkout."

"I just want to eat and take a nap when I do it," Jack said and smiled.

"You look like you have been doing it a lot lately," JT teased. Jack feigned like he was going to punch JT and he darted out of the way.

"I worked out on acid once," Don said and laughed. "Legs too!"

"No way!" JT said laughing.

"Yep. Me and my old workout partner who was kind of a druggie. We probably squatted for over an hour with minimum rest. The owner came over and asked us what was wrong with us. We were all freaked out because we thought we were acting stupid. He finally said he never seen two people squat with that kind of intensity for such a long period of time.

My legs, lower back, Jesus, my whole central nervous system was fried for days afterward. I could barely get off the toilet the next couple of days!"

"That's crazy," Jack said. "I thought I was nuts for working out drunk once."

"You girls can sit in here and work jawceps all day. I have arms to train," JT said and walked out to the gym floor.

"How are you feeling?" Jack asked.

"Eh, kind of a crappy day today. But I guess prep is going ok. I think I'm going to have to cut some calories, my weight seems to be stuck. I like to try and consistently lose two pounds a week."

"You're what, about two thousand calories right now?"

"No, I'm at twenty-four hundred still. This is the first real lull I've had and maybe the number on the scale isn't moving because I'm adding a little muscle. I am taking quite a bit of gear. Maybe I'm holding some water too." Don hated to worry about the number on the scale. Bodybuilding wasn't a fat loss contest or even a body-fat contest. It was supposed to be about how you looked. "How do I look? You see me every day; do you think I'm still progressing?"

"It's hard to tell. I think you look more defined for sure. Your waist is super tight. I mean from where we started it's night and day." Jack wanted to be more helpful, but he also didn't want to say he saw something he didn't. "I think you are still heading in the right direction."

"It's so freaking hard trying to hit that balance."

"Have you thought about increasing your walk time?"

"No, I'm happy with that. Besides I don't want to be out on the streets any longer than what I already am. I see a lot of weird stuff." In just the time I walk now I've discovered a haunted house and met the girl of my dreams who may or may not stay at said haunted house. Don was not yet ready to have that discussion with Jack. Especially when he still didn't really have any answers to the questions that would surely come.

Jack laughed. "I bet. You would think at that time of the morning everyone would be asleep."

"There is a whole nother world happening at that time." Don said and then quoted in a deep voice the opening of the television series Tales from the Darkside: "Man lives in the sunlit world of what he believes to be reality. But there is, unseen by most, an underworld, a place that is just as real, but not as brightly lit...a Darkside." They both laughed and determined enough talk, it was time to get going.

The workout was agonizing. Don's shoulder had been hurting lately and he hated training shoulders anyway. They had been focusing on the lateral deltoid head to give him more width and he wasn't sure it was working. It was difficult to get a good shoulder pump when your shoulders felt good; it was nearly impossible when your shoulders felt like it was bone grinding on bone with every rep. He gutted out the workout going as hard as he could on what exercises he could while trying to limit joint pain.

Don got home and was disappointed there was no note in the door. It had happened once so he didn't know why he thought it should happen again. For that matter, he had only seen Alless once if you didn't count their stare down in the middle of the road so why should he expect to see her again. He sighed as he checked his mail and got all of his food ready for the next day. He had so much hope but when he really thought about it, his hope was built on a very flimsy foundation. He cooked his eggs and was mad at himself for forgetting to put the white cheddar popcorn seasoning on them. He scarfed them down without the added flavor that made him feel like he was eating something good.

It had been a day and Don was ready for it to be over. He double-checked to make sure he had everything ready for the next day. He had been very forgetful lately and that was bothering him. He took his nightly cup of supplements in pill form and then swallowed his nighttime sleep cocktail of drugs. He added a Xanax in because he felt like he was going to have a tough time sleeping.

DFR, as his dad used to call him before he died, crawled into bed under a flimsy comforter. He liked to be cool when he slept, but no matter how cool it was he was likely to wake up in the middle of night covered in sweat. Tren sweats. At least he wasn't taking DNP. DNP made him sweat through a shirt every couple of hours. He had tried it just that one time and while it worked, the side effects were horrible. Besides the sweating it left you in a state of exhaustion. It wasn't just a tired feeling it was a can I just pee in this empty bottle so I don't have to get up type of exhaustion. He had literally had to force every single movement. There was also the danger that if it was misdosed it could literally cook you from the inside out. Not surprising from a compound that was found in dynamite.

He clicked on the television and found a recommended horror movie on Prime. His inner voice teased: *what kind of psycho falls asleep to a horror movie?* He liked falling asleep with the television on. It kept his mind occupied while waiting for the sleep drugs to do their thing and knock him out. He usually didn't get very far into or very involved in the movie before he started dozing off.

Don wondered where Alless was. Had her life ended up like a victim in a horror movie and that was why he had not seen her again. Had she decided that she didn't want to make her free as a bird life mesh with his very regimented routine? Did she lurk in the shadows watching him? Was she waiting for the right time to attack and kill him so she could steal his car and belongings? Did she want to stay in his house while his corpse rotted in the garage? Maybe she was going to feed on his corpse. Sleep washed over him and when he woke to the sound of someone banging on his door three hours later, he thought it must be close to morning. He was shocked to see it was still a few minutes before midnight. He donned a pair of shorts and walked out of the bedroom.

He looked out the window to see who was banging on his door hoping to see his hooded princess with green eyes outside. Instead, it was an old man Don found himself looking at. His ragged face and missing teeth told a story of woe. His pale skin was barely distinguishable from the scruff of white hair protruding from his head and chin. He wore an old army coat and ill-fitting jeans. He opened the door a crack and the man tried to push his way in. Don was clearly much stronger and held the door to a crack.

"What do you want?" Don said angrily.

"Help! They're after me. Let me in!" the man wailed and tried to push the door open again to no avail.

"Who is after you?" Don asked and pronounced judgment on the old man as a homeless paranoid schizophrenic.

"They are," he yelled and gestured towards the low hanging tree across the street. Don looked in that direction and didn't see a thing. The man pushed on the door a third time and made no better progress than his other attempts.

"You're not coming in!" Don said sternly. The man looked through the crack and Don could see he was truly terrified. A piece of discarded fast food trash blew across the yard and onto the porch grazing the man's leg. He screamed and took off running. Don looked down to make sure it was really garbage and not some creature of the night. The golden arches confirmed his original recognition. He watched the man run down the road like his hair was on fire. He was pretty fleet of foot and Don wondered if he was younger than he looked. Living on the streets and in a constant state of flux had a way of making one look quite a bit older than they were.

Don heard something rattle by his garage. He stepped on the porch and looked around the corner. He didn't see anything but had that same strange sense that he was being watched. He glanced back in the direction the man had run and could faintly make out his frail figure still running far down the street. He stepped off the porch and walked towards where he had heard the sound come from. It was probably just more garbage blowing around he thought as small pebbles dug into his bare feet causing him to wince. He looked down the driveway and beside the garage and there was nothing out of the ordinary. He stood in the driveway annoyed. He was about to check behind his garage just to make sure there wasn't anything of note when a bird struck him in the side of the head.

The large black bird had seemingly come out of nowhere and flew into the side of Don's head. It hadn't pecked him or scratched him with its talons, it just simply flew into him. He was reminded of a Seinfeld episode where a bird flew into Elaine's head. He also conjured up the image of a large black bird flying into John Travolta's face in the movie Wild Hogs. But the thing that rushed forward from the galleys of his mind was a 7th Century text called the Dialogues. With his uncanny ability to do so, thanks to a near photographic memory, he pulled up the text in his mind:

> "Upon a certain day being alone, the tempter was at hand: for a little black bird, commonly called a merle or an ousel, began to fly about his face, and that so near as the holy man, if he would, might have taken it with his hand: but after he had blessed himself with the sign of the cross, the bird flew away: and forthwith the holy man was assaulted with such a terrible temptation of the flesh, as he never felt the like in all his life.
>
> A certain woman there was which some time he had seen, the memory of which the wicked spirit put into his mind, and by the representation of her did so mightily inflame with concupiscence the soul of God's servant,

which did so increase that, almost overcome with plea-sure, he was of mind to have forsaken the wilderness."

Was this a sign that his gorgeous green-eyed goddess was a tempt-ress—a demon of the night? A succubus? He certainly wasn't overly reli-gious and barely spiritual. And really, did he need to be tempted for any reason? He hardly thought there was a battle for his soul. However, it wasn't lost on him that black birds and ravens were used throughout literature as an ominous sign, a harbinger of ill-fate, and even death. He reached up to double check and make sure he wasn't cut or scratched. There was no blood nor any lingering pain. He decided enough was enough and he needed to get back to sleep.

But sleep did not want to come. There were too many things to think about. Was the old man a sign? Was the bird a sign? What did signs do? They pointed to something or warned you of something. What could they possibly be pointing to? What was he being warned about? *Duh, Alless.* Don had a pretty pedestrian but successful start to his cut until he met her. Now things just kept getting stranger and stranger. Maybe it was better if he didn't see her again.

The image of her face and her perfect lips flashed in his mind and made him want to see more. He recalled her electric touch and wanted to feel more. He thought of how good she smelled and wanted to inhale her sweetness again. The remembrance of her dulcet tones made him long for her voice in his ear. And the taste of her lips made him crave her. He thought of another religious text about a young man who forsook his fam-ily for wealth and found himself in a dire situation. The text read "and he came to his senses." If Don came to his senses, he would find they were in agreement across the board: he wanted more of Alless.

He had to stop thinking about it or he was never going to go to sleep. He turned on YouTube and a science fiction podcast was recom-mended to him by the application. He clicked on it hoping it would be uninteresting and put him to sleep. To help the cause he took a couple of squirts of liquid melatonin As he drifted off to sleep he heard the "expert" imploring that they're not coming because they're already here. Don, half asleep, grabbed the remote and turned it off. The darkness embraced him and overcame him.

Don was restrained and the little green men around the table wearing lab coats watched with interest. The talked amongst themselves in a language he could not understand. One of them moved around toward where his head was on the table—they didn't walk, but appeared to glide from place to place. With a thin finger, that had at least twice as many joints as a human finger, the other worldly being tapped on his forehead. It then took a drill off an adjacent table and pointed the large drill bit right where it had been tapping. The drill whirled to life and roared in Don's ears as the sharp bit touched his skin...

Don woke up sweating with his heart racing. Thank God it was just a nightmare. He took a deep breath and went to the bathroom. On the way back he glanced out the window into his backyard and saw an owl. Funny, he had never seen an owl around here before. He watched as the owl came closer to the window. It's feathers melted away and its eyes grew bigger. He tried to scream "It's not an owl" but he could only produce a gurgling sound. He was still making that sound when he woke up from his false awakening. Then he wondered as Poe had in his poem "A Dream within a Dream" if he was still dreaming and everything in his life was just a dream. He closed his eyes and muttered, "often, every daybreak, alone I must bewail my cares" and he drifted off again quickly to a plethora of dreams that he would not remember.

Fourteen

July 20, 42 Days Out, 193 pounds

The raindrops were welcomed as Don set out on yet another morning walk. It had been warm even for July the last couple of mornings and the weather front would supply at least a little cool down. He didn't mind it at all unless it turned into a torrential down pour.

He was six weeks out and for the first time he started to be concerned he wasn't going to be ready. There was the matter of his weight. No, it wasn't a weight loss contest but to compete in the divisions he wanted to compete in he still had to lose another sixteen pounds. No one wanted to compete at the light end of a division. You wanted to just barely make weight and look bigger, fuller and more shredded than the other guys in your weight class. He knew he didn't stand a chance if he competed in light heavyweight at only one hundred and eighty pounds when the rest of the guys would be squeaking in under the bar at one hundred and ninety-eight pounds. Yet he didn't want to drop weight and lose muscle mass. It was inevitable he would lose some, but the key was to retain as much as possible while getting down below five percent body fat. That's why the gold standard was two pounds a week—anymore and you were likely burning up muscle rather than fat.

He did his first injection of Masteron that morning. It might help him get harder and look more grainy, but it wasn't going to help him burn fat. Maybe he had been ridiculous to think he could just rely on diet alone without doing any real serious cardio work. Maybe he should forgo the walks for long high intensity interval training on the step machine. He could do the work, that wasn't a problem. If it was a hard work contest, he liked his odds. It wasn't. It was a combination of hard work and smart work, gear and genetics, and diet and dedication. He thought he was working smart. Perhaps he did need a coach.

The old Buick had seen its share of rain and probably a lot of Michigan road salt as well. At one time it had been a powerhouse. It had been state of the art: fast and gorgeous. Now it stood on jack stands waiting patiently for someone to love it enough to restore it. He thought the same about his soul. It needed restored, It needed love. He resisted the urge, turned from the old car and walked toward Broome Park—in the opposite direction of the house where his love could be waiting for him. Probably was hiding from him.

He took a step and felt his ankle giving out on the cracked and uneven pavement. His instinct took over and all his weight transferred to the other leg and although he stumbled a bit he missed out on a nasty sprain or even a fracture. He had never broken a bone or even had a serious injury. His body naturally knew how to transfer weight and become limp or relaxed at the right time to avoid catastrophes of bone and tendons. He was thankful for the gift, thankful that he wasn't laying in a parking lot with a broken ankle. Thankful that his prep wasn't ruined by one small step.

The rain slowed and stopped. A mist appeared eerily over the parking lot as the rain water evaporated on the still hot asphalt. It reminded Don of old horror movies, when setting the ambiance trumped seeing the monster. Don, watching where he was stepping, crossed the parking lot and took the little trail that would lead him back onto Fenton Rd.

He passed by a long forgotten hot tub nestled barely in the woods on the far side of the trail. A ghost party sat in the tub enjoying their drinks and grab-ass as they had done while living. They had been laughing and complaining about contemporary mores and did not see the man approach with a gun. It was a jealous husband that shot them dead and rendered the hot tub trash. Next up on Donnie's Death Trail was the beat up couch that currently held a homeless man with a nasty looking blanket pulled over top of him. However, at one time the couch belonged to Archie Mast who successfully strangled seven lovers on the couch before dumping it along the trail as if time and weather could wash away the DNA. Finally on the Trio of Terror was the bridge to nowhere. The rusty steel structure that creaked and groaned in the wind had once given pedestrians safe passage above the highway below. A lack of people and lack of maintenance had rendered it useless and it was locked up with multiple warning signs gracing the gated entrance. The jilted, broken hearted, distraught lovers who hung themselves on the bridge found the warning signs easy to avoid. Six just this year and nineteen total found their release from the pain of a broken heart at the end of a rope on the bridge.

Don imagined the field day his therapist would have with that little fictional account of the trail. She would surely point out that all three tragedies had some type of connection to relationships and that he was manifesting his own guilt and grief in his adventures in storytelling.

"I will never make you want to use that bridge," said a beautiful voice. It was so captivating that he didn't once think about how she knew what he had just imagined about the bridge. He saw approaching from out of the shadows the hooded form of Alless. She ran up to him, grabbed his face and kissed him deeply. He thought he could get used to greetings like that. She withdrew and they shared a long, quiet gaze that seemed to be their calling card.

Alless took him by the hand and said "let's walk". They went back in the direction of the park. Don asked where Omega was and she replied that he was safe. He thought that was an odd answer to the question. He felt she was avoiding saying where the dog really was. Could it be at home with her husband, he wondered, but didn't push the issue further.

"So, I've missed you," Don said and right away hated himself for saying that. What a dumb thing to throw out on the first pitch!

"I've missed you too. And I know my soon was longer than you hoped for, but you must believe me when I say it was as soon as I could."

Don thought about unpacking that a little further and then decided to go in another direction. "Thank you for the note. It meant a lot to me and made my day."

"You're welcome and you're probably wondering how I knew where you lived." She paused and when Don didn't say anything she added, "I recognized your car from when we met in the street. It was in the driveway a couple of times so I deducted that was where you lived."

Her voice was magnificent. The second kiss had been every bit as magical as the first. He didn't want to ruin anything but did have a lot of questions that he hoped would not fuel the fire of his inner skepticism. "I don't mean to sound like I'm accusing you of anything but how did you know my name? You called me Don and you also wrote Don in the note."

She squeezed his hand and glanced at his face with a sad look. He didn't like that expression and didn't care to ever see it again. "I'm ashamed to admit that I have gone through your trash looking for essential items of need. I promise I wasn't spying on you. I just needed some things to survive. And in the process I saw some of your discarded mail with your name on it"

107

Don felt bad for asking. He paid cash for his house and was driving a Lincoln. She moved from abandon house to abandon house while pushing a shopping cart. No wonder she was ashamed and he had made her feel that way.

"It's ok," he said and squeezed her hand this time. He had to really think about the questions he asked and the things he said. The last thing he wanted to do was upset her. In the back of his mind he thought we should just kiss each other and that will keep me from saying or asking anything stupid.

"When you hugged me you felt strong. I guess you do more than just take walks," she questioned.

Don spent the next ten minutes talking about bodybuilding and his upcoming contest. It wasn't like him at all to go on a long monologue especially one where he was talking about himself. He wondered if it meant he was letting his walls down. He wondered if it meant that she was really the one. He was also worried that it sounded like bragging. The whole concept had to be foreign to someone who dug through other people's trash to survive.

"That's impressive. I'm proud of you," she said and swung his hand up to her mouth where she kissed it.

"Thank you!" He had a long list of questions he wanted to ask. He wanted to know all about her—what her story was, but he didn't know how to frame the questions without sounding like he thought he was superior than her. For example he wondered if she was homeless, but didn't think coming right out and saying, "are you homeless" was the way to her heart. Be intentional, break the cycle. He was about to ask her what she liked about him but she beat him to the punch.

"Don Ream, what is it that makes you attracted to me? Why do you seem to like me?"

He stopped and turned her to face him. "Everything I see is stunning. You stimulate my senses in ways I've never dreamed they could be aroused before. You have a *je ne sais quoi* that I couldn't possibly begin to pinpoint yet, it demands my heart and attention. I could so easily quote Elizabeth Barrett Browning to you right now, but it might seem a little forward and like I was jumping the gun."

"Please do it," she said and gave him a look he could not refuse. He cleared his throat and recited:

"How do I love thee? Let me count the ways.

I love thee to the depth and breadth and height

My soul can reach, when feeling out of sight

For the ends of being and ideal grace.

I love thee to the level of every day's

Most quiet need, by sun and candle-light.

I love thee freely, as men strive for right.

I love thee purely, as they turn from praise.

I love thee with the passion put to use

In my old griefs, and with my childhood's faith.

I love thee with a love I seemed to lose

With my lost saints. I love thee with the breath,

Smiles, tears, of all my life; and, if God choose,

I shall but love thee better after death."

She smiled and said that it was beautiful. It's from "Sonnets from the Portuguese" he told her and remembered another quote from it: "Quick-loving hearts...may quickly loathe." That one he kept to himself and hoped it would not be true in this case.

He kissed her gently on the forehead and they walked some more in silence. As they approached his house she asked him another question. "Don, does it bother you that our lives are so very different?"

He paused knowing he could answer this wrongly in a thousand different ways. He knew he could hurt her feelings or upset her wholly on accident by not being careful in his word choice. Finally he answered, "No, it is not that it bothers me per say, but I do worry about you all the time. I care about you and I want you to be happy. And I do wish we could spend more time together."

She smiled the smile that he loved. Her whole face lit up and her eyes appeared to dazzle like a multi-shaded green kaleidoscope. "Thank you for being honest. I want you to be happy as well. If I ever fail to make you happy you must tell me." He nodded in agreement. "Do you have any children," she asked while looking into his face.

"Good heavens no!" he blurted out. "God has mercifully spared any children from having to call me father. I am certain I would have destroyed their lives. I do have three ex-wives I'm ashamed to admit. If that causes you to run for the hills I would understand."

"No," she softly said. "Every situation is different. I too do not have any children." She paused for a moment and added, "I have to take my leave from you now. I will see you later and you have my word it won't be as long as last time.

He took the side of her face in his hand and saw that his palm had smeared a patch of mud on her cheekbone. For a moment he felt distaste well up in his gut, but when she reached up and touched his face it quickly went away. He wanted to push her hood back and run his fingers through her hair. He wanted to kiss her passionately until her knees buckled and she dragged him to the ground where they would make love until the morning light. A flickering streetlight reminded him that they were not in the golden meadow that his imagination had placed them in.

"Are you sure you don't want to come in?" he whispered in her hood covered ear.

"Not this time. I have to go and you need to stay on schedule. I want you to win this contest and couldn't forgive myself if you got distracted because of me."

They kissed good-bye and it was Don who felt his legs turn to jelly. It was astonishing that everything she did to him electrified him and made him feel like he was doing it for the first time. He could not wait to have that experience with her when they were making love. As if reading his mind she gently patted his chest with the side of her fist and said "very soon." Then she was gone.

He went into the house and collapsed into his Lazy Boy to decompress and rejoice. He looked at his Fitbit to see if he had gotten in his ten-thousand steps in. He had. Right on track. He checked his sleep score and it was good, although he noticed a large chunk of time where it said he was awake. He didn't remember being awake. That had been happening the last couple of nights. It always recorded him as being awake for slivers of time throughout the night, but the last few nights there had been a block of time that showed him awake for almost an hour nightly. He wondered if it was from the drugs. Probably.

He relaxed and unknowingly invited his worried inner thoughts to the stage. *Same clothes again. And I know that smudge of mud freaked you out a bit. You're ok that she went through your trash? You do realize that even though you walked with her for a good thirty minutes you still don't know anything about her. What could she possibly be doing that is keeping her from seeing you every day—it sure as hell isn't laundry. And did you notice the weird way she talks sometimes? It's like she is trying to act more educated than she probably is. There are just so many red flags for you to fling yourself at her like she is clearly the perfect girl you have always dreamt about. To quote Sue, "why do you think this is?"* Unlike Sue the inner voice didn't wait for an answer. *You want to feel loved and to reciprocate love so badly you're being delusional for the sake of that dream. And the calorie deficit, low body fat and the all the drugs make you the perfect storm of vulnerability. Now do I think she is taking advantage of that and somehow using you? No. I think, much like you are doing, she is riding the crest of a wave towards dreamland. But you both know waves go crashing into the shore where they die.*

The voice had said its piece and retreated back down into the caverns from where it had emerged, where it would wait again until Don needed knocked off his high horse. Don slapped his thighs and stood up. It was time to get ready for the rest of the day. He switched into auto-pilot mode and went about his business while his mind thought about all the ways he and Alless could indeed make it work. They after all weren't Romeo and Juliet. They didn't have a lot of resistance keeping them apart. *That you know of,* echoed from the abyss. She may not have any money but he certainly made enough to support them both and he had a house.

Their love was not forbidden by warring families. It was more like the forbidden love between Heloise and Abelard of France in the Twelfth Century where social construct kept them apart. Abelard wrote in a letter, "I saw her, I loved her, I resolved to make her love me. The thirst of glory cooled immediately in my heart, and all my passions were lost in this new one. I thought of nothing but Heloise; everything brought her image to my mind. I was pensive and restless, and my passion was so violent as to admit of no restraint." Whereas Abelard lost his passion for philosophy in pursuing the much younger Heloise, Don had to be careful to keep the North American Bodybuilding Championships as his prime focus. He felt like he was failing. Alless was literally all he thought about.

Fifteen

July 22, 40 Days Out, 191 pounds

The morning rays nearly blinded Don as he piloted his MKZ into the Clarkston's Growing Oaks Assisted Living Center. It was his first time there and he was visiting Jakob Latunski, whom had been recommended to Love Through Literature by his granddaughter. The file read: "Grandpa used to love books. He had several full bookshelves in his house. When Grandma died and Grandpa moved to an assisted living there was no room for the books. He told me in a recent visit that he missed reading and he would love to get lost in a grand novel again."

Don nervously rang the buzzer at the door. He was always nervous when he entered a new facility where he didn't know anyone. He waited and heard the door click. He pushed it open and walked in where he was promptly greeted by the manager. Julie was fairly young and had no formal business training. The only qualification she had for the job was that she had spent seven years there as a certified nursing assistant before moving up to assistant manager and then a year later manager. Julie had on light blue scrubs and her dirty blonde hair was pulled back in a ponytail. She was friendly and seemed genuinely glad to have Don there.

"Let me show you to Mr. Latunski's room," Julie offered and lead the way down a long hall. The building was very clean and bright. It was painted to look like a village block and each room represented a small bungalow. It had a certain charm that was warm and inviting. There were green street signs on every corner and streetlights dangled high above. She knocked on door number 107. A gruff voice yelled, "come in."

"Jakob, this is Don Ream," she said and gestured towards Don, "he is from Love Through Literature and wanted to talk with you about getting some books for you to read or even have someone come out and read them to you."

"I don't need anyone to read me a goddamn book! I know how to read and I can see if people would quit hiding my glasses!" Jakob had a mess of gray hair and wore a faded red flannel shirt with red lounge pants. He had brown slippers on his feet with no socks. He was hunched over in his wheel chair, but Don imagined when he was young and healthy he had been quite an opposing figure.

Julie turned to face Don, raised her eyebrows, gave him a tight lip grin and said "good luck". He returned the smile.

"Can I sit in this chair," Don asked motioning to a folding chair across from where Jakob was facing.

"And if I say no will you leave. Ah piss just sit down," Jakob said and Don sat..

Don was not sure he had the energy or patience for such an encounter. It was early but he was already tired and hungry. He longed to see Alless and between her and the prep he didn't have a lot left for anyone else. He felt bad about it and would focus more on his work after the contest.

"Well, what do you want? I don't have all day!" Jakob had a slight German accent that manifested itself when he said words that started with "w".

"I want you to love reading again like you once had."

"You don't know anything about me. How do you know I once loved to read? Are you a spy?" Jakob grunted angrily and raised his lip in a snarl.

"Well sir, it is my opinion that someone of your structure and intellect must certainly love to read. All the great men loved reading so why would I expect you to be any different?"

"Great my ass. I've never done anything great. I had a wife that despised me, kids that deplored me and a lot of mistresses that desired me. Ask any of them how great I was and they would spit on your shoes."

Don wondered if this would be him in twenty years minus the kids. He hoped Alless would save him from that and help him turn the corner from being regarded as a womanizing wreck that had wasted a life.

"Nonetheless in all that you didn't say you didn't like to read. I assume that you do. What, sir, is your favorite book?" Don locked eyes with him and didn't look away.

"What are you some sort of book expert? Or are you trying to sell me another goddamn set of encyclopedias that I will never get to read. I hate salesman. All salesman do is try to fuck your wife or fuck your bank account—either way you're fucked."

"I am not a salesman, I assure you. Nothing I offer you today will cost you one red cent. And I am somewhat of a book expert. At least certain books."

"What is your favorite book? You tell me yours and I will tell you mine." Jakob said and sat back for the first time in his wheel chair. He was a bigger man than Don had thought. Standing straight up he was probably six foot six on a big, thick frame. In his younger days, he probably weighed in near the 275 mark.

Don paused for a minute. He was asked this question often and most of the time gave a different answer depending on how he was feeling. He wondered which one of the ten or so books he considered his favorite would Mr. Latunski be most impressed by. Finally he said *Beowulf.* Jakob looked puzzled like he had never heard of it.

He grunted and said, "I had you pegged as a Brothers Karamazov type of guy. Maybe even Hunchback of Notre Dame."

Don smiled and said, "Those are both worthy of consideration. There are so many it's hard to choose one."

"It's not for me. I have a clear-cut number one. Care to guess."

Don did not care to guess. It was impossible. All you could do by trying to guess someone's favorite book was offend them or make them feel bad. He decided to go with a German author and used his own namesake as inspiration. "I'll say, *Doctor Faustus* by Thomas Mann."

"You devil you!" Jakob laughed and Don followed suite letting Jakob know that he got the pun. "That's not it however. My favorite is *The Modern Prometheus.* The greatest story ever told in my opinion and so far ahead of its time one has to wonder if good old Mary Shelley was a time traveler!"

"Do you prefer the 1818 or 1831 version?" Don asked demonstrating a rudimentary knowledge of the subject in hopes of gaining Jakob's favor.

"You would think the 1818 because it's the original, but I like how the 1831 gives more attention to what Victor's motivations are and his deeper thoughts on creating life."

"I tend to agree with you. I find the book to be an excellent commentary on grief. You know, what would intense grief motivate you to do. I wonder if Stephen King thought of Frankenstein when he wrote *Pet Semetary*?" Don stopped when he realized he was thinking aloud.

"I have not read any of his works, but I've seen a few movie versions of his books and they were not impressive by any means."

"Yes, his books don't translate very well into movies or endings in that matter," Don said and was the only one to laugh at his little jab at the Master of the Macabre. "You might not believe this but I have in my office a copy of the original handwritten manuscript by Mary Shelley with all of her notes in the margins."

"The hell you do!" Jakob yelled.

"I do and I will bring it and a magnifying glass in for you the next time I come."

"When will that be?" the excited old man asked.

"I'll tell you what. I have nothing to do tomorrow so I will drop it off to you sometime tomorrow and then sometime after you study it we can chat about the nuances of her notes and how the story could be different. Deal?"

"I feel like I am Faust and have made a deal with the devil. Yes you have a deal."

They said their good-byes and Jakob thanked him profusely. Don walked out of the room feeling pretty freaking good about himself, his studies and his program. Jakob had a genuine childlike excitement about getting a copy of the handwritten manuscript. He was smiling as he walked down the hallway and heard, "Oh my god, he does look like him."

Don stopped and let curiosity get the best of him. He wondered who he looked like and thought Paul Newman maybe. "I'm sorry," he interjected, "did you say I look like someone?"

The young aides giggled and the more mature of the two answered, "We used to have a chaplain that worked with hospice that came here to visit. His name was Mike Spear. You could be his brother you look so much alike."

Don laughed and said, "Does he still come by? If I have a doppelganger I'd love to meet him."

Both girls frowned and the same one that talked before said, "No, he was murdered by his ex-wife a few years ago. Horrible tragedy."

"I'm sorry," Don said outwardly and inside he said I'm surprised we don't also have that in common. Don took the next few minutes to tell them who he was and what he did. Julie then walked up.

"It must have went well. He seems in great spirits now."

"It did go well and I'll swing by tomorrow to drop the book off to him." He excused himself and headed toward the door. Behind him he heard Julie say, "he does look a lot like him!"

Don went about the rest of his day in pedestrian fashion. There was no excitement, no emergencies, no one complaining about the job he was doing and no interruptions to his eating plan. He was eating at three-thirty, five thirty, eight-thirty, eleven, two, five and seven. Some meals were only a shake, but he still felt it was extremely important to eat as close to the times he had planned for as possible (of course, some argued that it didn't matter). He liked being regimented and knowing what he was going to eat and at one time. He felt it made it easy for him to stay disciplined. It also helped with hunger because you knew, no matter what time it was, you were going to get to eat again soon.

Soon. That was a word he was beginning to dislike stemming from the flippant way Alless had been using it. He thought about how badly he wanted to see her and if he controlled when he saw her soon would mean in a few hours. However, she was in control of when they saw each other and soon for her meant days. He acquiesced that even a week was soon when you took it in the context of many years. He could remember people asking him when his end of time in service date (ETS) was when he was in the military and he had said soon when he was a month out. Therefore, it was relative in the scope of things, but Don still didn't like it.

He was a sweaty mess when he left the gym. The workouts had been getting harder simply because he felt tired all the time. He also felt he was starting to get noticeably weaker. Usually he could do more reps with more weight than Jack could do, but lately they were pretty even. He worried simultaneously that he was getting too lean too fast and also that he wasn't going to be ready in time. Contest prep was a mind fuck. You swung back and forth like a pendulum feeling you were going to peak too soon and that you weren't going to be ready in time. You lamented on one hand how weak you were getting and rejoiced on the other how good you were looking. You loved when you looked big and full and cried when you thought all your mass was gone and you looked like a swimmer. Your extra-large hoodies hung off you like you were an emaciated prisoner of war or homeless fella.

Homeless. Another word he would never feel the same about. You couldn't say he was dating a homeless girl because they had not exactly gone on a date. He was, however, seeing a homeless girl and he wasn't sure how to think about that. The inner voice quipped, *you don't even know for sure she is homeless.* Don reasoned she was. He said it aloud, "Alless is homeless."

She didn't have the characteristics Don stereotyped as homeless. She didn't stink (unless his olfactory was playing tricks on him). She didn't beg for money (at least that he knew of). She wasn't covered in sores (at least her face wasn't). Her breath was pleasant and her teeth were not rotted. Yes, she wore the same clothes and had dirt caked on her face and hair in places.

The inner voice of woe had been waiting patiently to get a foot in the door and saw an opportunity…

You are painting a very beautiful picture full of colors when your pallet only contains a few hues. You don't know any of this to be true and factual. Her body could be covered in sores and riddled by disease. Maybe she brushes her teeth and gurgles with mouthwash found in the trash before she sees you. The flowery fragrance that surrounds her could be simply oil poured over her body. You have not even seen her without her hood pulled up over her head. For all you know she could be another Edward Mordrake hiding a face on the back of her head. At best, she had been a waif who had learned to make her way over the course of many difficult years. At worst, she came from a good home but was lured into the streets after falling in love with dragon rock and now will do anything to get it. You just don't know anything about her!

Don retorted. Why can't I for once just get out of my own way and listen to my heart? Why does everything have to be analyzed, given probabilities and put into designated categories? I've always trusted reason and logic and where has it gotten me? Three failed marriages and a whole host of relationships gone south. Maybe it is time I throw caution to the wind and use bolt cutters to unfetter my heart so it can experience raw, untamed love.

A squirrel ran in front of Don as he turned down his street. He had to brake not to hit it and the squirrel stood in the middle of the street giving him a look. He was sure if a squirrel had a middle finger he would be getting it at the moment. I should have just fucking ran you over, he thought, and some would suggest that he was starting to have some roid rage.

Don didn't believe roid rage to be a real thing—it was a myth. He certainly believed that steroids magnified who you already were. And the fact was most people who took steroids were already Type A aggressive sorts so naturally those characteristics would be amplified on gear. But steroids didn't make an otherwise nice guy into a maniacal Cretan.

Don parked his car and carried all his stuff to the door. He saw a pink piece of paper jutting out from between his screen door and dropped everything. It was another note from Alless. This one was on pink stationary that was clean and crisp. Don smelled it and it smelled of vanilla and cherry blossoms. The next thing he noticed was that it didn't appear to be a hastily written note. Her penmanship was bold and flowing like her voice. The letter was much longer than the first. It was a Dear John letter he feared. Why else would it have been so long when her sweet loving note was so short. She was going to great lengths to explain to him why they shouldn't see each other.

He started to read:

Hi Don, I hope this letter finds you happy and fulfilled. I wanted to take a moment and let you know how I feel since I don't always express myself very well in person. I think I am falling for you. You intrigue me. I see the kindness in your eyes, but I also see the anguish and guilt that surrounds the kindness trying to suffocate it. I hope it never does. I love that you are not demanding and take from me what I give you. I know it's not much, but I do hope someday it is enough. I don't know how we can reconcile how very different our lifestyles are, but I'm not going to worry about that now. I want to live in the moment and enjoy this happiness that I currently have. Being with you makes me feel whole and complete. In your arms I feel safe. When you live a life like I have you can't quantify the importance of feeling safe. Thank you. I want to come over the day after tomorrow. It will be late evening or early into the night. I will have to bring Omega, my loving dog. If that is ok with you just leave me a quick note in the door. If I don't see a note I will understand and just keep walking. Love Always Alless (it's pronounced like your people's name Alice)

Don read it again and a third time before gathering up his belongings and going inside where he read it a fourth time. He sat in his lazy boy staring at it, smelling it and soaking the words in. She felt the same about him as he did about her. Sure things might get awkward and difficult, but like she said they should enjoy the moment. And in the moment they had each other.

During the fifth reading, a question came to his mind when reading about reconciling their different lives. What would he do if she wanted him to forsake everything and live on the streets with her? I mean it's preposterous, right? Who would live on the streets and be homeless if they didn't have to? But maybe for her it was her culture. She did reference him as "your people" at the end of the letter. If he met and fell in love with an Asian woman would he automatically assume she would abandon her culture and join his? Is it any different? They would be like the couple he saw picking through his trash—the couple that rummages through trash together stays together. He grinned.

That was a lot to think about and Don agreed with the letter that it would be something to consider and talk about at a later date. For now, they would just enjoy each other. He started thinking what he would write on the note he left for her.

Sixteen

July 24, 38 Days Out, 189 pounds

That Sunday was the longest day ever. He tried watching a couple of movies, but couldn't get interested in them. He cleaned his house and did laundry. He read from the "Mabinogion" where he mentally took a snap shot of the following quote and added it to the rolodex in his mind: "Then they took the flowers of the oak, and the flowers of the broom, and the flowers of the meadowsweet, and from those they conjured up the fairest and most beautiful maiden that anyone had ever seen." He imagined Alless was Blodeuwedd, that most beautiful maiden. Then thought better of it when Blodeuwedd turned out to be a conniving cunt of a woman. The inner voice echoed from the depth of his thoughts, *harbinger*.

And yes, he had been mentally pronouncing her name wrong. He had been pronouncing it like Ah-less. He was so very thankful she told him the right pronunciation before he called her by the wrong name in what could have been a very embarrassing turn of events. He wondered if that was the spelling given to her at birth of if she adopted the spelling or even the name sometime later. She was still shrouded in so much mystery

123

it amazed him that he could even imagine them as a couple. But he could, did often and loved the thought of it..

He went to the gym and had to do thighs on his own since Jack had a family wedding to attend. It was really difficult to get up for thighs on your own. However, if there was a body part Don could coast on a little bit it was his thighs. They were thick, wide and vascular. He had always dreamed about having legs like the legendary Tom Platz who was on the cover of the very first muscle magazine he ever bought. And while his legs were nowhere close to that they were very impressive for someone his size.

Don decided to do a lot of volume with counter supersets. He would do a quad exercise and then immediately do a hamstring exercise. His reps and sets were going to be higher than his normal leg routine allowed for. He felt he didn't have the motivation to go heavy in the empty gym without a workout partner nor did he feel safe doing so. If something happened he would not be found until Monday morning. Not to mention he would miss his "date" with Alless and probably never see her again. He, without a doubt, put more concern on missing out on seeing Alless than he did getting some type of injury.

It was clear that this prep and contest were not his sole area of focus. Alless had equal if not more of his attention. Big deal, he thought. Hundreds of thousands of contest preps have been done by someone in a relationship—it wasn't out of the ordinary. He had done prep in absolutely self created shit shows before. It could be done. From deep down: *but this was supposed to be different. This was supposed to be your sole focus. You set everything up so you could give this contest prep your undivided attention. Now you're going to settle with bringing in a subpar package like you have in the past all because you found some homeless floozy to be cute?*

Don dismissed the voice. He plugged his phone into the gym's sound system and cranked out his workout play list that contained a heavy dose of Motley Crue, Five Finger Death Punch, Halestorm, Eminem, Guns

N Roses and Ted Nugent. He might not have been going heavy but the intensity was there. He focused on the muscle contracting on every rep, squeezed and then lowered into the negative very slowly. Every repetition was purposeful, every set was taken to the limits of muscle failure. Sweat trickled from seemingly every pore.

He went to stand up after a set of lying leg curls and the room spun and twisted. He reached out to grab a nearby machine to steady himself and missed. He swayed on uncertain legs while the lightheadedness made him feel like he was falling down drunk. Don managed to keep his feet and the moment passed. He had to be careful about standing up quickly after a max effort set or for that matter standing up quickly in general. His body was rebelling. It liked being in homeostasis at a comfortable body fat with a slight surplus in calories. Don was forcing change, entering extremely low body fat levels and had been in a calorie deficit for the better part of ten weeks.

He finished his workout with four supersets of good girls/bad girls on the abductor machine continuing the slow grinding method of pumping out reps. When he was finished he felt wiped out and didn't think he could do another set. He laid on a bench and stared up at the ceiling. Don felt like he could take a nice nap if it wasn't for the increasing pain in his hips. It wasn't a sharp pain, just a gnawing dull ache that made him feel like the joints were slightly out of place. He moved his legs around hoping that if his hips were out of place they would slide back together properly. It didn't work and made the pain worse. He got up and walked around and the ache seemed to level out.

Don gathered his things, clicked off the lights, and wobbled his way out the door to his car. It was hot outside and the inside of his car was like a furnace. It made him feel lightheaded again. He needed to really hydrate before Aless came over. He didn't want to cramp or have any lightheadedness when he was with her. He wanted to be his best.

125

He got home and stepped into the Edgar Alan Poe decorated bathroom. It was really the only room in the house that he had decorated since moving in. The decorations consisted of a black and white portrait of Poe in an antique oval frame on the wall. A picture of a raven with the final few lines of The Raven written below it in fancy script mounted on a beautiful wooden plaque on the adjacent wall. On the over-the-toilet vanity was an early twentieth century ten volume set of Poe's Collected Works. The orange covers were worn and the pages in betweened yellowed. On each side of the Collected works was a raven shaped book end. The final piece was a shower curtain that featured a raven in front of a blood red moon. Don loved it all.

He stripped down to his birthday suit and applied a heavy coat of Nair all over his body. He set a timer and waited. He was tired of waiting. He wanted to be with Alless. He wanted to be done dieting. He wanted to be done with the competition and competing in general. Six of the longest minutes later the timer went off and Don stepped in the shower and completed the defoliating process. He was afraid to shave his body this close to the contest. A deep razor nick could really stand out distracting the judges eyes. It wasn't like he had perfect success with the Nair. Before his first show he wanted to make sure his body was as smooth as possible and he left the Nair on a little too long. It burned a patch of his skin in his lower abdominal area. That patch wouldn't hold the spray tan correctly and looked like a giant annoying birth mark when he was on stage. A dumb mistake.

He dried off and looked at himself in the mirror. His waist was tiny and his shoulders looked wider than ever because of it. He flexed his abs and each little muscle popped leaving a crevice between. They looked etched in stone and his obliques rippled with feathery muscle striations. He flexed his glutes and made a face. They were still almost smooth and he noticed a swath of fat around his lower back. He thought he looked good, but saw where he still needed a lot of improvement.

He shaved his face. Don didn't want to tear up Alless' face with coarse stubble. Yes, he was planning on kissing her a lot. When he was done he threw on some nice sweat pants and a t-shirt. He laughed when he thought about his "nice" sweat pants—going to Sunday meetin' sweat pants he said in his best Elvis voice which did not sound like Elvis at all. He did have levels of sweat pants he was afraid to admit. Nice ones consisted of fairly new sweat pants that fit him well. Workout sweat pants had a loose fit, were comfortable, worn but not torn and had deep pockets. Then there was garage sweat pants which were old, stained and perhaps even had a few holes.

Don didn't just have categories for his sweat pants he had a whole system for his workout clothes. Things that went together. Shirts that he wore only on chest day or arm day because they made that body part look bigger or more defined. He even had designated hoodies for designated days of the week. And of course for every outfit he had a corresponding pair of No Bull athletic shoes. His ex's always gave him a hard time about the particular way he arranged workout clothes. They couldn't just leave him be. He hoped he would never find Alless to be nagging or bitchy.

Don was all ready for Alless. He was sitting on his couch when he realized he had not written the note and therefore had not placed the note. "Fuck," he yelled and hoped she had not been by yet. He grabbed a sheet of typing paper and wrote neatly on it the following poem he had created just for her.

My heart beats with love

Whenever you smile

Your eyes light up and so does my life

He folded it into quarters and carefully placed it between the screen and door frame. He stared at it intently making sure it wasn't going to slide out. When he was certain it wasn't going anywhere he shut the door. After a minute or so he went out the other door to look and see if the note was still in place and visible from the road. It was both still in place and visible. He thought it was out of his hands now and went back inside where for the next hour he worried that she had come by earlier, didn't see a note and walked away from his life forever.

Don relaxed on the couch watching a series of YouTube videos about which horror novel is the best. They argued for It and Pet Semetery. They dissected Hell House and Amityville Horror. They over analyzed Ghost Story and House on Haunted Hill. They forget The Castle of Otranto and The Monk. And Don drifted off to sleep.

The knock on the door was light but Don had not taken his sleep cocktail and therefore slept on just the other side of consciousness. He ran to the door never doubting that it was Alless and not some crazed old man fleeing from an imaginary group that was after him. And he was right. Through the window on his porch he saw Alless wearing the same clothes that she had worn every time he had seen her previously. Tethered to her was Omega who seemed a lot less intimidating under the warm porch light.

Don panicked and realized he had only seen Alless in the dark and in the shadows. What if under a bright light she was not so captivating? The light would serve to spotlight her flaws and the homely features of her face if any existed. Maybe she was like the two-face girl from a Seinfeld episode. That girl, however, had been pretty in the light and homely in the shadows. He pulled the door open and was relieved. He invited her in and when she walked into the brightly lit living room she was every bit as beautiful and alluring as she had been in the darkness. He hugged her and kissed her. It was, again, electric and stimulating.

"Thank you for the note. Is that a Don Ream original?" she asked a slight blush rolling into her cheeks.

"I wrote it just for you. I love your smile and it lifts my spirits."

She bent down and freed Omega from his rope. He wagged his tail, ran and jumped on the couch. He curled into a ball like he belonged there and was familiar with the warmth and comfort of a soft place to lay his head. "I'm sorry," she whispered, "He has no manners."

"No, don't be sorry! I love it and want you both to feel comfortable and welcome."

"Don, do something for me," she said in a voice that was as pleasing as angelic harps, but also demanded obedience. It was a combination that both excited Don and made him a tad bit fearful. He knew she had control over him; yet he didn't care. It wasn't hypnotic or even the power of suggestion. It was something else entirely. He wanted to say it was the power of love and Huey Lewis and the News would agree with him.

"Anything, Alless," he said saying her name aloud to her for the very first time. It warmed his heart.

"Please get me a towel and a wash cloth, show me to your bathroom and then wait for me in bed," she whispered and her voice seemed more sultry and deep. He looked at her eyes. They not only appeared lined but she had naturally long eyelashes that added more depth to her high cheekbones and slightly upturned nose. The randomness of mud streaked on her face looked like war paint and she could have played Boudica in a movie if she were taller.

Don did as he was asked (told). She kissed him and beckoned him to go wait for her. He left her to the privacy of the bathroom and noticed on his way to the bedroom that Omega was snoring comfortably on the couch. That made him smile. He was a dog lover at heart and that Omega had a warm safe place to sleep for at least a little while made his heart dance happily.

He heard the shower turn on as he stripped down naked and slid between the sheets. He killed the lights except for the little faux lantern on his nightstand. He hoped he wasn't being presumptuous and didn't think he was. He opened his nightstand and swallowed down a couple of the small pills from the ForHims bottle. No taking any chances he thought and then grew worried. What if it didn't happen? He was after all fifty-six. The pill was no guarantee. He knew, from experience, the more he thought about it the more of a problem it was going to be. He prayed, "God please don't let it fail me now." Then felt like he was going to be cursed for praying for such a thing.

He heard someone talking, no singing. It was Alless. She was singing in the shower. He wondered how long it had been since she had taken a shower. He listened closer and heard her singing:

"A moment like this, some people wait a lifetime for a moment like this

Some people search forever for that one special kiss

Oh, I can't believe it's happening to me

Some people wait a lifetime for a moment like this"

His heart soared and he felt like this was the real thing. The real thing he had been waiting for since reading Love Story by Erich Segal in middle school. "Love is never having to you're sorry," he remembered without having to pour through his cerebral rolodex for the memory card.

The shower stopped and Don became increasingly nervous. He was going to be so embarrassed if she looked shocked to see him naked and in bed. What if she meant they would just lay on the bed in their clothes and watch television or talk? He would look like a horn toad!

The bathroom door creaked open and Don realized he had not been this nervous since the breaking of his virginity some forty years earlier. He wanted it to be special. He wanted it to be perfect. Most of all he didn't want to disappoint her. It dawned on him at that moment that he didn't have any protection. Mr. Preparation was not prepared. Fuck, he thought and saw her silhouette approaching. She stood in the doorway and he saw how voluptuous she was. Her curves stood out with the light of the television behind her.

Alless stepped forward. Her curly auburn hair was free from the confines of the hoodie and danced playfully on her shoulders. In the hoodie it had come down and covered some of the "Detroit" on the sweatshirt. It now bounced down her breast which stood firm and full. A lock of hair caught on her erect nipples and it took Don's breath away. She was hairless from the neck down Don noticed as she strutted towards the bed.

Her right leg was completely covered in bright colorful tattoos. In the instant he had to see it in the light he recognized a mermaid, a shark and a treasure chest of gold. She stepped again and he saw a purple octopus tentacle wrap around her upper thigh. Se pulled the covers back and she put one knee on the edge of the bed and moved her face towards his.

She was stunning. Her full rounded red lips stood in contrast to her fair complexion in a way that made her look goth. He felt a stirring before she even touched him and knew that was not going to be an issue.

Their lips grazed and Don was certain sparks must have flown as she slid into bed next to him. Her body was warm, soft and smooth. She kissed him deeply and their tongues played an erotic game of tag. Their hands began to explore each other's bodies in a slow graceful massage that was on the verge of turning into a frenzied groping. He kissed her neck and she smelled of vanilla and tasted of sugar cookies. He gently slid his thick thigh between her leg and she gasped as the muscled quadriceps touched her clit. It was the catalyst needed to start the frenzy.

She thrust her pelvis into his thigh and grinded hard against it. Their hands grabbed and groped at whatever they touched. She dug her nails into his glutes and pulled him closer to her. Their bodies were tightly smashed together rubbing and gyrating to the rapid beats of their heart. He went

CLEES

to roll her onto her back and she resisted. She, instead, pushed him to his back and mounted him. He was as hard as he had been since he was in his twenties. They locked eyes and she smiled that sly girlish smile that made his heart flutter and pushed him to the brink of orgasm.

He wanted inside of her. He wanted to feel her wetness and softness embrace him. She raised her hips for him to enter her and whispered in his ear, "It's ok my love, I can't get pregnant." Somewhere far away the inner voice was going nuts, but Don couldn't be bothered by it. He began to slide into her slowly. The head of his cock spreading the soft folds of her lips apart. She squeezed him as he went in further. He could feel her muscles tightening around his shaft. She moaned and Don thought it sounded like a symphony reaching its climax. Once he was fully in her she relaxed and started riding him. Slowly at first, but harder and harder as he squeezed her breast and let his fingers caress her nipples.

He felt like he was about to explode. He couldn't imagine feeling better than he did in that moment. And just before he reached the point of no return she lifted off of him. She walked her knees up to the side of his head and pinned his arms down with her lower legs. He noticed her vagina glistened in the light before she lowered it on to his mouth. He licked and sucked her. She moved down ever so slightly and he found her clit with his tongue. He swirled his tongue around it several times before flicking it gently. He took it between his lips and massaged it back and forth. He was in ecstasy with how she felt, tasted and smelled. He was sure she was created just for him.

She pushed down into him and he could feel the spasms ripple through her as she came hard on his face. She grunted and groaned as wave after wave of orgasm flushed through her body. She jumped off of him and got on her hands and knees on the other side of the bed. He didn't need to be told what to do. He entered her deeply from behind and her gasp was loud.

132

Don thrust into her hips making a slapping noise and she bucked back into him urging him to go harder. He reached up and grabbed a thick handful of her mane and pulled her head back as he slammed into her. And once again as he neared climax she moved away. She pushed him back onto his back. "I want you looking into my eyes when you cum" she demanded.

She stradled him again and he slid into her easily this time. She lowered her body onto his and their faces were only inches apart. Her long locks dangled down into his face and in one sweeping motion she pulled her hair away and Don could see her soft rounded features. He could not believe how gorgeous she looked. In that moment she was everything he had ever desired and imagined. Her hips began to move in ways that bordered on unnatural. He had reached the point of no return. He closed his eyes and was about to let loose.

She grabbed his face in her hand and told him to look at her. Her eyes seemed to be glowing as he emptied himself deep inside of her. His body shuttered and jerked. Before he could finish she covered his mouth with hers and they kissed until he went limp inside her. She rolled beside him and in the quietness of the moment, Don knew he was in love.

He wanted to say it. Hell, he wanted to shout it and if he hadn't been struggling to not die of a heart attack he probably would have. She laid beside him tracing his veins with the tips of her fingers. She followed the cephalic vein from his shoulder down to his wrist. She let her finger tips cross the many veins in his stomach as if she was strumming guitar strings. She was purring.

He quoted a line from Victor Hugo's Les Misérables, "The power of a glance has been so much abused in love stories, that it has come to be disbelieved in. Few people dare now to say that two beings have fallen in love because they have looked at each other. Yet it is in this way that love begins, and in this way only."

"How do you know and can recite so many quotes," Alless asked while still tracing the roadmaps.

"My degrees are in literature so that helps. But I can also…it's hard to explain. If I read a text that I want to remember it is as if I take a picture of it. Then it gets filed away in my mind. When I want to recall it, I pull the picture from the files. It's not like I have it memorized, but I'm able to see the file in my mind and read the quote from the snapshot. It's nothing I do with any skill, it just happens."

"It's impressive she said," now tracing the thicker rope like veins in his thigh. She seemed mesmerized that they were so big and stuck out like they did. "The quote you just said, what do you think about it?"

"Do you mean in regards to love at first sight?" Don asked while he played with her soft, luxurious hair.

"Yes, do you believe it to be true?"

He took a deep breath, "I never used to. But now I'm not so sure. Maybe one has to experience it to believe it."

She rolled back on top of him and looked down at his face, "Are you saying you experienced it with me?" He was silent and wanted to say absolutely. She laughed, "I'm just teasing you." She kissed him deeply again.

Something jumped on the bed and scared the crap out of him. It was Omega. He had completely forgotten about the dog. Omega pushed his head into Don and rolled onto his backside so both the man and the dog were on their backs in submissive positions to the female. She laid on top of Don and rubbed Omega's belly. Don thought he could stay like this forever. They were a happy family. He dozed off.

Seventeen

July 25, 37 Days Out, 187 pounds

Don woke up alone. He was groggy and it all seemed like a dream. He checked his watch and saw that it was ten minutes before his alarm was supposed to go off. However, it wouldn't because he forgot to set it. He wasn't entirely sure the whole night had not been a dream until he found the note on his kitchen counter. It read: I didn't want to wake you. Let's do something fun on Saturday. Omega and I will come over in the morning and we will spend the day together until you have to go to the gym. Love Always, Alless.

The note made him smile and then frown. He was ecstatic to get to spend the majority of the day with her, but at the same time disappointed that he wouldn't see her again for almost a week. Be positive. Be intentional. Let it happen. He was thankful the inner voice of dissident must have still been sleeping. He was sure that when it woke there was going to be a long lecture.

Don weighed himself and was pleased to see he was solidly below one-ninety. At 187 and just a little over five weeks out if he lost two pounds a week he would hit his target weight nearly perfectly. He loved when his plan seemed to go perfectly. He loved it more because it was his plan and not some coach he paid through the nose for. He loved it because people always doubted he could do it himself and thought he was crazy for not getting help. But doing his own plan was all part of the experience—he actually loved that part. The researching and playing with the numbers gave him a sense of ownership and helped push him on when temptation came calling.

Her scent lingered in the bathroom, in his room and on the sheets. He laughed out loud when he thought he would never wash those sheets again. She made him feel like such a teenager who was having his first experience with love—and that was a great thing. She bedazzled him in every way.and what a relief to have seen all of her and not be disappointed. She was more than he had imagined and dreamed.

He sat on the bed and caressed the sheet where she had laid. He wondered what time she had left. Don had slept hard. His shoulder and bladder, both antagonist that woke him up several times a night, didn't even have the power to rouse him from his slumber. He checked his Fitbit and it said that he slept from eleven to one, then was awake for an hour before sleeping again from one to three-twenty. He knew the sleep monitor on it wasn't 100% accurate but it sure had been giving him some strange recordings as of late. He ignored the reading that said his resting heart rate was still steadily climbing as he pulled out his treasure chest of gear (she had a treasure chest on her leg).

Monday was not a fun gear day. It was the one day that he injected all three compounds: test, tren and mast. The leaner he got the more the inter-muscular injections hurt. He combined the test and tren into one syringe so it was only two injections instead of three but he was starting to really hate giving himself shots. He thought back to when he tried to really bulk hard and was taking a ton of shots daily. He did four site enhancement oil injections in each arm for a total of eight, two insulin injections, two growth hormone injections, two injections of MK-2866 and one injection each of test and NPP for a grand total of 16 injections a day! He had felt like a pincushion. And to make matters worse it didn't seem to provide much in the way of muscle gain. Shots were tolerable when you got some result from them, not so much when you didn't see the fruits of the injections.

He pinned both thighs and headed out for an uneventful walk that was filled with the berating of his inner voice that kept calling him *"her baby daddy"* and urging him to go get an STD test. He pushed the voice down with memories of how good she had made him feel. The voice fired back in its best Monty Python voice, *"You're suppressing me!"* He smiled as he relived the moment they locked eyes and climaxed. That was special.

His work day was a struggle. He was really feeling the disruption to his normal sleep schedule. He didn't mind. He would lose a couple of hours of sleep every night to have amazing sex like that. He even loved that after they had sex Omega came in the bed and slept beside him. He couldn't recall feeling drowsy. He felt like he went from heart racing wide awake sex to being asleep in the manner of five minutes. Then there was the awake time that he didn't remember and maybe that was why he was so exhausted.

Don contemplated skipping his workout. He was exhausted. His shoulder ached and it was shoulder day. He sat in the gym parking lot for several minutes with his phone in his hand ready to text Jack that he wasn't going to make it. *You might as well just cancel the contest plans, his inner voice argued. You would have never dreamed of missing a workout before. You can't half-ass this. You're either all in or you're out. Save yourself a little money and just end it. It's not like you were going to get your pro card anyway.*

Maybe dropping out of the contest wouldn't be such a bad idea. He could replenish his energy, make love all night and really get to know

Alless. If things worked out between them wouldn't that make dropping out of the contest worth it? Would he trade a stupid bodybuilding contest for true love? Of course, that was a dumb question. But what if things didn't work out? What if things were only working now because he was preoccupied with the contest? If he had his full attention to give Alless would he simply find himself becoming increasingly frustrated with not seeing her? Would he resent her because he didn't follow through on his dreams after carefully preparing for the contest?

Don put his phone down and walked into the gym. He was hesitant to take Cracked Gold on shoulder day, but felt like he needed it. What he didn't need was the way his prostate swelled when taking DMAA too often. It caused him to feel like he had to urinate all the time and when he did try to go he stood in front of the toilet with a burning sensation as a few drops dripped out. It was altogether unpleasant. He decided on 2/3 of a scoop instead of a full scoop or two scoops. That would give him some energy and focus without, hopefully, the urinating issues.

The locker room was quiet. It was a hot summer day and people were forgoing the gym for an afternoon at the beach. The gym was traditionally dead from the 4th of July until Labor Day when it picked up again. The new membership promotion had spiked interest for a few weeks but it had died down rather quickly. Even with the influx of kids home from college the gym still felt empty. Don liked it that way. It made it easier to plan his workouts and it motivated him that he was there grinding away and so many other people were out partying.

Don had always been one to find motivation when people told him he couldn't do things or when he felt he was slighted by someone. "He would show them" had been his lifelong calling card for just about every one of his accomplishments. It fueled him. It gave him reason to go on. It strengthened his motivation, discipline and resolve.

Jack walked in and just stared at Don.

138

"What?" Don said with a grin spreading across his face.

"You had sex last night." Jack said pointing his finger at Don.

"How the hell do you know what I did?" Don said trying not to laugh.

"Who is she? Someone from the gym? A worker from one of the businesses you visit? Oh my god, you broke down and got a prostitute!" Jack exclaimed.

'No on all accounts. What makes you think I had sex?"

Jack smiled at him. "Well you look like you were up half the night, yet you don't seem pissed about it. And dare I say you look content, maybe even satisfied. Com'on! We are workout partners. I see you almost every day. I can tell when something is out of the ordinary."

Don was really impressed with Jack's perception of events. Don did not have that ability. Jack must be an empath Don reasoned.

"Spill the beans, boy! What's the scoop. Who is she?" Jack pleaded.

"Just a girl from the neighborhood."

"You have to give me more than that! Is she hot? What does she do for a living? Is this a one-time thing or could it turn into a relationship?

"This is all I'm going to say," Don said holding out his hand as if to signal Jack from stopping the questions, "She is hot. It could turn into something more. But she knows I am doing this contest and that is where my focus is."

"Did you have any problems?"

"What?" Don said incredulously.

"You know some guys on trenbelone say they can't get hard; others say they can get hard but wear out their girls pussy because they can't cum. Did you experience any of that? Any issues with you being too lean or depleted. I bet it looked big to her because you don't have any groin fat!"

"Jesus, Jack! No, I didn't experience and problems. Everything worked just fine."

"Did she massage your prostate?"

"Oh my God!"

"She pegged you didn't she?" Jack said laughing so hard he was almost crying.

"I'm going to work out. If you need a moment or two to go in the stall and fantasize about my sexual exploits I'll be warming up doing military presses on the smith machine."

Jack yelled after him, "Did you warn her you don't always look like that. She shouldn't expect the six pack forever!" Don just kept walking and Jack understood the cue that it was time to get serious.

The workout was agonizing for Don. His shoulder and elbow ached with every exercise they tried. It didn't matter if it was a compound movement or an isolation exercise. It didn't matter if they used light weight and high reps or heavy weight and low reps—it still hurt. Don kept trying to roll it out and stretch it out. He swung his arms back and forth. He rotated his elbows. Nothing helped.

"Fuck it," Don said and dropped the twenty pound dumbells he had been doing laterals with. He walked down the rack and picked up the forties and started repping out side-laterals using a ton of momentum. He grunted out six reps before dropping them and doing the same with the thirties. He found the twenties and did about ten reps before lifting them over his head for ten behind the head dumbbell presses. He rereacked them and collapsed on a bench.

"Nice set," Jack said and gave him a light pat on the shoulder.

Don laid there and thought it wasn't worth it. Maybe if he was healthy and his shoulders weren't killing him it might be. But this was crazy. He pushed and pushed and pushed and for what? So some judges who barely paid attention could tell him he wasn't big enough or he wasn't conditioned enough. The cost of the contest was insane as well. Why was he doing this to himself?

"Come on. Get up. You think you're the only one fucking hurting. There is someone in their basement training harder than you right now. They're hurting but they're gutting it out because they want to be a fucking champion. Is that what you want to be? Or would you rather lay on a bench and feel sorry for yourself. The Don I know wants to be a champion and will do whatever it takes to have his hand raised on stage. Who are you? Who do you want to be? There are fucking people in this gym who look up to you because you're fucking fifty-six years old and out training people half your age. You're not a quitter. You're not soft. Make the people who love you proud of you and get off this bench and attack the fucking weights, bitch!"

Don sat up. Jack was usually philosophical when trying to motivate him. It was Don who usually raged and swore at Jack to reach new levels. Don stood and growled. He did a drop set of side laterals starting with sixty and going down five pounds at a time until he was shaking while holding the fives in a crucified position. The whole time Jack was yelling at him, pushing him, willing him to do one more rep. He dropped the fives and started to walk away. Don didn't know if it was the Crack Gold or Jack's motivational words, but he went back and grabbed the twenties and did as many rest pause reps as he could. The pain in his joints and tendons was unreal, but he finally felt the pump in the muscle themselves.

They finished with a monster drop set of shrugs before calling it a day. They were both soaked in sweat. Don barely had the strength and energy to shake up his post workout shake. He wondered if he could put the shaker bottle in one of the paint can shakers he had seen at Home Depot. He sucked the orange creamsicle concoction down in two gulps feeling like he needed the carbs to replenish his glycogen stores in the worst way.

"That was some workout," Jack said. "It's not often we can jack up that kind of intensity for some shoulders."

"Thanks for pushing me through it. I was being a big fucking baby."

"Dude, you have been in a calorie deficit for a while. You're up at the ass crack of dawn walking for an hour, working all day and then coming in here and still killing it. Most people, including myself, don't have the heart and guts to do what you're doing. Don't ever forget that."

"I don't know…there are so many people who compete as a bucket list item now," Don lamented and hated people who haphazardly entered a contest just so they could check off an item on a list. He hated that they called themselves bodybuilders. He wasn't ashamed to call himself an elitist when it came to bodybuilding.

"Those people aren't doing the same work you're doing. It's like comparing the Christian Motorcycle Club to the Hell's Angels. One is the real deal and the others are just posers. How did the leg workout go yesterday without me holding you back?"

Don laughed. "Man, you don't hold me back. If it wasn't for you I probably would have skipped today. I almost texted you to say I wasn't coming."

"Well just so you don't think I was slacking, it was a Catholic wedding and I probably did a hundred reps of bench squats. Up, down, up, down. It was ridiculous. I had an actual pump in my quads."

"I just did a few supersets to get the blood flowing. I was kind of on cruise control. I mean I'll have the best legs on stage anyway so I didn't feel the need to crush them at this point."

"You are the Quadfather!" Jack said and stood up. The gym was starting to get more crowded with people filing in after their nine to five jobs. "I've got to run and take my daughter to soccer practice. I'll see you tomorrow!"

"See ya." Don was thankful Alless couldn't have kids. *Or so she says*, quipped his negative Nancy inner voice. Don envied people who had kids and had great relationships with them. He didn't think he would have one of those type of relationships. He imagined if he had ever had kids it would be a tumultuous relationship that would end with a hospice social worker contacting them to tell them their dad was dying. They would tell the social worker ok and never give it another thought.

Let's just say she was telling the truth about not getting pregnant, the voice reasoned, *what about the other thing. It wouldn't be shocking if she had some type of venereal disease. Good heavens what were the statistics on the percentage of homeless people that had AIDs? Hepatitis? Did you throw out the towel and wash cloth she used? Has your scalp been itching today? Thankfully you both are shaved down below. I hear crabs are nasty little critters.*

"Enough," Don unexpectedly said out loud.

"I'm sorry, were you talking to me," a passer-by asked. Don waved them off and decided it was time to get out of there. He wanted to get home, get everything ready, eat and get to bed a little early if that was possible. It had been an emotional twenty-four hours and he was beat.

Eighteen

July 28, 34 Days Out, 184 pounds

Don pulled the door tightly shut behind him. The string on his hoodie got shut in the door and Don almost choked himself. He had to unlock it, open it to free himself, and pull the locked door tightly shut again. A neighbor had warned him the night before that criminal activity was increasing in the neighborhood and he should make sure his doors were locked and he didn't leave any packages on his porch for very long. Don got a bunch of packages. He ordered all his protein powders and some of his food through Amazon. Really, he ordered as much as he could because he hated going to the store.

It was another ridiculously hot morning. He had not expected it to be this warm this early in the morning. When he decided to walk at this time he envisioned he would have to wear a sweatshirt of some kind most mornings because it would be cool. That had not been the case. The hoodie was not needed, but he had grown use to wearing them, almost as a security blanket, and if he sweated a little bit so what.

He walked towards Fenton Road. There was a lot of trash on the side of the road. It almost looked like the garbage truck had sprung a leak and left a wake of trash behind it as it maneuvered through the neighborhood. Don would never stop taking notice of how some houses looked neat and clean and then the very next house would be in shambles. He guessed most of the nicer houses belonged to retired GM workers who were determined not to move.

He got to Fenton Road and turned north. Nearly every business in this direction was closed down. He had counted three business that still looked open: a convenience store, a barber shop and oddly enough a comic book store. The rest had chains on the doors, windows broken, signs torn down, debris piled up in front of the door or aged signs noting they were having a going out of business sale. He thought about how cool it would have been to live here when businesses were open and thriving.

Most of the buildings were home to either gang symbols spray painted on them or a mural of some sort covering a whole side. Some of the murals were really quite spectacular. They were tastefully done and showed a considerable amount of talent and skill. Others were haphazardly done and depicted scenes from inner-city life that was not quite so tasteful.

A woman rode by him on a bicycle giving him a wide berth as if she were afraid that he was going to attack her, He said hi. She did not respond and peddled faster. He wondered if all her belongings were in the small cart bolted to the handlebars. He wondered if Alless had a similar bike or had a similar bike at one time in her life. Were all her belongings now in a yellow shopping cart parked outside a burned out house where she slept on a nasty mattress on the floor? He hoped not. He remembered that she seemed highly educated. Clearly she could find nicer shelters and soup kitchens.

He turned towards the park and was startled by a family of raccoons knocking over a metal garbage can. They stood their ground and hissed at

145

him when he walked by. Like the other creatures of the night, they claimed other people's trash as their own treasure and guarded it. Was Alless considered a creature of the night?

He walked across the broken concrete of what had once been a tennis court. In the corner of the tall fence a man slept sitting up using the fence as a back rest. There was a black garbage bag in his lap. Don moved quietly so not to wake him. The man stirred when a bird landed on his leg. The bird looked around, determined there was nothing to eat and flew off.

Don went around the far side of the baseball field where he heard someone grunting. He heard a voice saying "oh my god" over and over. He crouched down and scanned the area where the sound was coming from. He saw two SUVs parked by the tree line, barely visible to him and completely hidden to the road or parking lot. At the back of one of the SUVs a person was bent over at the waist and another person was behind them. They were having sex. Don didn't want to move for fear of being seen.

His eyes adjusted better and he concluded it was two men. The bigger of the two was bent over taking a pounding from the smaller one. He heard one of them grunt followed a short time later by, "you fucker, you shit all over me." He thought of Justin and the Ron LeFlore story and found it amusing that you didn't have to be in prison to see that "shit". His pun caused him to laugh out loud and both men jerked their heads in his direction. He stayed still and he could tell they were looking in his direction. "Let's get out of here," the bigger of the two said. They jumped into their separate SUVs and were off and moving down the cow path out into the street in a blink of an eye.

Don stood up and shook his head. Motherfuckers be driving fifty thousand dollar SUVs but couldn't afford a No-Tell Motel. Maybe it was more exciting doing it outside in public. That was probably part of the rush. He would miss the weirdness and randomness of these walks when the contest was over. There was always something to see. He thought Vickie

Stringer could spin a hell of a tale just based on the things he had encountered on his walks. *She could spin a hell of a tale about you and Alless* he heard in that not so small voice.

Don walked up the park driveway and saw someone sleeping in the grass. They didn't have a garbage bag with them but clutched a brown bag that hugged the curves of a bottle of some sort. There were many empty liquor bottles on the street he had noticed from all the walks. If he had to guess, he would have said at least half of them were empty Hennessey bottles. He did a little commercial in his head: "When you have no one else and the streets are cold and lonely you can count on Hennessey to warm your heart, mind and soul.:Cheers!" *Good god, you're losing it!*

He started to cross the senior citizen complex when way down the street he saw a figure pushing a yellow cart. He yelled out, "Alless!" The figure kept going and disappeared out of sight. He thought about giving chase and then his pride told him if she wanted to see you then she would see you. You can't go running down the street chasing after someone when you can't even be sure it was her. He wanted to offer his pride a rebuttal but behind him a voice boomed.

"Hey, hey. What are you yelling at? I'm Dan Dan the Dancing Man," the voice said. Don turned in time to see a skinny, long haired white dude with a scruffy looking beard. The man shuffled his feet like a boxer and rotated his fist like he was trying to pedal a bike with them.

"What is up, Holmes. How are you?" When Don didn't reply he continued, "Baby, you don't remember me? We used to knock them back at the Copa in days gone by."

"I'm sorry, you must have me mistaken for someone else," Don said and started to walk away.

"I don't think so. Your muscles are hard to forget. Maybe you remember me by my other name, Nunchaku Ned. I use to dress all in red, looking for ladies to bed, I ran into jealous Fred and had to bust his head, now he is dead, in hiding went Nunchaku Ned."

Don made the huge mistake of replying falsely indicating he was interested, "Maybe you should have changed your name to Rapper Dan Trapper."

The man bent over in laughter. "So you do remember me? I knew it was you. I bet you wondered what happened to me. The state I had to flee. But I'm back you see. It's really me! Your muscles are big like Mr. T. You know me Gee. I slap my knee you can't believe what you see. I hid out in the D. I'm a parasite like a flea. Now I got them Flint keys. You feel me?"

Don thought Dancing Dan was pretty high on some crack and smack. "I gotta run"

"Wait you got a smoke? I just want a little toke. Ain't no joke. Be a good bloke."

"For the love of God stop the rhymes! You have me mistaken for someone else and I really need to get home."

Dan Dan the Dancing Man did a little pirouette and said, "I'm at your service. How can I be of assistance?"

"Sorry, I don't really need any help. I just need to get home," Don found it hard to be rude even to someone on drugs who was annoying him. Sue would have cited it as a prime example of him being a people pleaser.

"I know these streets like nobody's business and for a taste of your whiskey I'll give you some advice." Dan sang the last part of his sentence.

"I don't have any whiskey. I don't have any smokes and I don't have any money!"

Dan looked at him with a curious look. And just when Don thought the conversation was done, Dan added: "I'll give you a freebie. You need a heater? I know where to get one. You need some rock? I can lead you to some. You need a little sweet poontang, I know where the hot ones are that will suck you off until your toes curl. Ain't no one know as much about these streets as Freaky Friar Tuck. That's me and you're in luck."

Don gave him a dirty look and held out his hands indicating he didn't want anything.

"Come on baby. Try me out. Ask me anything."

Don had a sneaky suspicion that he wasn't going to get away without asking him a question of some sort. "Now, I don't have anything to give you but I do have a question. Again if you want to answer it for free that's on you. I can't give you anything. Do you understand?"

"Now you're talking, baby? Fire those questions my way," the man said and moon walked a few feet before stumbling.

"Ok. But you understand you're giving me this information for free. I cannot pay you in any way."

"Get on with your bad self and test my knowledge. You're not going to be disappointed."

"Fine," Don said and asked the man the only thing he thought the man could answer for him. "What do you know about the girl who pushes a yellow cart?"

The man literally jumped back. "You're asking about The Yellow Cart?" he stated and immediately covered his mouth like that would some-how keep his words from going anywhere.

"Yes. I want to know about the girl."

Dan, Ned, Friar Tuck and whoever else he might be put his finger over his lips and shushed Don. "Woo-wee. That's a doozy."

"Do you know anything about her or not?"

"I know enough not to be talking about it. But I'm desperate. If you got a five spot I'll tell you what I know.

How about I grab your scrawny ass neck and choke you until you spill everything you know and if I'm satisfied I won't rip your head off and shit down your neck. "I told you I don't have any money."

"What about that hoodie. It looks really warm and comfortable. Cool design." It was his gray and blue Monsta Clothing hoodie with a faux Superman logo on the chest. Instead of an "S" was the outline of a muscular guy in the diamond.

"Jesus! You want me to give you my hoodie in exchange for information?"

He spun around and said, "I just want everybody to be happy."

"Fine," Don said and took off his hoodie revealing a tight t-shirt underneath.

"Damn Holmes! How much you bench? You looked big with that hoodie on but you're jacked like a mofo."

Don threw the hoodie at him. "What do you know?"

The man leaned in close, "She is one bad bitch and that's all I know."

"What does that mean?" Don was doing his best to contain his frustration and angry.

"It means you go the other way if you see her and you sure shit don't talk about her. She is like the Candyman. You talk about her and you end up in trouble. And by trouble I mean dead. She causes more fear in us than the serial slasher did in his hay day. And that's all I know and all I'm saying. Don't ask me anything else about her because I don't know anything." The man mimed zipping his lips, put on the hoodie and walked away. He turned around one last time and told Don, "Be careful." Then he was gone. Well now there were two homeless people wearing his hoodies, Don mused.

150

Don hurried home. He plopped down in his chair and the thought that struck him was: what the fuck? Maybe Alless and this so called yellow cart person were not one in the same. I mean, really he had only seen her pushing a yellow cart the one time. And there were an abundance of carts on the street. And the Dollar Store was just around the corner and they had yellow carts so there was a good chance there was more than one yellow cart being pushed around by homeless people. Maybe he should be worried about her running into the person who pushed a yellow cart and scared people.

He knew about the legend of Candy Man. It was similar to the bloody Mary legend where if you said their name five times in front of a mirror they were to appear and kill you. Don had personally never tried it, but he was familiar with it. However, he had to Google "serial slasher". It turns out he was an Israeli man who stabbed and slashed random people in Flint and the surrounding area some twelve to thirteen years ago. He was a big man and Don could see why he struck fear in the hearts and minds of those who roamed the streets of Flint.

Out of curiosity Don googled "The Yellow Cart". The only thing that came up of note was a store in California that called itself The Yellow Cart. No links to a murder or anything of that nature. No conspiracy theories. He had to believe if there was any merit to it there would have at least been something on the internet about it. But there wasn't and Don breathed a sigh of relief.

He had to force himself to get up and out of his chair. It was much too early in the prep to be this tired and lightheaded. He felt like he was carb depleting during peak week, but he was still taking in over one hundred and fifty grams of carbs a day. There was no reason for him to be that tired. He thought maybe he needed a refeed or cheat meal and decided to have one on Saturday when he would spend the day with Alless. It was going to be a relief not having to carry his lunch bag around with him.

He started fantasizing where they would eat and what he would have. He thought it was going to be a great day!

Don pulled into the parking lot at Planet Fitness. He was in-between visits and needed to tan. He had been trying to tan two to three times a week to maintain a good base tan. He got a room with a tanning bed and went inside. He stripped down to his birthday suit when the overwhelming urge to urinate came over him. If he threw his clothes on and went back out to the restroom he would miss most of his tanning time since the beds came on automatically. He was too much of an introvert to say anything at the front desk.

Don looked at the bottle of cleaning solution and considered he could pee in it and then throw it out when he was done tanning. He determined there was too much solution in the bottle and he would over fill it. God knows once you start you can't just stop on command. He was running out of time to make a decision because he had to go and it was on the verge of just starting to come out on its own.

He finally decided to just go on the floor a little bit behind the tanning bed. They clean the rooms all the time he thought justifying his actions. He probably was having a false alarm anyway since the prep was jacking up his prostate. Don started to go a little bit and then couldn't stop. He went more than he had in a long time. Much to his surprise the small electronic box behind the tanning bed started sparking and smoke rolled out from under it. He saw a little flame and that was when his "fire hose" quit working.

Don grabbed the bottle of cleaning solution without once considering it might be flammable and poured it on the electrical box. The flame went out, smoke rose from the box and the tanning bed shut off. The lights were still on so he had not tripped the main fuse. Don jumped back into his clothes in what had to be world record setting time and bolted from the Planet Fitness.

He sat in his car breathing hard and sweating. *Really? Can your life get any more bizarre? You got some dancing freak doing his thing this morning and now you want to see if you can go to jail for public urination. Do I need to remind you that this prep is supposed to be stress free? You're like some jungle cat hopping from stress tree to stress tree. Get your crap together before you mess up everything!*

Nineteen

July 30, 32 Days Out, 183 pounds

Don walked. He assumed Alless would meet him somewhere on his walk or else she would show up at his house when she was ready. What did that mean "ready". Was she going to have to shower at his house? Did she have any clean clothes to put on? And what exactly were they going to do? He would have been happy just lying in bed with her kissing and making love all the day long. However, if she did want to go out he had some plans and "couple" things they could do. He started worrying that she wasn't going to shower or have clean clothes to change into. He was not at all comfortable with going somewhere with an obvious homeless person. Be intentional. Be different. Think differently. Love her for who she is, not who you want her to be.

So, the annoying little fuck of a voice began, *now you're embarrassed to be seen with her if she doesn't clean herself up and pretty herself up? That's a fine start to a relationship you have. I can't wait for her to meet all your friends—wait you don't have many. How about your one friend. Will she meet Jack's approval if her hair is matted and her face has streaks of mud?*

Will you have to go roll in the mud before you meet her friends? You do realize this is a failed relationship before it even started, don't you? You had your little fun and stress release. She was a nice little bang. Nevertheless, isn't it time for you to tell her that it's just not going to work? Your worlds are too far apart. Maybe have your fun with her again today and then let's put an end to it.

A stray pitbull jumped out of the shadows barking at Don. He imagined the inner voice running away afraid. Don wasn't afraid. He stopped and made himself as small as possible and whispered sweet nothings to the dog. It stopped as well and its barks turned into deep growls. It didn't have a collar but it's ears were chopped so at some point it had belonged to someone. The dog's head was large and looked out of place on the thin frail body. "If you follow me home I'll give you some food and water." It growled and had learned to be distrustful of human beings. "You're a good boy," Don said in a soft voice. The dog whined once and took off running in the other direction.

"You are so sweet!" came a voice behind him and even though it dripped with honeysuckle it scared him because he wasn't expecting it. He turned to see Alless wearing his Monsta Clothing hoodie.

"Where did you get that hoodie," he asked with a hint of exclamation.

"Well, it's nice to see you too," she said in a voice that lacked the sweetness he had been accustomed to.

"I'm sorry," and he was, "You scared me and then I was shocked to see you wearing that hoodie. Some guy conned me out of it the other morning on my walk."

"Oh," she acted shocked. "He must have not liked it after all. I found it at the bus stop enclosure just lying on the bench."

For the first time Don had the horrible feeling that she wasn't telling him the truth. It made him feel sick to his stomach. Be intentional.

Approach it differently. Don't be distrustful. Give her the benefit of the doubt. "Can we start over?" he asked and held out his arms to her.

"Of course, my love," and the sweetness was back. She embraced him and they kissed deeply.

"That sweatshirt looks great on you," he said switching gears and they both smiled. He noticed she carried a WalMart bag in the hand that she normally held her dog's leash. "Where is Omega?"

"He is at home, sitting on your porch."

Maybe she meant nothing of it, but what she said made Don's inner being all warm and fuzzy. She had called his house home and even though she followed it up with "your porch" the first part bombed his negative feelings into oblivion.

"Well let's go see him," he said grabbing her hand.

On the way she explained to him her plans for the day. She wanted to shower and then she had a surprise to show him that she thought he would love. She would say no more about it other than "you will love it". Omega wagged his tail when they approached. As soon as Don opened the door he ran in and found his spot on the couch. I hope you feel at home puppy, Don thought and the giddy feeling kept rolling through his body.

When he was sure she was in the shower Don stripped down and joined her. "What took you so long," she said and started kissing him. It wasn't long before she was pressed up against the tile wall with her legs around his hips and her arms around his neck. She moaned loudly and the audible stimuli combined with everything else made him orgasm hard. He shuddered, as she seemed to draw every life giving seed he had in him into her. Alless washed him off and then playfully kicked him out of the shower so she could finish.

He dried off and fell into the bed with the towel covering his genitals. He whistled once and Omega came running in and jumped into the bed.

He fell asleep rubbing the dog's belly. When he woke up he saw the most beautiful woman his eyes have ever had the pleasure to grace staring at him from across the room.

Alless' hair was even more full and more curly than before. The auburn color was accented by streaks of strawberry blonde highlights. It framed her face perfectly. Her green eyes sparkled above her little nose and full red lips. She could have been a model in any era and in any culture. Don's eyes followed her hair down to her cleavage. Her ample breast pressed together and stood pronounced above her green sundress. The dress hugged and flowed in all the right spots drawing attention to the voluptuous nature of her curves.

She smiled that slow, sly smile that he could never get enough of. "Do you like it," she said treating him to more of that coy smile. His heart was hers. It was all he could do not to say right then and there that he loved her.

"You look absolutely stunning," he said truly in awe. He couldn't help thinking again that she was the perfect woman for him.

"Thank you, my love. Now get dressed we have an adventure ahead of us. Is it ok if Omega stays here? He is housebroken."

Don would have agreed to anything in that moment. Just when he thought he could not possibly be more attracted to her she did something that proved him wrong. Sometimes all it took was a look. The way she moved. A change of clothes. A smile. "Of course. I love him (you), he is such an awesome dog. Does he need some food? A bowl of water?"

"We ate this morning and will eat again this evening so he doesn't need any food. I am sure he will appreciate a nice cold bowl of water."

Don jumped up, realized he was naked and threw on some shorts and a t-shirt. "Am I dressed for the occasion," he asked as he walked to the kitchen to get Omega a large bowl of cold water.

"You look perfect as always," she said and came up behind him at the sink. She kissed his neck and ran her hand up the inside of his thighs stopping just short of his manhood. She let her hand graze it as she moved away. Teasing him. Promising him of things to come.

"Do you know where Cronin Derby Downs is," she asked.

"I have no idea."

"I'll give you directions. We will drive there and then walk the rest of the way. Your car will be fine in the parking lot."

"Sounds great," he said completely unsure whether it was great or not. He was beginning to feel a little trepidation for whatever it was she had planned. "Are you sure you don't want to stay here and make love all day?"

"Oh honey, we have already made love in the bedroom and the shower. Lets go somewhere a little more exciting and make love."

He smiled and hoped they weren't going to be like the two gay guys he had encountered in the park the other day. She told him to grab a couple of good flashlights and he thought lucky for her I have one and I just charged the battery. He explained how good the flashlight was and how long it held a charge. She seemed skeptical before finally agreeing it would have to make due.

They walked out under the watchful eye of Omega. He wagged his tail when she told him to be a good boy. They walked to the car where Don opened the door for her and she slid in.

"What kind of music do you like," he asked.

"Just turn it off and let your heartbeat be the only sound I hear." In another context he might have thought that was creepy or corny, but the way she said it and the situation they were in he thought it was extremely sexy.

They drove to the park largely in silence. She struggled giving him directions for she clearly was not used to navigating in a car. The sun had cleared the horizon and promised another hot day. The park looked desolate. Don thought it was a lot of wasted space as he looked down the long track where many soap box cars had raced down to the finish line.

Alless made sure he had the flash light and then took his hand and walked down the track. This is probably not going to be fun to walk back up when we come back he thought. They got to the end and she followed the turn off. They walked off the southern corner and into the woods for about fifty feet before she stopped. Alless looked around and Don thought they were lost. She moved the dry pine needles with her foot and uncovered a manhole cover. Buried in the dirt next to the cover was a crow bar. In a matter of seconds, she had the cover off and stood above it smiling.

"Ready for your adventure?" She grabbed his flashlight and went down first. He followed and when he reached the bottom he grimaced as he realized his shoes were going to be ruined. He should have grabbed an old pair, but he had no idea they would go spelunking, although given the nature of things he shouldn't have been surprised.

She moved through the tunnel with ease and he struggled to keep up. It was dark, damp and smelled the musty odor of stagnant water. There were spider webs everywhere and the thought of having spiders all around him made his skin crawl. He was shocked how far the tunnel went on. They walked for quite a ways before she took some steps on the right that led up to a closed door. Alless pushed against the door that resisted her efforts before swinging open revealing a dry corridor. She seemed to know right where she was going so much so that it made Don wonder if she played in these tunnels as a child.

Don thought about rats, spiders and bats. These walkways seemed like they had not seen anyone pass through them in years. She looked back and told him they were almost there. It felt like they had been walking a long time. At least he was getting in extra steps today. They took a couple of more turns and took stairs both up and down. She was taking his "I'll follow you anywhere," attitude a little too literally. Don was getting a really bad vibe about this adventure business. But she was so beautiful and sweet that the bad vibe only bounced up and down on the surface never sustaining a completely uneasy feeling.

They came to a locked door and paused. "We are here," she said smiling and a little out of breath. You brought me to a locked door. This was the surprise. Don was feeling just a tad bit annoyed when she added, "Boost me up to the light fixture."

He cupped his hands and she stepped in and reached up to unscrew the light cover. Don thought it was a small miracle that it was not broken. After completely unscrewing it, she turned it upside down and a key fell out into her hand. She screwed it back in, dropped down and held the key up like she had just rescued the Holy Grail.

Very slowly she unlocked the door and pushed it open. He thought she was doing it for dramatic effect for his benefit when in reality he just wanted it to be over. He wished they were in his bed making love.

She shined the light in and he was astonished to see a car. There were no big doors. The room had been built around the car like it was entombed. He stepped in and took the flashlight from her. The metal had dulled over the years and all four white wall tires were flat, but the car itself was not in horrible shape. He marveled at the pointed front end and how the back looked like a rocket ship thruster suspended between two large tail fins. It was a convertible and the top was gone revealing a small two seater cockpit. He had never seen a car like it. It was amazing. It reminded him of a car out of an old science fiction movie.

He whispered, "oh my god" and followed the long design of the car. He came across some lettering on the side. Le Sabre. He had no idea what year it was, but he couldn't help but wonder if it was the very first Le Sabre hidden away for posterity's sake. Or maybe it was some kind of prototype hidden from the public view so no one could steal any of the engineering aspects.

"Let's get in," she said and climbed into the passenger side. He followed suite in the driver's side. It was incredible. It felt much more like a rocket ship than a car. He looked over at her and could tell that she was thrilled that he was excited about the car. Don reached his arm around her and kissed her. He couldn't express the joy of kissing the woman of his dreams in the front seat of a super cool car that he thought very well may be the unicorn of cars. Their kisses became more passionate and before long he was stretched out on the trunk with his shorts around his knees while she grinded into him.

She looked down into his eyes. "Isn't this better than making love in your bed again?"

"This is absofuckinglutely amazing," he said. She took both of his wrist and pinned them together above his head. She held them tightly, He looked up at her and she winked at him. He lost it and came harder than he could ever remember cumming before. She came a moment later and squeezed so hard she pushed him out of her. Alless collapsed on top of him.

Once she caught her breath she told him he was amazing. He kissed her cheek and said "ditto". She pulled back a little bit so she could look in his eyes. "You know you want to say it."

He smiled and said, "what?"

"You know what I'm talking about. Just say it." Her voice had that curious way of being sweet, angelic, but yet demanding.

Don laughed and saw the she was looking at him intently, seriously. He felt her drawing him in with her eyes. It was that helpless feeling, but not in a bad way. A feeling that he would submit to her every wish, not because he was coerced, but because it was his desire. He felt his eyes and expression screaming I love you—I'm devoted to you. Then his lips moved and he whispered, "I love you." She kissed him passionately, looked at him playfully and then told him she loved him as well.

The dam was broken and he found himself telling her he loved her at every turn with every kiss. He needed her to know that he loved her, afraid she might forget or not feel loved. He did his best to make her understand it wasn't a rote saying—that every time he meant it from the depths of his soul.

They traced their steps back through the labyrinth and had to be nearing the end Don thought when she pushed him against the wall and held a finger to her mouth in the universal sign of "be quiet". She looked worried. Don had never seen that look on her face.

She turned off the flashlight and they pressed against the wall in the darkness. He could hear water dripping from a pipe overhead. He could hear her heartbeat. He could hear the faraway sloshing of someone walking followed by a scraping noise. There was a shuffling. Was there someone coming. Someone she knew to be afraid of. Maybe it was a security guard, but Don knew by her look that it was much more ominous than just a security guard. He wanted to step from the shadows and show her he could and would protect her. He was strong and was a good wrestler. He had extensive combat training. He could put up a good fight.

The shuffling grew louder and every now and then was followed by the splashing of water. There was a loud whistle that hurt his ears. Then there was a bang with a flash of light that ruined any night vision he had developed. He was completely in the dark and realized the whistle had stunted his hearing. He thought Alless was trying to communicate with him but he couldn't see her or hear her. He felt her leave his side. There was a blood curdling scream. He thought someone yelled "no!" More splashing.

Another flash of light. The sound of something ripping and tearing. Then an eerie silence that was more frightening than anything else.

A moment later and Alless was back beside him. She grabbed his hand and quickly led him away from where the light and the noise had been. They weren't running but they were close to a trot. After a few minutes she turned the flashlight back on and Don expected to find them surrounded by a horde of homeless zombies. They were alone. She hugged him tightly. He hoped he was comforting her. He wanted to ask what had happened, but knew it wasn't the right time. It was another question for later. A growing long list of questions he wanted to ask, but was holding out until she felt she could trust him with any information. *Jesus Christ, you're really not going to ask her what the unholy fuck that was all about? You've got to be kidding me! What happened to the little dude who had to know everything? I miss him! Did you also pick up on her not wanting you on top of her when you're having sex. That might be another little question to sling her way when you grow a pair.*

They found their way out of the hole and in the light Don noticed she had a splatter of mud up the front of her dress. Her hair was also askew; she looked tired. They went back to his house and slept until it was time for him to go to the gym. He asked if she was hungry and she said no. He made himself a shake and downed it. He felt like he was starving. He had missed the cheat meal with her and wasn't sure when he could now fit it in.

She kissed him and clung to him tightly. He felt like she wanted to tell him something. He held her and hoped he was making her feel safe. He had no idea what had happened in the tunnel. He really wanted to ask her, but he felt she would tell him when she felt comfortable to do so. He was slowly realizing there was a lot more to the homeless world than what met the eye. It was almost like an alternate reality and he wasn't sure how someone could fit in both worlds. Ultimately one would have to choose—ultimately he or Alless were going to have to decide if their love was bigger than the bond to the world they knew.

She pulled him tighter and pressed her entire body into his. She couldn't get close enough to him. After a few minutes she pulled back and looked at him, "Don, I love you and all of this is going to be difficult. Our roads are not easy. But whatever happens I want you to know how much I cherish being in your arms. How much I adore your presence. How much your love means to me. Promise me you will never think badly of me just because I am different than you."

Don kissed her forehead and said, "I promise you with everything I am."

Twenty

August 3, 32 Days Out, 183 pounds

Don ducked into Barnes and Noble hoping to look at a few magazines to keep him from just staring at the clock and waiting until he could feed again. He would check out the last remaining non-digital muscle magazine, Muscular Development, look at Writer's Digest, thumb through World Literature Today, and casually peak at the pages of Fangoria magazine. Magazines, the printed variety, were dying a slow death and that made Don sad. He had always looked forward to getting a new issue of a magazine in the mail. He would usually go through it quickly and then at a later date read it cover to cover. The internet was making it increasingly difficult for in-print magazines to turn a profit and be viable. The magazine racks at Barnes and Noble wanted you to believe otherwise. They were full of hundreds of different magazines. Don was walking around the racks when he heard someone talking quite loudly for a bookstore. His curiosity got the best of him and he walked towards the back of the store in the direction of the voice. He was surprised to see someone beginning a book reading and signing.

Don walked over and sat down with the seven other people in the audience. There were a few standing nearby who were curiously watching, but didn't want to commit to having a seat. Don wished he had remained standing, that way if it was boring or went on too long he could just casually walk away without anyone noticing. By sitting, he would nearly cause a scene if he decided to leave in the middle and would draw attention to himself by standing and walking away. He felt his anxiety creeping up. He tried to relax and immerse himself into the author's world

Greg Hubris, a local author, set his hardcover book on the podium and pushed his glasses further up his small nose with his right hand. An old girlfriend had once commented that it was a shame to hide his gorgeous slate eyes behind glasses, but the thought of wearing contacts made Greg sick to his stomach. His dirty blonde hair was cut short and styled in a way that a dab of product and thirty seconds was all it took to have his "do" ready for show time.

Greg took a deep breath. He was comfortable in his blue jeans, blue t-shirt and black, casual sport coat. The coat was tailored to fit him and sat on his shoulders perfectly. It didn't hang off his slim build like off the rack coats tended to. The left sleeve was empty and sewn to the coat in a way that kept the sleeve from flopping around. It also made it appear that there was an arm filling out the sleeve. But there wasn't.

He scanned the crowd once more looking to see if there was anyone he recognized—there was not a familiar looking face in the bunch. There also weren't any women that he found attractive. Oh, Greg knew authors were not rock stars, but he still couldn't stop fantasizing about a hot blonde in a short skirt sitting in the front row crossing and uncrossing her legs as she looked longingly at him. That would happen when he had truly arrived he mused.

"Thank you all for coming," Greg offered weakly and cleared his throat. "I'd like to begin this afternoon with a little reading from my new book." He said new book like there were old books, but there wasn't. Just one measly offering that he invested his life savings in writing and if it wasn't for the attack no one outside his family, if they even did, would have read it. He looked down at his hard cover book on the podium and it still made him smile to see his name on a book. The dust jacket was flat black. The title "Abducted, Abused & Abandoned" was in neon green at the top while his name was in the same color near the bottom of the book. In the middle were two neon green, leaf shaped eyes that were easily distinguishable as the eyes of a generic alien. He opened the cover and looked up once more before beginning to read.

"My name is Greg and I'm a survivor of life long abductions. I know the popular misconception is that your memory is either erased after your abduction or completely repressed and you need powerful hypnosis to find out what happened. That is not my situation. I remember every detail and every abduction perfectly. I wish I didn't remember it. I wish there was a metallic pen I could look at and my memories of the abduction would be gone. But that, is simply not my experience. I even recall the first time I encountered an alien being and I was at an age where most have no memories whatsoever.

"It was early fall in 1970. I was two years old and my three older brothers were at school. My dad was at work and my mom was in the kitchen making dinner. I was in my playpen in the living room. I don't know how the two small slender alien beings got in the house—they were just all of a sudden standing outside my playpen. They had thin, frail looking, sexless bodies with big heads and big dark eyes that dominated their facial features. They had a tiny mouth and tiny noses and no ears. At least then I didn't think they had ears. I would later learn that the three horizontal slits near the top of their head was what they used to hear with.

"Even at two years old I knew to be afraid. I started to cry out for my mommy and one of the beings held his finger to his very thin lips to

167

'shush' me. I remember thinking when someone does that it's important for you to be quiet. I tried to stop my crying but instead it manifested itself as hitching sobs. But at least I wasn't crying out. I was afraid but also remember being curious. There was a thought that these were new playmates or maybe a new pet like the brown dog 'Charlie' that occasionally ran by and brushed my face with his tail. I wanted to not be afraid. But I was afraid because I was always afraid. My older brothers took joy out of jumping out of nowhere to say 'boo' so that I would jump and draw my face into a frown before starting to cry. The little bit of rational I had as a two year old told me that although I was momentarily frightened I was never hurt or injured by the scare. Maybe these new things were harmless too.

"Right when I was letting my curiosity win the day the one who shushed me reached out and grabbed my hand. He jerked me to the edge of the playpen and held my chubby little hand like it was in a vice. I tried to pull away. I tried to sit down. I started to scream. The other being took out a small silver tube that looked like a crayon and stuck it into my wrist just below where my hand was being held. It hurt so bad. It was like the pain I felt when I accidently ran into my daddy's cigarette. The being held the tube against my wrist for a few seconds before pulling it away. Then the other being let go of my hand and I plopped down on my behind. I was now full on screaming for my mommy. I heard her yell from the kitchen 'hold on pumpkin, mommy will be right there.'"

Greg paused there and looked up from his book. He wasn't the best reader, but felt that because he was reliving a moment from his life the authenticity could be heard in his voice. Most in the small audience seemed to be captivated and that pleased him. He took a deep breath as he often did to reset his nerves. It was still difficult to tell others what he experienced and if it wasn't in black and white in front of him he didn't know if he would be able to tell the story. He went to look down at the scar on his wrist that served as a lifelong reminder of that first encounter. But that scar and most of that arm was gone somewhere in the woods of Michigan's Upper Peninsula. He continued.

"My screaming became hysterical wails as the nerves in my wrist frantically told me something was wrong. 'Oh my goodness,' I heard my mom exclaim and heard her running into the living room. Tears flowed like a waterfall down my little cheeks. She scooped me up in her arms and pleaded over and over, 'what's wrong baby?' I couldn't stop sobbing. She became frustrated and screamed: 'stop crying! What's wrong.' Through the sobs I whined 'hurt' and 'hot' and held up my wrist to her eyes. She pulled back and saw the puncture mark.

"She sat on the couch with me in her lap and inspected my wound in the light pouring through the window. 'Oh honey, did you cut yourself on the edge of the playpen?' My wailing had subsided and I shook my head no. She kissed my hand above the wound and took me in the bathroom where she poured something from a small green jar on it and it made it hurt worse. She apologized mentioning it was necessary to keep me from being infected. Little did we know that it was too late, I was indeed infected." Greg looked up from the book and adlibbed: "infected until an ape like creature tore my arm from my body." There was a guffaw and some chuckling. Greg felt anger rising up and knew he should return to the book before that rising rage got the best of him.

"She dried it off and put a band aid on it. I kept looking around to see where the little beings were hiding. There was no sign of them. She put me back in the playpen and I watched as she inspected the places were the playpen folded up. She ran her hand over them looking for sharp edges. I wanted to tell her about the beings but I did not yet have words for monsters.

"Satisfied that there were no sharp edges and that my wound must have been a freak accident she started to head back to the kitchen. 'No' I screamed and the hysterical crying came back until she picked me up

169

again. I said 'ascared" over and over between the great hitching sobs. She took me in the kitchen with her and I felt momentarily safe in her arms. She whispered to me that there was nothing to be scared of and that she would be right there with me. I resisted when she put me in the highchair, but took comfort in her telling me everything was going to be ok. It turned out that was the biggest lie she had ever told. I spent the rest of the day in my highchair screaming hysterically whenever she wasn't in my sight. I vaguely remember her telling my daddy over dinner about how I had cut myself and it must have really hurt because I did a lot of screaming all day and acted terrified. Daddy looked at me, was about to say something, but then just went on with eating his dinner. That night was the beginning of me crying myself to sleep every night out of sheer terror."

Greg stopped and closed the book. He paused for dramatic effect and said the next line from memory: "I was five years old when I encountered them again."

"How old were you when you saw the Loch Ness Monster?" someone yelled from the back of the room. The crowd chuckled and Don's curiosity was piqued.

Clearly flustered Greg gave a tight lip smile and asked if anyone had any questions about the book.

A middle aged man stood up near the front and said, "In the book you talk about having sex with aliens as a teenager. Do you think this was just your mind's way of masking your homosexual activity?"

"What?" Greg stammered. The heat of anger made his face flush.

The man gestured broadly with his hands and replied, "you were brought up to think homosexual activity was wrong so to sidestep parental disappointment you created the illusion of having sex with aliens instead."

Greg was dumbfounded. "I am not gay," he blurted.

"Clearly you want to believe that and you want your parents to believe that, but please it is 2022. It's quite all right and dare I say normal if you would like to now come out of the closet."

"What kind of bullshit questioning is this!" Greg fumed. "I am not and have never participated in any gay sex. Jesus H. Christ!" Greg saw his publicist start to get up out of the corner of his eye. He took a breath and regained his composure. "Any other questions?"

Don wanted to raise his hand. He had a few questions, but asking a question in this format was a little bit out of his comfort zone.

A young man with more piercings and tattoos then Don could count stood up. "Do you think anyone would have published this nonsense if you hadn't got attacked by a bear up north while writing it?"

"I know what a bear looks like and it wasn't a goddamn bear!"

The young man feeling even more bold continued, "After all this made up shit do you really think anyone will believe anything you ever say again in your life? You're a classic case of crying wolf." Don chuckled to himself and thought clearly you have no idea what a classic case of anything is.

"Fuck you!" Greg Hubris screamed and pointed his only index finger at the young man. "You're a scumbag piece of shit!" A man in a suit who was obviously associated with Greg grabbed the author and turned him away from the crowd,

"I'm sorry. We are going to have to cancel the rest of the Q&A and the book signing. Thank you again for coming." The suit offered and led an angry Greg away from the crowd. The meager audience were making jokes about little green men among themselves. Don felt bad for the author. In a way, writing a book was very similar to a bodybuilding contest. You worked hard for a long period of time to put your finished result out there for all to judge and critique.

Neither Greg nor the suit saw the young man with the piercings and tattoos come up. Don noticed him and the young man threw his hands over his heads and roared like a monster, "I'm a CHUD! Are you going to write about this encounter in a book?" The pierced and tatted man laughed and turned his back on Greg who lowered his shoulder and charged him. They both went sprawling to the ground knocking over a couple of tables and an expensive looking lamp. Greg came up on top and threw a punch into the young man's jaw before being hauled off by onlookers.

"I'm going to fucking sue you!" piercings and tat man screamed at Greg. "You're a fucking psycho. You're finished!" Several men led him away from Greg as the suit made sure he stayed in between Greg and the young man.

Don watched intently as the suit spoke with several Barnes and Noble employees. Order was restored and Greg Hubris sat in a chair disheveled and embarrassed. Don decided to approach him and ask a legitimate question about the book.

"I'm sorry," Greg said, "the signing has been canceled."

"I'm intrigued by your book and have a real question. I also would like to purchase a copy of it," Don said hoping his harmless intentions were showing through.

The author looked him over and realized he could use some positive publicity even though the muscled man didn't look like he was one to share a story on Instagram. "Sure. What's your question?"

"Where are these aliens? I mean do they fly back to their home planet after such an encounter or are they somewhere on earth and if they are how do they avoid the fact that almost every square foot is monitored by cameras." Don saw Greg's brow furrow and quickly added, "I'm not doubting you I am just curious."

Greg ran his fingers through his hair. "I honestly don't know. A lot of people believe they have stations deep within our oceans that they operate out of. Some even believe they have a massive underground system of cities. I think they have motherships that orbit our earth and if they have the technology to come here then they probably have the technology to remain invisible to our radar detection systems."

Don nodded and was about to ask why they come here and what do we have to offer when Greg continued. "There is a local guy who calls himself Sir Grave the Ghoul that runs a podcast. He believes aliens inhabit the tunnels under big cities. He has done several episodes from the utility tunnels under Flint and claims to have video proof of an alien in a tunnel under the old Oak Grove Sanatorium. If you want to check him out just enter Sir Grave the Ghoul in your search engine and he should pop right up."

"Thanks," Don said sincerely and purchased an autographed copy of the book. He looked at his watch and even though his stomach had already told him so, it was time to eat. He wanted to get home and check this YouTuber out anyway. His mind kept going back to what had happened to him and Alless in the tunnel. Did they have an alien encounter? Did the homeless community know more about extraterrestrial beings living on earth than anyone else? He wondered if there were scores of homeless people who tried to tell stories of otherworldly visitors only to be mocked as crazy.

Don had no trouble finding the guy's YouTube channel. He saw he had just over a hundred subscribers and each video had less than a thousand views which meant he was not really popular in that community considering every video featuring Giorgio A. Tsoukalos had hundreds of thousands of views. He searched through Sir Grave the Ghoul's collection and found the video "Video Proof of an Alien in the Tunnels under Flint, MI". Don clicked on it.

There was a lengthy political commercial that played before the episode that Don found annoying. Does anyone really change their mind because of an attack ad? He hoped not. The video started and Don thought he was looking at someone trying to pull off a Jim Ignatowski, of Taxi fame, Halloween costume. He sure hoped Sir Grave wasn't trying to enhance his credibility through his appearance, but then again that he called himself Sir Grave the Ghoul should have told him everything he needed to know.

"I finally, after months of setting up in the tunnels of Flint Michigan, have video proof that extraterrestrial beings are living here on earth under our cities. This is not an original idea of mine but something I learned about when I became a member of MUFON. It is now my area of expertise."

The man droned on and on about his qualifications including being abducted by aliens as a young child. Don was skeptical when it came to extraterrestrial life on earth, but was something he wanted to believe was true. He and his brother had seen an unidentified flying object one summer night while looking out their living room window. The boomerang shaped object tumbled through the night sky and left them both wide eyed and scared. They had no idea if the object was extraterrestrial in nature, but it was certainly something they had never seen before.

Don also was not so elitist that he believed humans were the only intelligent beings in the entire vast universe. When he laid under the stars at night, he knew there was something more out there. Something his mind couldn't comprehend but just as real as himself. But again, his skepticism reigned because of our technology not producing any evidence. There was also the fact that nearly everyone ran around with a camera in hand and there was literally no more photographic or video evidence than there was before smart phones—at least not authentic evidence.

Sir Grave kept reiterating he had just such proof. Don became annoyed as the video was winding down and he had still not produced the goods. Then came the kicker. He had the extensive proof on his OnlyFans page and for a measly ten dollars a month, you could gain access to that "astonishing" video and many others that would erase any doubts you might have. Don went over and clicked the thumbs down icon. He read through the comments and universally they complained what a bunch of bullshit it was and how the video in question was basically a shadowy figure moving in a dimly lit tunnel. There were no discernable features. And even at the end of the video when a bright flash happens all you see is an outline of a smallish shaped figure with so much glare that it could be anything.

Don decided to take the reviewers' word for it and save his ten dollars to buy a giant ice cream sundae after the contest. That would probably be way more satisfying than a dark video of what could be anything. Don looked at the book on his table and hoped it would be half as good as Communion by Whitley Strieber or Contact by Carl Sagan. The guy seemed interesting enough and was clearly passionate about what he wrote. Don thought he should check out the story about how he lost his arm, but got distracted by a YouTube video discussing the merits of going to failure in your workouts. He drifted in and out of sleep while he watched.

Twenty-One

August 5, 26 Days Out, 177 pounds

Don stepped on the scale and was astonished that he had lost another pound. He calculated that he had averaged losing a pound a day for the last ten days. He had cut 50 calories a day from his diet and slightly increased his T3 intake, but that should have just given him a little bump—not a pound a day! A pound a day was a crazy number and meant that he had to be losing muscle as well as fat. He had worried a few weeks ago that he might not be able to get down to weight for the contest; the worry now was that he was going to lose too much.

He looked in the mirror and went through the mandatory poses. He thought his arms looked small and wished he had more detail in his back. It wasn't that his arms were small, they were in proportion with the rest of his body, but standing on stage with a bunch of guys whose arms outshined the rest of their physique was going to make his look small and underdeveloped.

Don loved how tiny his waist appeared from the side. From the front his well developed obliques made his waist look a little thick. He thought about how Johnny Fuller was criticized for having a wide waist back in the eighties, but in reality, he just had properly developed obliques. Don would take the thick obliques any day over the insulin and growth hormone bubble gut that most guys had. He thought they should be penalized for a bubble gut but that never seemed to be the case.

His chest was thicker than it had ever been and didn't flatten out completely when he hit a front double bicep pose. It also looked fuller and had more depth when he hit a side chest pose. The side chest pose was quickly becoming one of his best poses and showed off his strengths while minimizing his weaknesses. Overall Don felt like at twenty-six days out he was in as good or better condition than he had been on show day his last few shows. He was excited to see how the final package would look. He was simultaneously afraid that the final package would look too small. It was a struggle to not find faults in your preparation. He hit one more side chest when he saw the mark on his right glute.

The mark looked like a scab or maybe even a rash. He wondered if he had cut himself in the tunnel or been exposed to something that was causing him to break out. He looked at it from several angles in the mirror and thought it was almost undetectable unless you were looking extremely close. However, any blemish to his physique might draw the judges attention away from looking at the shredded muscle and focusing on a flaw. He thought twenty plus days was plenty of time for it to heal.

Don got dressed and could really tell that his clothes were not fitting him well any longer. He felt like he was swimming inside his hoodies. Maybe he should just give them all to the homeless and buy smaller sizes.

Do you really believe she just found your hoodie at a bus stop? The inner voice was awake. *That would be one hell of a coincidence. You give it to a dude who really liked it and probably had some need for it and he accidently leaves it at a bus stop? He didn't look like the type who would be using bus stops did he? And let's just pretend that he did and did indeed leave it there. Alless just happened to be the one that walked by and found it. And best of all she just threw on some random hoodie and started wearing it? That is a lot to buy.*

Let me also remind you about the whole tunnel shenanigans. That was some far out shit that really does need to be explained. That's what I don't get. You would badger a girl for answers if she wore something green on a fall Saturday but with this chick you're just sweeping everything under the rug pretending it doesn't exist. What gives? Don't throw the love bullshit out there either. You are acting like you are scared to death to find a flaw in her. Like one little blemish would blow up your whole worldview of her and you would see her for what she really is.

Don concentrated. Be intentional. Be different. Do things differently and maybe you will find happiness. Do things the same and be your old miserable self, living with righteous indignation and guilt.

He walked out the door and into the humid blast furnace of an August morning. The contest was less than a month away. He was already good on his weight and his condition was very close to being spot on. He normally liked to peak for a contest and not be ready until the final week. This was going to be more difficult. He was going to have to hold top conditioning for a couple of weeks. The biggest problem was that he was already completely exhausted. This was a feeling he didn't usually have until the last week,

Don was also experiencing mental problems associated with being in a calorie deficit for a long time and also being at a very low body fat percentage. He was forgetful, struggled to concentrate, lacked patience, and had difficulty problem solving. It was the perfect storm of problems to sabotage a blooming relationship. He thought about dropping out again. He didn't want Alless to think this was who he really was. He was better than this. He was a romantic, at least in the early stages of a relationship.

He saw the old Buick and decided to just quickly walk by the house without paying much attention to it. He told himself he wouldn't stop no matter what. It would be ok as long as he didn't linger in front of it. He would pretend it was just another old abandoned house and confidently walk on by. He got close and that smell put up a warning wall that told him to stay away.

"Often, for undaunted courage, fate spares the man it has not already marked." Don quoted Beowulf aloud and pressed forward through the shield of vile smells. He didn't necessarily believe in fate and surely didn't believe in predestination. It was a topic that kept him out of religious circles where people ignorantly claimed tragedy "is all part of God's wondrous plan." Don liked to think God had better plans and worked within our poor decisions to help guide us to the best possible outcome. If tragedy was God's best laid plans than as a deity he didn't deserve to be worshipped.

The smell was becoming overwhelming as Don bravely (or stupidly) pressed forward. He glanced at the house and he felt the urge to explore it. It had a magnetism to it that drew you close when you looked at it. It was like a giant trap. You knew the spring was going to be sprung and snap your back in two but you couldn't resist the allure of the stinky cheese. Don forced himself to look away and was almost passed the house when he saw the yellow cart nestled on the porch out of the corner of his eye. He stopped. The pull to come closer was incredible despite the stench.

Go in and look for Alless, a new internal voice hissed. *She is in the house. All your answers are in the house. Go in and be enlightened. Everything you want to know about her is inside. Now is the time to find out the answers to your questions. Once inside, the smell of death and decay will be replaced by Heliotropium. You will feel like you're in a dessert shop where they are baking you a fresh cherry pie. Just go in and seek out her beauty in the ugliness of decay. She awaits you. She beckons you. She desires you.*

179

Don felt himself leaning towards the house. He wouldn't say he was in a trance but considering his prep state of mind he was completely focused on the entrance. He started to take a step in the direction of the door when he felt something grab the cuff of his sweat pants and pull. It was Omega tugging at him away from the house.

Don felt like he was being pulled apart. The house wanted him inside, Omega wanted to pull him away. He wanted to do both at the exact same time and felt his soul being torn asunder. Omega gave a hard jerk and Don tumbled away from the house. He would swear it felt like he was pulled from a magnetic field and could then resist the urge to go inside. Omega let go of his sweat pants and ran a few steps away from the house and barked. Don thought he would just take one last look behind him, but he heard Alless' voice shouting in the distance.

He followed Omega to the sound of her voice and found his love sitting at a picnic table near the soccer field. He kissed her before sitting down across from her. She had her Detroit Lions hoodie back on.

"I was calling to you for a long time," she said sadly. Don looked at his Fitbit and was shocked to see what time it was. He should have finished his walk fifteen minutes ago. He had completely lost over thirty minutes of time. Had he really been standing in front of the house that long or was he just miscalculating what time he left.

"Don," he heard Alless say in the distance. "Don," she said again and jerked him out of his stupor.

"I'm sorry, I was just momentarily confused. This prep is really starting to wear on me and it is so not fair to you."

"It's ok, I'm just worried about you. Why do you do it?"

"Do what," Don asked completely clueless as to what she was inquiring about.

"Why do you put your body through so much? What do you really want to accomplish by all this." Alless stared across the table at him with wide eyes.

"It's mostly my competitive nature with a lot of goal driven mentality thrown in. I also like working out. And I am in my comfort zone when living the regimented life."

"I'm sorry if I am a disruption to your regiment. I don't mean to be."

Don had never seen Alless feeling melancholy before and he didn't like it. He took her hands in his. "You are not a disruption to me at all. If anything you inspire me to be better so I can make you proud. I would never look at you as a disruption."

She offered a weak smile and shook his hands up and down ever so slightly. She was acting very unlike her confident and happy self. They sat in silence for a few minutes before she said, "Can I ask you something and you will do it."

Don's gut reaction was to say sure. However, he was feeling a little different towards this version of Alless. It was like there was a pall over their relationship all of a sudden and she lacked the ability to pull them into the sunshine as she had done in the past. He finally answered, "Of course" and knew he wasn't being completely honest with her as she had not been honest with him about the Monsta Clothing hoodie.

"I want you to stay away from that house. There are a lot of bad things associated with that house. It is where a lot of drug deals, robberies and prostitution happens. It is dangerous for homeless people, but much more so for someone like you when it's dark."

Don wondered what she meant by someone like him, but decided not to ask because he knew it would lead somewhere he was not ready to go.

181

"I try to avoid it. It gives me some weird vibes. But I'm also curious about it and some of the things I've seen in it. What do you know about it?"

"I know enough to stay away and to warn people I care about to stay away. There is nothing good in that house. I need you to stay away from it. I can't protect or help you in any way except to warn you not to go near that house. That is my contribution to your wellbeing. That is all I can contribute," Alless said looking defeated.

"Ok. I will stay away from it. Curiosity killed the cat, right?" Don quipped. He felt again like he was being dishonest with her. He wanted to learn the secrets of the house. He wanted to learn her secrets. He desperately wanted all the answers to his questions. He pulled up a quote from Michel de Montaigne and read it silently: "Pride and curiosity are the two scourges of our souls. The latter prompts us to poke our noses into everything, and the former forbids us to leave anything unresolved and undecided." He felt the idea in that quote was going to be the ruination of his and Alless' relationship. He longed for that head over heels in love feeling that made him disregard all the red flags and simply be mesmerized by her. He wanted to be drawn in by her again.

She said, "Thank you," and her countenance was uplifted. Don was quick to notice the change and wanted to continue the upward trajectory.

"I love you," he said, "and despite the obstacles in our way I feel I will always love you. My connection with you, in just a short time, is a stronger bond than I have ever had with anyone. You truly have my heart and I trust you with it and only you."

She squeezed his hand and asked if she could walk him home. He told him he would be thankful and honored if she accompanied him. On the way they talked about squirrels and birds, trees and trash, the weather and the street lights—neither mentioned the house again.

"Do you want to come in," Don asked when they arrived at their destination. She declined the offer with no explanation. "Can you wait here? I have something for you." She agreed and Don bounded into the house and was back outside in a moment. He was relieved to see her still standing on the sidewalk. Part of him thought she would have been gone.

Don took the diamond cut gold necklace and put it on her over the hood she was wearing. The shiny gold colored key dangled between her breast. She looked confused and he explained, "It's the key to my house. You can come and go whenever you please. It doesn't matter if I'm home or not you can come by and hang out, take a nap, get something to eat... whatever."

She smiled and her eyes brightened. Alless threw her arms around him and thanked him over and over. It meant so much to her that he was willing to do that. She kissed him deeply and Don felt like the temporary malaise in their relationship was behind them. They looked deeply into one another's eyes as their arms held them together. It was a look that would have left no doubt in a passer-by's mind that they were in love. It was a look that belonged to them and could never be shared with another.

Twenty-Two

August 8, 23 Days Out, 176 pounds

Don was embarrassed to have only kept his word for three days. He had decided the night before that he would swing by the house after the gym. He had spent the better part of the previous evening researching about the house. He had made quite a few discoveries.

The two story house with a basement was built in the 1950s when General Motors were hiring people off the street and the economy in Flint was booming. The original owner lived there alone for fifty-three years. He died when he fell down the basement stairs, broke a hip and could not get to a place to call for help. He laid at the foot of the stairs unable to move for over a week before death over took him. Dehydration was listed on the death certificate as cause of death. Don thought it was a horrible way to die but nothing fantastical that would give the house a strange haunted house feel. He never saw or felt anything that he could tie to the old man's fall or death.

The house sat vacant for three years as the courts tried to determine who inherited the house. The man had no wife or kids and appeared to have outlived any parents or siblings. It was eventually put up for auction where a young man purchased it only to allow it to go into foreclosure without ever making a single payment on it. Some say he went into hiding after it was discovered that he was not who he said he was. Others say he just turned up missing with no explanation.

It sat for another year until an investor purchased it and rented the house out. Julio Jackson was the first and only person to rent it. He had served time in prison for sex trafficking in Ohio and then did another stint in Indiana for selling drugs. He convinced the landlord that he was rehabilitated and needed a fresh start.

The neighbors reported signs of drug dealing and prostitution almost immediately after Julio moved in. "There was a constant stream of shady looking men going in for a few minutes and then coming out. Not to mention all the harlots hanging out in and around the house," a neighbor told the Flint Journal after the house burned down. A couple of times gunshots were reported coming from the house. The day before the fire a couple of neighbors filed a complaint about a horrible smell that came from the house. The police did not get a chance to check on it before a small explosion and fire was called in.

The fire was confirmed to have had started when a small meth lab exploded in a back bedroom. Nine bodies were found dead in the aftermath, four of the bodies belonged to children. It was later proven that two of the people had been dead long before the fire started as the result of gunshot wounds to the head. All the victims in the house had been males except for one female who was reported to have been the mother of the four. She was also reported to have been a long time known prostitute.

After the bodies were removed and inspections performed the house sat as it currently is. There was an insurance issue over the situation of the fire and what would be covered that was holding up the house being torn down. However, it was at this time that things really got strange.

There had been nine calls to the police department in the last year regarding the house. Five of them had been about homeless people going in the house. Two were about strange lights and noises coming from within the house. One was about two people having sex on the front porch. And the final one was "I saw a monster enter the house just after midnight. It was small in structure and had fish like scales covering its body. It had two enormous eyes on its lizard shaped head. It looked right at me when I saw it out of my kitchen window. I'm afraid its going to come across the street and attack me."

The police report filed in response to the call was equally as strange and certainly seemed to warrant a follow up call. It read, "Arrived at the scene to discover a burned out house. I walked up to the porch where I heard some very strange noises. Nothing like I had ever heard before. I went to investigate further but the condition of the house led me to believe it was unsafe to go any further into the house. I called out and a female voice replied 'squatter's rights'. I inquired as to the safety of the female and she said, 'everyone is fine'. I started to exit when I saw a series of flashing lights coming from what I assumed was an upstairs room. I called out again asking if everyone was safe. The same voice told me yes and I exited the premises concerned for my own safety. I determined that homeless squatters were in the house and that the neighbor had been mistaken about what she had seen due to the poor lighting and her failing eyesight. This was confirmed by previous reports of homeless people going in the house."

Don thought it extremely strange the officer left people inside an unsafe house. Maybe there were legal issues with squatters he knew nothing about, but it sure didn't seem right. He thought about all this while he battled insomnia and that icky feeling you had when you took too many sleep aides. It felt roughly like a panic attack and a dream running head-long into each other at a high rate of speed. Somewhere in the night, he determined he would have a look at the house in the daylight.

The house was harder to find in the car and in the daylight than he had anticipated. He finally rolled up on the soccer field and the picnic table where he had vowed to Alless that he would never again go near the house. The inner voice suddenly seemed to be on Alless' side. *Really? You can't keep your word for more than a few days? She must mean a lot to you for you to be shitting on a promise you just made to her. And for what so you can satisfy some sense of curiosity that has nothing to do with your life. Maybe you hope to find her there shacked up with some homeless dude so you can end this sham of a relationship and get on with your contest prep without all the added stress. I think you're realizing this was just some cute little fantasy and its not coming to fruition like you had hoped and you're now looking for a way out. If you don't find something damning in the house you will tell her you looked and broke your promise which would make you untrustworthy and the façade will be over.*

I don't want to end the relationship with her. I love her and I want to do everything to keep her safe. She has lived on the street so long she doesn't know how to depend on someone else for her safety. She doesn't know how to receive help. I need to unravel this mystery so I can be the best boyfriend possible.

Oh poppycock. To paraphrase Pascal you want to satisfy your curiosity so you can have mastery of it—its vanity. You can't stand anything mysterious. It hurts your soul to think something is knowable but someone is keeping that knowledge from you. You take it as a slap in the face. You feel like she thinks she can't trust you with that knowledge and you're going to show her, relationship be damned.

"Fuck off," Don said and felt an uneasiness pulsate through his veins. He was irritated, tired and hungry. He wanted this contest to be over with so he could get on with his life without being shackled to the clock and a lunch bag. He was no longer having fun and he blamed everything on being in contest prep. His whole body ached. He was tired of it hurting when he urinated and tired of jabbing himself with needles. He was tired of taking stimulants and sleep aids. He was tired of it all.

He parked at the soccer field and got out of his car with his clothes still sweaty. He walked up to the house with a renewed confidence that wasn't there in the dark. In the light the house looked very different. It didn't look menacing and evil. It looked broken and beaten. Yes, it still smelled but nothing like it had in the early hours of the morning. Don walked up the sidewalk. Gone was the magnetic pull and almost hypnotic like suggestions. The yellow cart was nowhere to be found. For the first time he stepped up on the porch and peered in the doorway.

There was all sorts of trash strewn on the floor and wallpaper flaked off the walls like bark on a birch tree without any of the hope of renewal that mythology afforded the birch tree. The ceiling was the color of a badly burned cookie sheet. Don took a step inside and narrowly averted stepping on a used condom. Several trial sized liquor bottles dotted the floor. He took another step and saw a tattered mattress on the floor in one of the backrooms. The charred remains of a door resting on the bottom hinge hung open enough for Don to see stairs leading downward. He took a step in that direction and felt like he had been Venus Flytrapped.

The overpowering stench dropped him to a knee. The room swirled around him and he reached out to grab a fallen chair to keep himself upright. The chair felt sticky to the touch and he thought it was the same glue used in a mousetrap. The more he tried to pull away the further entangled in the glue he became. He thought his arm was coming apart at the elbow as he pulled with all his might. He vomited on his pant leg. The odor became a real entity that moved like a smoke monster into his throat gagging him. He would vomit it out and it would jump right back in. He was hyperventilating. He was panicking.

Don's muscles felt weak and ineffective. He realized he couldn't hear anything. It was like his ears had popped and now were stuffed with cotton.

He tried to call out but the wider he opened his mouth the thicker the smoke monster became in his throat. He was gagging and choking. He felt his bladder cut loose and he fell to his butt. Every point of contact was immersed in the sticky glue substance that was taking on a life of its own like in the movie The Blob. It was spreading up his arm and wrapping around his waist. It burned to the touch and Don wondered if it was eating his flesh and would soon dissolve his bones.

He closed his eyes and couldn't reopen them. The house was closing in around him and a vision of Alless flashed in his mind's eyes as he thought about how much he was going to miss her. They had barely begun their relationship and because he didn't listen to her it was now going to be over. All his hard work for the contest down the drain. He regretted he would never taste pizza again. He was about to submit to death when he felt the blob loosen its grip. He made a herculean effort to get to his feet and stumble towards the door. The house reached for him and he lunged out onto the porch, rolling down the steps and landing on his backside on the sidewalk.

He crawled out to the street and wondered why he couldn't open his eyes. He then realized they were open but it was now nighttime. He looked to his wrist to check his Fitbit only to realize it was gone. It must have come off in the house. He got to his feet and didn't look back as he ran to his car. He brushed off the dirt and debris from his clothes and fell safely into his car. He almost fainted when he realized he had been in the house for over three hours.

The shock wore off after a few minutes and Don pulled his vehicle away from the house. He drove home anxious to get in the shower and wash the house off his body. It disturbed him. It was the antithesis of Alless. For all the reasons she made him feel good and loved the house had just as many reasons to make him feel nasty and scared. Don thought it odd that her positive presence in his life was counter balanced by the negative presence of the house. And even more odd he couldn't seem to stay away from either one. The real kicker was he somehow felt they were connected—they had a bond. It felt like a love triangle gone horribly wrong.

The hot water cascaded over his body cleansing him both physically and metaphorically. Don had lost time on several occasions in the past, but every one of those occasions had been because of alcohol and drugs. Maybe someone had slipped a mickey into his post workout shake. And while he thought that was absurd was it really any more absurd than what had happened at the house. Normal…reasonable…were words that no longer applied to him. His life had become a series of sideshow acts shaken up with a haunted attraction. He could not make heads nor tails on what was going on. His life was spinning recklessly out of control when it should have been perfectly predictable and mundane. Was Alless to blame? Was the house to blame? Were they connected—were they one and the same?

Anxiety caused him to sit in the tub and water washed over his body. Was the tub sucking him in like the house. He watched the drain and expected to see his foot being pulled down the drain with a Pennywise on the other end. He reached up and shut the water off and sat in the tub shaking.

"Often, every daybreak, alone I must

bewail my cares. There's now no one living

to whom I dare mumble my mind's understanding.

I know as truth that it's seen suitable

for anyone to bind fast their spirit's closet,

hold onto the hoards, think whatever…"

He bolted from the empty tub and downed a couple of Xanax. He closed his eyes and wished all the feelings and sensations away. He stumbled to the couch and put his feet up. The pinpricks danced up and down and zigzagged across his legs. He wanted to somehow crawl out of his skin. He imagined kissing Alless. Oh, how much he cherished every kiss. How her lips perfectly covered his and in sync they puckered and opened and lingered...

Don released the negative feelings as he inhaled deeply through his nose and exhaled out of his mouth. Alless' kisses pushed the house away and Don started to feel almost normal again. He wished Alless were there so he could hold her and feel her gentle heartbeat. He needed her touch. Breath in and exhale... He longed to feel her hair on his face. He felt like he was really missing someone for the first time in his life...another feels like the first time.

He felt himself drifting off to sleep. Don forced himself to get up and get everything ready for the next day. He took his nighttime pills that consisted of Yohimbe, taurine, chromium picolinate, vanadyl sulfate, winstrol and his sleep mixture of trazodone, Tylenol Pm and liquid melatonin. He already had a double dose of Xanax and expected to fall asleep quickly.

Don laid in his bed wide awake. He took enough sleep aides to put down a bull, why weren't they working? Had he taken a nap inside the house and that explained why he was in there so long? He let his hands roam over his body feeling the definition and cuts. He marveled at the thickness and length of some of the veins sticking out against the skin. He felt his lower back and was pleased that the fat was finally melting away from that troublesome area. He felt very hard to the touch all over. The masteron was clearly working. He touched a spot on the side of his lats and winced. There was something there that hurt. It felt like a chunk of skin was missing. He entertained the thought of getting up and checking it out when sleep covered him like a crashing wave and he was off into dreamland.

He dreamed of hanging out with his ex-girlfriend, the one who finally made him realize how horrible he had been. She was nice to him in the dream and he was happy. Then she ran off and left him alone. He chased after her in the tunnels under Flint. Water splashed up with every footfall and he wished he had worn some nice water resistant shoes. He heard a scream so close that it rattled his very being. He came across his ex's upper torso and head. She has the very readable expression of "why" on her dead face. Don looked ahead. A giant lizard like creature was eating the rest of her. He ran away and experienced the carnage of every girl he had ever hurt strewn about the path in front of him. It was a macabre and gruesome trip down memory lane. He looked back to see where the monster was and it was gone. There was no sign of a monster and he took a bite of the apple in his hand. His conscious told him he was the monster and he realized the apple was his first wife's heart. Don jerked awake. He thought what the fuck kind of dream was that? Fell back asleep and forgot the dream forever.

Twenty-Three

August 10, 21 Days Out, 175 pounds

Don thought, at three weeks out, it was too close to his contest to have a cheat meal or even a slice of birthday cake. Therefore, he spent his birthday quietly going about his business without much fanfare. They had played some silly Happy Birthday song at the gym and that was about all the acknowledgment he had received. The only present was the new Fitbit he had bought himself to replace the one he had lost in the house.

He had checked his phone often thinking that someone might text him Happy Birthday, but it was just another day. He hadn't seen Alless in five days and wasn't sure when (or if) he would see her again. He hated that part of their relationship. He was not a fly by the seat of your pants type of guy. He liked planning and being regimented. He liked to know what was going to happen and when. Not knowing when he would see a girl he was in love with was agonizing. Part of him told him he deserved all the agony he was getting.

Don went to turn on the television and relax for a few minutes before turning in for the night. Instead, he picked up the novel he had purchased at Barnes and Noble. He started to read where the author had quit at the book signing.

"I was a scared little kid. Maybe it was a hangover from the encounter at two years old but a lot of it had to do with my upbringing. I had three older brothers and like older brothers do they took joy in scaring me. I was terrified to go in our basement because I had been told that a monster lived in the tiny hole where the sump pump sat. It would crawl out of that hole and eat me if I ever found myself alone in the basement. I imagined it all slimy and green with a giant mouth and enormous teeth. I was also afraid of helicopters. I was conditioned to believe that if I was outside when a helicopter flew over that it would land on top of me and squash me. If it didn't squash me then surely it would chop off the top of my head with its blades like what happened to the zombie in Dawn of the Dead. I was certain that a disembodied hand roamed the house and waited for me to be alone so that it could choke the life out of me. My brothers had models of all the famous monsters in their room: Dracula, Gillman, The Mummy, The Wolfman. I was terrified of them. They even had little figures of the Beatles that scared me because they reminded me of the Zuni Fetish Warrior from the movie Trilogy of Terror that I had somehow managed to watch. Therefore, it was no wonder my parents thought it was my brothers being mean to me when I had my second encounter with the aliens.

"Once again, this memory is very vivid. It was a Saturday afternoon in early spring and a gentle breeze was blowing through the windows. I had just finished eating a bowl of SpagehttiOs and was looking out the open window to avoid watching an episode of the Outer Limits that everyone else in the family was watching. I know the armchair psychologist among you will proclaim "no wonder you thought you encountered an alien, you were listening to The Outer Limits!" And if this had been my only encounter I might tend to agree. However, it was the second in a long line of encounters.

"I looked out and saw the mail lady in her station wagon bouncing up and down as she drove the uneven path of our dirt road. She reached our box and I strained to see what she was putting in the old rusty box across the street. It looked like a magazine. Maybe it was the new Sears catalogue I thought or the TV Guide. I watched her pull away and turned to ask my mom if I could go get the mail. She said I could as long as I looked both ways before crossing the street. I bolted out the door without a care or concern in the world other than finding out what was in the mailbox.

"I started to run across the street and remembered my mom's directions. I looked both ways and there wasn't a car in sight. I bounced across the road leaping over holes like a jungle explorer. I opened the metallic box that was mostly orange with rust and saw that it wasn't a catalogue or even a TV Guide. It was car magazine addressed to my oldest brother. I was so disappointed. I walked back to the house without any of the bounce or excitement in my step that I had on my way to get the mail. I started up the small flight of concrete stairs when I saw it nestled amongst the rosebushes beside the porch.

"It was my height and my build except that its head was much larger. And its eyes were bigger and seemed to glow—they reminded me of the lens of a Magic 8-ball but much larger. It was wearing some type of metallic suit that was silver or grayish in color, like the color our mailbox was before it rusted. The exposed flesh had what appeared to be light scales covering it or maybe it was just the pattern of their skin I thought at the time. Its mouth was tiny and it beckoned me to come to it without moving its mouth. I wanted to run and I wanted to scream. I could do neither. I nudged closer to it hoping someone would look out the window and save me. I moved closer and wondered how it was not being scratched up by the thorns on the rosebush. I pulled against the force driving me towards it when out of the corner of my eye I saw a second being come from behind me and push me off the porch into the rosebushes.

"The alien that had beckoned me grabbed my wrist in the same fashion that one had when I was a baby and jabbed a silver cylinder into the exact same spot. It hurt so bad that I finally found my voice and screamed out. I was screaming hysterically when my family came running out on the porch to see what happened. My mom pulled me out of the bushes and my dad frantically searched for the monsters that I said had attacked me. My brothers laughed and made jokes, but my dad didn't think any of it was funny. He yelled at my brothers and told them they had better stop scaring me and that if they didn't he would give them something to be scared of. My mom took me in the house and cleaned up my scratches and cuts. No matter how many times they told me that I probably saw a piece of paper blowing in the wind and that was what scared me so that I fell off the porch and into the rosebushes, I would not believe it. I knew what happened then just as well as I know it now.

"One thing you might be surprised to note is that these first two encounters took place in broad daylight. It's our fear of the dark that prompts a lot of fictionalized alien sightings, but many of my encounters took place during the day. Day or night seemed to have no impact on when the Landy would come for me. Landy is the name I gave them from a sound they made when I asked them who they were. I don't know if it's a planet or not; hell it may even mean to be quiet. But it stuck and is what I have referred to them as since I was a teenager. The Landy are real and they live among us."

The novel slipped from Don's hand as he momentarily found sleep. It falling startled him awake. He took his pills and stumbled off to bed nearly asleep before his head hit the pillow.

He woke up to the sensation that someone was dragging their fingernails up the inside of his thighs. He looked down to see a dismembered hand with bright red fingernails doing exactly that. His heart jumped in fear, but then he realized the hand was not dismembered at all. It was attached to the most beautiful girl he had ever met.

"Happy Birthday," Alless said in a voice that reminded him of Marilyn Monroe singing Happy Birthday to President Kennedy. Don smiled. He wasn't exactly sure how she knew it was his birthday, but was happy to see her nonetheless.

She continued stroking his thighs with her nails. "Do you like them," she asked waving the shiny red nails for him to see.

"Oh my God, I love them!" And he did. Red nails, red lips…it was all swoon worthy!

"I did it just for your birthday, honey," she said and then traced up and down his thighs with her tongue while her hands brought him to a full erection. She moved upward taking him in her mouth. He had thought her lips and tongue were perfect for kissing; now he realized just how talented she was. He was so close to exploding when she gently pulled down on his scrotum and waited for the feeling to pass him by. Then she went back to performing fellatio on him until his testicles drew up tight again. She edged him over and over like this until he was panting and out of breath.

Alless climbed up on top of him and guided his full length into her. "I love you," she said as she rhythmically rolled her hips back and forth. He clutched her ass as she leaned down flicking his nipples with her tongue.

Don wasn't sure if his nipples were so sensitive because of the increased estrogen (when taking large amounts of testosterone some of it is converted to estradiol) or because Alless had pushed him to an unknown level of arousal where she could have licked him anywhere and he would have felt the most pleasurable sensations. Whatever the case was he arched his back and she rode him harder. She sucked his nipple and he could feel himself ready to erupt. She almost came completely off of him before slamming back down on top of him. He gasped and she repeated it over and over until he felt his semen spraying inside of her. He jerked and hitched through the longest orgasm of his life.

Don was spent. Completely exhausted. She smiled down at him and he whispered, "I love you so much."

"Was this the best part of your birthday," Alless playfully asked.

"Best birthday present ever!" She laid next to him putting her head on his shoulder. He played with her hair thinking how silky it was to the touch. He wondered if her hair was so soft and silky because she didn't wash it all the time like most women did. He twirled the curls between his fingers and she purred like a satisfied kitten. They drifted off to sleep together and in the moment Don was sure he had never been happier.

His dreams had been increasingly vivid as his prep wore on. Some experts claimed anabolic steroids didn't necessarily make you dream more, but allowed you to remember more of the dreams than you normally would. Others suggested that most users of performance enhancing drugs stayed very hydrated and therefore woke up more frequently to urinate and would naturally remember more dreams.

Don dreamed he was in the seat of the yellow cart. His legs had been crushed to fit in the little leg holes. Pushing him into the house was Alless except she had yellow eyes, scales and great big fangs. He looked to where she was pushing him and saw the flames of an enormous furnace. She yelled at him, "For crimes to the heart you have been sentenced to everlasting burning so that you might know the pain you have inflicted on others."

He tried to get out of the seat and felt the heat of the flames. She gave him one last great shove and the cart tumbled into the fire.

"Wake up, wake up," he heard Alless saying over the crackling of flames. He sat up in the bed and realized he had been screaming. He was covered in sweat, yet felt cold. He saw her naked next to him. Omega was standing beside the bed. He barked once and went back to curling up on the couch.

"You were yelling out and flailing your arms," Alless told him. "I tried to wake you up gently but you wouldn't come out of it. I raised my voice and shook you until you woke up. You scared me."

"I'm sorry. I was having an awful nightmare." Don told her about it and she hugged him tightly.

"I hope I don't give you nightmares," she said and the melancholy look dragged down her lips.

"No. No, not at all. I always have vivid nightmares the closer to contest time I get. They always seem so real. Sometimes it takes me several minutes to realize it had just been a dream. I'm so thankful you were here to wake me up." Don kissed her on the forehead and walked to the bathroom. He feared he was still dreaming and some hideous monster was going to jump out from behind the shower curtain while he was peeing. He was awake and there were no more monsters.

Don crawled on top of Alless and kissed her. He sensed that she was uncomfortable and he rolled off her. *Aha!* They kissed passionately side by side. He felt he was once again rising to the occasion but his exhaustion had other plans. Don fell asleep kissing her. Sometime in the night before his next trip to the bathroom she had slipped out of his bed and out of the house. She had left a card in the bed where she had been. It read:

"Happy Birthday, Lover! I hope that you have had an amazing day. I'm sorry I could not buy you anything of value, if I could have I would have. I hope it was acceptable that I came over without telling you. I hoped to surprise you and make you happy for a little while. I need you to know just how much I love you and how much I hope for a day where we are more like a real couple that sees each other daily and knows everything there is to know about one and another. Until that day please understand I want it and miss it more than you could know. I long to fall asleep in your arms after lovemaking every night. I want to wake up feeling your body next to mine. I want that and am working to make that happen. You will understand everything soon and I hope you will still love me. I love you! Love Always, Alless"

Don read it again and his tired eyes tried a third time, but the words were losing their focus and his mind was pulling him back to dreamland. He tried to resist and clawed to stay awake. It was futile and he fell asleep clutching the card to his breast.

TWENTY-FOUR: August 15, 16 Days Out, 173 pounds

"What do you make of this?" Don asked and dropped the card on Sue's lap. He had a million and one things to talk about with her and wanted to get right to it.

"It is good to see you also," she said and picked up the birthday card. After a minute during which she read the card several times she added, "Don, I have no context in which to make anything out of this card. I am guessing it was given to you recently. Could you share a little more detail with me?"

He stared at her and hated her and the off-white unassuming pant-suit she was wearing. Could she be any more conservative and proper? He wanted to scream at her to let her hair down and to stop acting like a goddamn robot. He couldn't explain the anger rising up inside him. "A girl that I've been seeing gave me that for my birthday. What do you think?"

She looked at him and for a moment he thought she wasn't going to speak. Finally, she offered, "I think that this relationship is in a battle with your contest over your attention. I also think you do not feel like the woman is giving you enough attention."

Don became annoyed. "I know how I feel. How do you think she feels about me?"

"I cannot possibly answer that question. I do not know anything at all about the woman and certainly cannot glean enough about her from a birthday card to make a judgment. Does this card make you unhappy? It seems pleasant enough."

"It's not the card! It's everything. I feel like I'm losing my mind. Everything is all twisted and jumbled." He waited for her to say something and when she didn't he continued, "I feel like I'm losing my mind. It's like I have a million things going on, but really I have two things going on and nothing else. The contest and the relationship."

"Don, those are not two small events. Both of them can be very demanding. Are you fearful that you will fail at both of them?" Sue said and leaned forward ever so slightly.

Oh, you're clever, he thought. You think this all boils down to some inner fear I have and if I just open up and talk about it everything will be hunky dory. I got news for you sister they don't prepare you for the shit going on in my head right now. "No."

They stared at each other, neither willing to draw their words first. Sue tried to make her face soft and not intimidating. She wanted to come across as the wounded listener who could ultimately sympathize with his problems. Don clenched his jaw and resisted the awkward feeling rising in his throat. He could sit in the silence as long as she could. In fact, he could not, and blurted out, "I don't know what I want anymore. Everything I think I want seems to be out of reach and out of my control. Happiness seems like a longshot and misery is right there for me to embrace."

Sue looked at him. He was more animated than at any time previously and was all over the spectrum with his thoughts. "Don, you have said before you do not think you deserve happiness. Do you still feel that to be true?"

"I could have had happiness with a couple of different ex-girlfriends, but I threw it away with my poor decision making. I treated them like crap so I guess, yes, I still don't think I deserve happiness. I've hurt so many people." Don could feel the tears welling up in his eyes. Guilt and regret were taking advantage of his weakened state of body and mind.

Sue reached out and handed Don the box of Kleenex from the table. He waved it away and then took it. "Don, I cannot help but to think you are allowing your guilt to sabotage this new relationship. I think you can be happy with this woman. I think you want to be. But you will never be if you do not turn loose your guilt."

"How? I've tried. I've worked at it. It just won't go away. It won't leave me and maybe it won't because I deserve it."

"That is not true."

"How is not true? I've ruined people's lives and nonchalantly went on with my own like it was no big deal. I deserve everything I'm getting. And yes I feel like I am failing at everything right now. I'm throwing away this contest to chase after a woman who is everything I don't deserve. And she sure as hell deserves better than the human wrecking ball of relationships. I wanted to feel love like I never felt it before. Well here it is and I can't handle it. I feel completely overwhelmed." Don put the Kleenexes on the table, sat back in his chair and sighed.

"Don, it is unreasonable for you to punish yourself for something that happened in the past. It is beyond your current self's control. You are not that person anymore. Do not shoulder their guilt and regret."

They sat in silence for a minute. Don thinking this was a waste of his time and money and Sue giving Don all the safe space he needed to talk. She looked at Don and said, "Don, are you ok?"

"No, I'm not ok! I am a relationship fuck up. I like to think of myself as a cowboy walking off into the sunset leaving the damsel who had been in distress in a much better place. Instead I'm walking off while her ranch is burning."

Sue studied Don a moment longer before replying, "I am worried about you. Physically you do not look well. Your face is skeletal, your eyes are sunken in, your clothes are hanging off of you and you have developed a tremor. Are you certain you are not pushing this contest prep too hard?"

"Probably not hard enough because I'm all jacked up inside emotionally. I even miss this girl's dog. It's stupid and illogical but I do," Don went to pull up a quote from Giovanni Boccaccio but he couldn't pull the quote from his mental files. He drew a blank. For the first time ever his mental capacity to pull up a quote he knew he had filed failed him. He sat in shock.

"Don, what is wrong," Sue said noticing the distress sweep across Don's countenance.

"I'm losing my mind. I'm losing my memory. I feel like I'm getting early onset dementia. Nothing feels right."

"You might feel that way because your life is in flux right now. You have entered into a new relationship at a time when you were giving all of yourself to the bodybuilding contest. These new emotions are being stirred while your body craves all the energy it can muster to do simple mundane tasks. I am not a coach or trainer but do you think you might benefit from taking a day off from training and dieting. It would be like a hard reset for both your mental and physical capacities."

"No, no, no. I'm way too close for that now. I don't want to throw away all the hard work and dieting now with such a short time left. I am fine. I'm just venting and you're supposed to be the safe place for me to do so, right?" Don held up his hands waiting for her to confirm.

Sue smiled at him. "Yes. I am a safe place for you to do so. However, I do not do it in a vacuum. The goal is always to help you feel better about yourself and your situation in life. I think it is important that in the next couple of weeks that you keep my phone number handy in case you need someone to talk to at any time. You are perilously walking a mental tight-rope right now with severe physical limitations. To use a racecar metaphor everything about you is redlining right now. Your engine might explode or it might carry you across the finish line. But you need to be keenly aware that you are in the danger zone."

Don interlaced his fingers behind his head and winced when it felt like someone was sticking a knife into his shoulder joint. "Doc, I am aware. I'm also aware how close I am. I feel like I am about to bust through a plateau and be the best version of myself physically and mentally. Or as you said I am going to crash. I don't think I can stay in the same place anymore. It's just too difficult." He thought of a Nick Hornsby quote, but it too alluded him. "I just want to be happy he said," and broke down crying.

Sue let him cry without interjecting herself into the situation. Don took a Kleenex wiped his eyes and blew his nose. "I'm sorry, I'm just super emotional."

"It is quite all right. Don, can I ask you a question?"

"No more questions," he said and laughed.

Sue laughed with him and when he finally told her to go ahead she asked, "What do you do for a living?"

He looked at her puzzled. She knew what he did, why was she asking him? "I use literature as a tool to facilitate the healing process in anxiety, depression and loneliness," he said giving her his rote definition for the question.

"Therefore, you help people. How many people do you estimate that you have helped?"

Don exhaled strongly and shrugged his shoulders, "thousands, I would guess or at least hoped I had helped."

"What do you like doing in the gym that stands out beyond the ferocity of your work outs?" Don had told her several times how he prided himself in working out hard.

He thought for a second trying to figure out what she was getting at. "Helping people?" he said in more of a question than a statement.

"Yes! You have mentioned many times how you like answering people's questions or helping with their exercise form. How many people have you helped at the gym over the years?"

"Countless," he replied right away.

"Don, you hold doors for people. You greet people in every situation with a friendly greeting and a smile. You say please and thank you. You go out of your way to help people in the gym. You help people as a profession in a very unique way. You are not a bad guy. You are not genuinely evil like you tell yourself you are."

"But, I've really hurt a lot of people."

"A handful. You have helped exponentially more!"

Don thought for a second and said, "What is that quote that says a man who goes out of his way to help others is trying to make amends for all the people he has hurt?"

"Do you really believe that is what you are doing? Do you imagine a judicial scale in your mind when you do something good? Do you add a weight after every act of kindness to try and balance out the scale? I do not think you do. I think you are a genuinely great guy that has made some really poor decisions on occasion that has affected the people closest to you."

"I honestly have never wanted to hurt anyone on purpose."

"I believe you. Think about that when you say you are no longer worthy of love or happiness."

They sat in silence. Don did think he was too hard on himself at times. Then he thought how much pain a broken heart must deliver. He, himself, wasn't quite sure he had ever experienced a broken heart before— at least not to the magnitude that he had caused in other people. There was that girl, Lynn, in high school that had broken up with him and he still thought about it. But it wasn't life destroying like some people lamented about a broken heart. And he was truly sorry for hurting anyone. It was never his intention.

"Thanks," he said. He did feel better now than he had when he walked in and that was saying something.

"I know you want a quick fix in this journey of healing, but you don't expect someone to feel less lonely after reading one paragraph of a book do you?"

"Oh my God, I hope we are further along in my healing process than just one paragraph!"

"Let us say we are half the way through, but the book is Atlas Shrugged," Sue said and winked at him.

Don rolled his eyes and said, "Who is John Galt?" They both laughed.

"Don?"

"Yes," he replied as he stood up.

"Be careful and remember I am just a phone call away."

Don got out to his car and had to admit he was feeling much better about his life. Sue was good at pressing the right buttons to get him to share more than he wanted. He realized he had forgot the card in her office and ran back in to get it. She was holding it up when he walked back in as if she was expecting him. Good luck she told him and he wasn't sure if she meant it for the contest or for the relationship.

Don decided to take the rest of the day off work and get to the gym early to work on his posing. He was just over two weeks out and really should have had his posing routine finalized two weeks ago. He had a good idea how it should look, but still needed to sync the poses with the music. He was posing to Electric Light Orchestra's Rollover Beethoven. The plan was to hit some slow classical poses during the prelude and once the guitar rift starts hitting poses faster and harder.

He was in the mirrored posing room practicing when Jill walked in. "You look great," she told him. Don was huffing and puffing from excursion and barely had the energy to say thanks. Jill was epitome of what one thought of when hearing the phrase "gym bunny". She was blonde, blue eyed, big breast, small waist, and always wore the latest popular gym attire. On this day she was wearing light blue leggings with a scrunch butt. Don had thought before that her ass was a wonder of the world, but in the scrunch butt leggings it took it to a whole new level.

"If you need help with anything and I mean anything, please just ask me," she said, waved and then sashayed her way out of the room.

The inner voice, that had been much quitter as of late, decided to take an opportunity to pull Don down from his post therapy heights. *You're thinking about taking her up on that offer aren't you? What about Alless? Are you ready to cheat on her? Or would it not be cheating because you're really not in a relationship with her? After all no one has actually seen you with her. You haven't gone to any public places with her. She is more like your sex doll than a girlfriend. Is that how you're going to justify this little affair with the hot gym bunny? You really are that guy aren't you. You just can't resist any girl who would have anything to do with you. A few days ago you were thinking about dropping out of the contest to be with Alless and now you're considering another girl to have sex with! You are one class act.*

Don went back to posing and he let the effort and loud music silence the voice. But it had made him wonder and distracted him from the task at

207

hand. He sat in a fold-up chair and turned off his iTunes app. He was happy to see it was time to start warming up. Don left the lonely room behind and went out on the gym floor where his mind wouldn't be left to wander. But it did wander. He had so many things to wonder about in his relationship with Alless. *Too many!*

Twenty-Five

August 17, 14 Days Out, 172 pounds

Don laid in the sauna. It wasn't because he needed to sweat out some pounds; his body was still losing weight at an alarming weight. He laid on the wooden bench because he was cold and was waiting for Jack. He had been getting cold often lately—even with taking thermogenics and the fact that it was a hot and humid August. It was an odd sensation to be cold yet to be still sweating. He also seemed to be constantly waiting on someone and that put him in a foul mood.

He heard Jack walk into the locker room and Don exited the sauna. "You're late!"

"I'm here at almost the same time every day. I'm not late, you just got here early."

"I'm going to go get started," Don snapped and walked away. Everyone always had an excuse for why they were late. Time was important. Don respected other people's time why couldn't they respect his. He walked over to the Nautilus curl machine made famous by Dorian Yates in the black and white documentary, Blood and Guts. He took his time warming up each arm slowly. He used a light weight, paused at the bottom, curled the weight slowly and squeezed at the top. His biceps had a nice little split in them and were more vascular than they had ever been. But they looked small to him. It made him more angry.

An old guy whose face he recognized but had no idea of his name walked up and told him how good he looked and wished him good luck on the contest. Don smiled, "thank you I appreciate that." Jack walked up and Don barked, "are you fucking finally ready to go." A far away female voice echoed in his mind: *you're doing that thing again where you are the nicest guy to strangers and a complete dick to those closest to you.*

Jack knocked out a set and declared he was indeed ready. They pushed hard doing a super set of one arm machine curls, dumbbell twist curls and hammer curls. Don looked in the mirror. His arms were pumped and still looked tiny. Jack's arms were swollen and looked enormous. It wasn't lost on Don that Jack was now using more weight than he was on nearly every exercise.

They attacked the weights in silence. Don forcing himself on. Jack driving the workout forward with energy and strength. Don resting on a bench between sets. Jack spotting and doing everything to encourage Don between sets. They decided to finish with barbell curls.

"Quarters?" Don asked.

"That might be a little heavy considering…" Jack trailed off and watched as Don put a twenty-five pound plate on one side of a forty-five pound Olympic bar. He reluctantly followed suite. Don grabbed the bar a little wider than shoulder width and tried to squeeze out a strict rep. The bar only moved a few inches. He tried again with the same results. Don slammed the bar back in the rack and yelled, "Fuck!"

Jack went to pull off the 25s and Don yelled at him. "Leave it the fuck alone. If I'm too much of a pussy to do this weight than I shouldn't be in the fucking gym!" He grabbed the weight and using mostly momentum and madness swung up five reps before dropping the bar back in the rack. He reached up and grabbed his right bicep in pain.

"What are you? Fucking stupid," Jack yelled at him. "You're two weeks out and you want to do some ego lifting to satisfy some sense of accomplishment. Those reps were awful and now you hurt your bicep. You're lucky it's not torn you dumbass."

"Fuck you! You don't train hard all year just to lighten up before a contest. That makes you look soft." Don said in a rage with spittle flying everywhere.

"You train smart. If you tear something you did all that hard work for nothing. Be fucking smart for once."

"Fuck off! Go back on the assembly line and show me how smart you are," Don yelled.

"What did you just say? You think because you have a bunch of worthless degrees it makes you smarter than me? Which one of us will be down at the plasma center in a few weeks because they can't afford their bills including a giant student loan payment?"

"You know what? I don't need a fucking workout partner to drag me down."

"Nope, you have a make believe girlfriend to do that for you."

"Fuck you. She is more real than your fake ass will ever be," Don screamed embarrassed by the quality of his so called insult.

Jack laughed at him. "Just because you're depleted and drained doesn't make it ok for you to be a prick to me. If you want to go the rest of the way on your own then that's fine with me. Just says so!"

"Fine. I don't need you. I don't need anyone!"

Jack was first to realize that nearly the entire gym was staring at them. Everyone looked shocked and their mouths hung open in disbelief. Most people at the gym loved and respected Jack and Don. They were two of the nicest guys in the gym. This outburst was completely out of character for either one.

Jack didn't want to continue on, especially considering everyone was watching. He gave Don a look of disgust, said good luck with the contest and walked out.

Don looked around. People were still staring. He wanted to scream, "What are you looking at?" but that would have made everything worse. He stripped the 25s off and did twenty-three reps with just the bar. He had lost his mojo and decided to call it a day. He went to the locker room and was happy to see Jack was already gone.

He was upset about the argument. Both with himself and Jack. He was mad at himself because Jack was just looking out for his well being and he had to be a jerk about it. It didn't matter that he was already thinking he wanted to train by himself the last few weeks. He could have simply told Jack that and he would have understood. It didn't have to turn into a whole gym drama type of argument. Instead he took the cowardly way out and created a fight to get the desired result of training alone.

Don was mad at Jack for the comment about Alless. That was an area where friends, no matter how pissed they were, should not tread. You left family members, wives and girlfriends out of it. He didn't care what Jack said about him, but to even insinuate anything about Alless was out of bounds.

Don sat on the bench and the far away female voice cheered, *Bravo! You managed to break the unbreakable bond of workout partner relationship!*

Again, you always hurt the ones you care about with complete disregard. He shook the voice off and opened his Fitbit app on his phone.

The new Fitbit was reporting similar sleep scores and had him awake for a straight chunk of time in the middle of the night just like the old one. He was still getting over six hours of sleep a night and that made him feel like he was getting adequate rest even though he was completely exhausted.

Don's resting heartrate was still tracking upwards. He laughed at the spike that just occurred because of his argument with Jack. He didn't find it so amusing when he realized his average resting heartrate was three beats a minute higher than it had been yesterday. His family had a history of heart related problems and he didn't want to become another statistic. He sat for another minute finishing his postworkout shake before heading home.

He was hopeful to see Alless. It had been a week since she surprised him on his birthday. However, he felt good about where they were. He had analyzed the card over and over before finally coming to the conclusion that he was finishing up contest prep and she was also finishing something up, whatever it may be, and afterwards they would be together more like a couple. It was beneficial for both of them and she was worth the wait.

Don almost turned on the television when he got home; he had been binge watching the cooking network's show Chopped. It was bizarre, he never watched it when he could eat whatever he wanted. But in his depleted state it interested him. He wondered about the psychology of it. Was it like when you weren't having sex and you watched a lot of pornography. However, if you were having regular sex porn wasn't as interesting. Could you compare sex and food in that way? It made sense to him.

Don would love to see a psychological study on prep brain. It would make one hell of a paper. There were constant emotional fluctuations. You did bizarre things while prepping. There was the constant war between looking small and feeling weak against looking shredded and more

defined. Sometimes you even looked bigger when there was great definition. The head games were unreal and you mind could change in a manner
of seconds.

Instead of watching television Don picked up Greg Hubris' book and
started reading where he last left off.

"I had been abducted enough by this time to know when it was about
to happen. It rarely took me by surprise. There was always a little swirling wind whether I was inside or outside. It was just enough to feel and
make you wonder what was that. I was always alone; they never took me
in front of someone else. The tell-tale sign was I felt a chill and got very
lightheaded. I might miss the swirling wind or even the chill, but that I'm
not drunk but I feel like I'm passing out from drinking too much feeling
was unmistakable. Oddly enough, there was always a smell associated with
their abduction of me. It is hard to describe but reminded me of burnt
sugar. It was also overwhelming as if the smell was being forced into my
nostrils. In almost every case the overwhelming power of the smell forced
me down on a knee in my lightheaded state. It was crushing. That may be
hard for you to relate to unless you've experienced a smell so thick and
strong that you couldn't escape it.

"I always became nauseous when I went to the ground. It was as
if I were drunk and the room spun around me. The floor would seem to
open up like a whirlpool and slowly suck me into it. I could not pull away.
The more I struggled the harder the sucking sensation worked against me.
Then there would be an audible pop and I would find myself in a different
place. I assumed it was aboard their space ship, but I never had any way to
confirm that. They always took tissue samples even when I thought they
were conducting a social experiment. I learned that the cylinder they stuck
me with on my two very first encounters was a way for them to collect
tissue samples.

"The return was always similar as well. I would wake up on the ground feeling hungover and exhausted. The entire encounter was like a dream begging to be forgotten and wanting to fall away like eye crust in the morning. However, for some reason, I would not forget it. I remembered it all every time.

"I always found it odd that to me these abductions seemed to last only a few minutes, but when I returned I found I had been gone for hours. It was a strange sensation and made we wonder about time being relative or circular rather than linear as we know it. It is hard for us to comprehend time as anything but being a straight line with the past at one end of the line and the future at the other end and our present somewhere in the middle. But when I was abducted the line felt like a figure eight. I am told that a line such as this accounts for our feeling of déjà vu. We don't just feel like we have been there before, we have been.

"I am not ashamed to admit that later in life when I felt the cool swirling wind I urinated out of fear. It was a Pavlov's dog reaction. These abductions were so horrifying that it is a wonder that I did not die of fright as people have been rumored to do so. You can't imagine the level of fear that grips you when you are taken into the complete unknown and subjected to horrors that haven't even been imagined yet."

Don drifted off to sleep and into a dream so real he was surprised he did not piss himself. He was at a carnival and wearing a clown costume. He tried to walk only to realize he was tethered onto a large spinning wheel. He looked over and saw Jack dressed as a game show carny. "Come on up, spin the wheel and give him a whack," Jack hollered down the runway.

A large cluster of women approached and Don recognized them all to be women he had dated and broke up with during his life. Each one came up and taunted Don, then they spun the wheel and Jack handed them a baseball bat. Depending on where the spinning wheel landed, they got between one and five whacks at Don.

215

The first woman called him a pig and broke his arm in two places. The next one called him a cocksucker and hit his thigh hard enough to cause an immediate bruise. The third one called him a loser and cracked some ribs with her five swings. They each expressed a level of glee that sent shivers up Don's spine after they took a turn.

"You're not looking so ready for that contest now are you bro?" Jack hissed at him and gave him an elbow to the chin. Another woman, another name, and another broken bone. It continued for hours and each spin became more agonizing than the last because of his crushed skeletal system.

He woke up drenched in sweat. He felt his body for broken bones and bruises. There were none in the awake version of himself. He walked on shaky legs to the bathroom, took his pills and stumbled off to bed. He thought such a horrific nightmare might keep him awake but he fell back to sleep as soon as his head hit the pillow.

Don was back on the spinning wheel, a bloody and bruised mess of torn tissue. Compound fractures poked out of his arms and legs. A rib had found its way through the skin as well. One of his eyes had fallen out of the socket and dangled precariously on his cheek. With his good eye, he watched as Alless walked up.

She got as close to his face as she could. Her voice was no longer angelic and was the stuff of haunted house ghouls as she hissed, "You couldn't wait for me. You had to fuck the hot gym bunny. Was she worth it? You could have had everything with me. I'm not homeless. I'm a millionaire who was trying to find a guy who loved me for who I was and didn't know about the money. But you're just a cheating pig and only care about your carnal desires." She moved the wheel one click and out of his dangling eye he saw it had landed on one hundred. She was going to get one hundred swings.

She reared back as far as she could and swung with all of her might hitting him in the neck. He felt it snap and lost all feeling from the neck down. "See. I still love you and removed the majority of your pain with one swing." She stepped out of the way of the charging bigfoot who tore off one of Don's arms. "Oh don't worry lover, Greg Hubris has a jacket you can borrow," Alless said and laughed a maniacal squeal. Jack and the bigfoot joined her in laughter.

Don jerked awake. The sheets were plastered to him with sweat. He wiggled his fingers and toes and they worked. He was still terrified and tried to stay awake. He thought of all manner of things that usually kept him awake. He begged for the inner voice of woe. He cried out to the far-away female voice. They ignored him and the darkness hugged him.

Jack was cutting him down off the wheel. Don had no control of his arms and legs. He was like a broken and crushed marionette. Then the strings made him dance. He looked up to see Alless operating the cross brace. But her face was drawn out and she looked more like a lizard than the beautiful creature he had fallen in love with. "Dance for me, my cheater boy!" He tried to say he didn't cheat but he couldn't get his mouth to work. "Are you trying to talk, my cheater boy? Jack will help you."

Jack walked up still wearing his carny outfit. Alless made Don bend over and Jack jammed his arm all the way into his rectum. Don wanted to cry out in pain but the signal to scream died on a broken neuron pathway. He made Don's mouth work with his hand as if he was a ventriloquist and Don mouthed the words: "I am a cheater boy. I deserve all of this. I am not worthy of love."

Don felt soft perfect lips touch his neck. He felt his body hurling through a vortex. The lips kissed his and he heard the sweetest sound delicately dance in his ears. "It will be all right, my love." He felt suspended between the nightmare and reality. But it was a safe place and he remained there until the morning alarm told him it was time to walk.

217

Twenty-Six

August 21, 10 Days Out, 170 pounds

Don felt Alless get out of bed. They had made love and fallen asleep in each other's arms. She comforted him. Without her, Don felt like a volcano on the verge of erupting. He hadn't spoken to Jack since the fight at the gym. He really felt like he owed everyone in his life an apology. Then he realized there were so few people in his life to actually apologize to.

Alless leaned over and kissed Don so delicately, yet so passionately he felt ready to make love to her again. "You sure you can't stay," he asked with heavy eyes, reaching out and taking her hand in his.

"I would love to and soon we will spend every night together, but for now I must go."

"Why," he asked half asleep and surprised himself. He was so used to just letting her do her thing without question. Not that he wasn't always wondering why, but he chose to focus on the time they were together instead of why they were apart.

"I have a few more loose ends to tie up," Alless said. "And soon you will have all your answers. There will be no more mystery."

"Ok, sweetheart," he said already falling back asleep. He felt Alless sit on the edge of the bed. He sensed she was looking at him. He loved looking at her while she slept. Marveling in her beauty…

The alarm went off. It was one of the rare occurrences when he wasn't already awake when it sounded. He thought of an old quote but couldn't remember who wrote it: "To the insomniac is the morning alarm a sweet song of release from the fleeting goal you seek or is it the wail of a funeral march to another night's sleep forever lost?" It was troubling him that he couldn't pull up quotes with ease like he had just a few months ago. He felt like his memory was going fast. He felt like his mind was going fast.

Alless was long gone. A small Hershey's kiss was on her pillow and that made him smile. She might not do the big relationship things, but she certainly had her finger on the pulse of the little things that gave him joy. He thought about popping it in his mouth. A few extra calories at this point wouldn't kill him. Instead, he walked to the scale. One hundred and seventy pounds. Jesus, he was going to be in the one-sixties. He knew he was more shredded than he had ever been, but he also found it disturbing that he was going to be as light as he had ever been. He wondered if Father Time was catching up to him and no matter how many drugs he took he was losing muscle mass. It was a losing battle.

He looked in the mirror. He still had those little splotches, for lack of a better word, appearing in random places. They were barely noticeable and once he went to the Earl Scheib paint shop you wouldn't see them at all. He wondered if he was having skin breakdowns from being in a calorie deficit for so long. He had heard of people having bleeding gums or losing their hair from being in a deficit for a long time. He guessed those things were worse than a couple of skin blemishes. He drank a shake, dressed, and headed out the door.

219

Don walked with a sense of purpose. He only had a few of these walks left before it was showtime. He would miss them. Even though he hadn't actually met Alless on a walk he associated everything about her with being on these streets. He thought about himself, Alless, and Omega being a nice happy family. He wondered if it would ever happen. He wondered if when the contest was done if his relationship with Alless would also be over. In a way it didn't matter. He had always dreamed of finding true love. He had found it—the dream never included sustaining true love. He would get his pro card at the contest and that would be that. All his hopes and goals checked off.

A black Charger with its windows blacked out and the same windows rattling from the music pulled along side him. Don thought whoever was inside was a douche bag for playing his music so loud this early. The passenger side window rolled down and Don could smell the weed immediately. "What are you doing out here, vanilla," the passenger asked and showed Don the pistol in his lap. Don ignored it and kept walking.

"Hey, man! I'm talking to you!"

Don looked at him, turned straight ahead and kept walking. The passenger laughed and told the driver to stop. He got out of the car. He was a skinny six foot African American wearing baggy jeans and a wife beater tank top. "Dude, Ima bout to put a cap in your ass if you don't answer me."

Don stopped and the man raised the gun and pointed it at his head. Don held out his hands and finally spoke. "I'm going for a walk. If you want to kill me for walking down the street go ahead and pull the trigger."

"Don't fuck with me. I'll kill you and no one will give a rat's ass. You'll just be another dead homeless man. They're a dollar a dozen," he said waving the pistol in the air.

Don thought about charging him. He was pretty sure he could take him out without getting shot, but he wasn't sure what the driver would do.

That was a heck of an uncertainty to leave dangling in the air when guns were involved. "Shoot me," Don growled suddenly not caring whether he lived or died. The suffering would all be over if the man shot and killed him. This way he could experience true love without having to experience the heartache that would inevitably come. It was a win-win situation for him. "Well, what are you going to do?" Don said nonchalantly. "If you're not going to shoot me then excuse me, I have a walk to finish."

The man's hand began to shake. Don's heart felt like it was beating out of his chest. They stared at each other without blinking and neither saw the large black bird sweep down until it hit the man's hand and knocked the gun flying.

"What the fuck," the man yelled and went to retrieve the gun when the bird swooped down and attacked his face with its beak and claws. It scratched and pecked at the man. Don turned and walked away. His life was getting stranger and stranger every day. He wasn't even sure what was a dream and what wasn't. What was reality and what was paranoid delusion. *Jesus sometimes it feels like paranormal delusion!* He smiled to himself and continued on his walk. The Camaro rolled by him and he heard the passenger yell, "next time, cracker!"

The old Buick welcomed him like a long-lost friend and Don paused at the corner. "Sorry pal, we are not friends. I want no part of your street. I want no part of that house ever again." Yet the pull was almost irresistible. *What do you have to lose? You already stared down the barrel of a pistol this morning, what is a house going to do to you? You said it yourself if you die you are spared the heartbreak that eventually comes with true love. Why not get your questions answered now instead of waiting for Alless to get around to telling you. You deserve answers!*

Don took a step up the Buick's street and a large black bird gurgled a deep throaty croak from an electric pole. He looked at the bird, "Are you the one who attacked the man with the gun? Are you my familiar?" The

221

bird turned its head to the side and looked down at Don with curiosity. "Did you run into my head by my house to save me from doing something? Are you all one in the same?" No answer. "What's the matter, cat got your tongue?" Don said and laughed at the image of the cartoon cat, Tom, pulling on Tweety Bird's tongue that flashed on his silver screen of imagination. He was truly losing his mind.

The house made another pass at getting his attention when the streetlight near it turned a bright white and then exploded into several hundred sparks. It looked like a fireworks display. It wanted Don to come and investigate.

"Not today, house. I have prep to finish and a contest to win." Don walked in the other direction of the house and didn't look back. He expected to encounter a talking raccoon or a two headed homeless person. The only thing abnormal about the rest of his walk was that it was normal. He shook his head and walked into the house to get ready for his day.

Don's work day wasn't going to be too taxing. His first and only stop of the day was Heavenly Acres; a little home for the elderly ran by a mother daughter combo. The mother was a retired nurse and the daughter a former nurse who had lost her license due to a paperwork mistake or so they said. Don liked them both and they seemed very receptive to his program. He was there to meet the six residents and determine if literature might be beneficial to them.

They met in the living room. The six elderly women were herded in like cattle from the dining room where they had just enjoyed breakfast. The elderly women sat on two couches with floral patterns while Don sat in a high back chair with a similar floral pattern. The cozy room had a fireplace on one end and a door wall on the other. The paneling seemed to be of the same time period as the furniture. There were two pictures hanging on the wall that suggested they came from the same living space as the furniture had. Miss Shirley, the mother of the combo, clapped her hands and said,

"We have a wonderful guest with us today. Let me introduce Don Ream, professor of literature. He wants to talk to us about books and reading and if everything goes well he may become a regular visitor here."

Don noticed that Sally, the daughter of the combo, stared at him the whole time her mother talked. It wasn't a mindless unintended stare, but the stare of a predator watching its prey waiting for the perfect time to attack. They made eye contact just as Miss Shirley was finishing. Sally flashed him a big smile that said "you bet I'm interested in you". Don smiled back hoping he wasn't sending the wrong message. Sally was very attractive and took great care of her figure, but Don already had a girlfriend. *Do you really?*

"Thank you for having me," Don said loudly. He was used to speaking to groups that were hard of hearing and adjusted the volume of his voice accordingly. "I would like to start by asking each of you what one of your favorite books are." He had tried to remember the names of each of the women, but with his diminishing memory he was worried he would mess it up. "Dorothy," Don said unsure if that was the name of the overweight lady that sat closest to him, "let's start with you."

"My husband used to cheat on me with the neighbor. I put arsenic and mercury in his coffee every morning until he died," the woman, who was indeed Dorothy, said in a deadpan voice.

"Dorothy," exclaimed Miss Shirley and then seemed lost for words.

"Thank you for sharing Dorothy," Don said filling in the lengthy pause. "Does anyone have a favorite book they would like to talk about?"

"It gave him cancer and he died. I don't regret it," Dorothy said very matter-of-factly.

"I don't know how to read much," Thelma said and pulled her stocking cap down to hide her face.

"That is perfectly ok. I like coming to small facilities like this and reading aloud to the group. Would you like me to do that?"

In unison they all said yes with the loudest yes coming from Sally. Don looked at her and she was biting her lower lip. *Oh boy*, the inner voice said, *here we go*. Don shifted in his chair feeling slightly uncomfortable when Helen spoke up, "I would have shot the bastard!"

"Oh my goodness," Miss Shirley said, "let's focus on books please and keep our words respectful."

"I read a book," Ruth, the skinny frail looking woman on the end said, "where the husband kills the wife. I think it was called Becky."

"I think you might be referring to Rebecca," Don added and said it was one of his favorite contemporary novels—at least contemporary to the group he was currently speaking to.

"What is one of your favorite books, Mr. Ream?" Sally asked.

Don felt like she wanted to let him know she was interested in books and interested in what he liked. "Please call me, Don." *I want to hear you scream Don when I have you bent over one of these couches after the women go to bed.* "That is a really difficult question for me because there are so many across so many genres that I struggle to pick just one."

"Let me ask it another way," Sally said and in a not so subtle sultry tone, "If you and I were stranded on a deserted island what book would you want to have with you?"

Tropic of Cancer. Hands down Tropic of Cancer. "Oh, I don't know, how about Les Misérables. It is long and intricate."

"I like the long ones," Sally said unabashed. Miss Shirley shot her a disapproving look.

Don swallowed hard and smiled. *This is really going to be a test of your relationship* the voice said mockingly.

"Are you sick?" Ruth asked.

"Excuse me?"

"You look sick. You're so skinny and your face looks pallor."

"Ruth!" Miss Shirley acted appalled but she couldn't wait to call her sister and gossip about this little group conversation including the hussy like behavior of her daughter.

"Oh," Don said, "I'm getting ready for a bodybuilding contest and I have to be very lean." His phone buzzed and he saw a text from Sally saying "I'd like to see what that body looks like under those clothes". He looked up at her and she winked like a hot pinup model. Don stammered as he tried to steer the discussion back to books. Sally smiled devilishly. "Um, so what type of book would you all want me to read?" Don was finally able to ask.

Veronica, seemingly the youngest woman in the group raised her had. Don called on her and she said, "A hot steamy romance with lots of sex!"

Miss Shirley started laughing. It was contagious and the whole group, except Don, was laughing. Don shook his head, waited for the laughter to subside and then added, "I think I have the perfect book for this group. I will come back in a few weeks and begin reading it to you."

"You have some color in your face now," Ruth chimed in.

"He is all hot and bothered," Veronica said and laughed.

"He will probably go sleep with the neighbor and we will have to poison him."

"He is certainly a Flutter Bum."

"He has nice teeth."

Everyone was talking at once and Don was feeling out of his comfort zone. The room started to feel heavy and he wished had taken a Xanax.

"I want to spank him."

"Me too."

"He sure is a cowfyne."

"I want to eat him all up."

"Where is my arsenic?"

Don said, "Thank you for all the nice words" and started to stand. He got about half way and knew he had a serious problem. The room tilted on him and he felt his quad muscles go slack. It felt as if he were quickly being pulled down a dark cave. The light was getting further and further away. He put his hand out to steady himself but there was nothing there. He could feel himself clawing at the air. Frantically reaching for something that was not there to keep him upright.

"Don!" Then there was a gentle slapping of his face. "Don, are you ok?"

His eyes fluttered open and Sally was looking down at him. His first thought was did we just have sex. No, they were both dressed. "What happened," he managed to get out.

"We were all talking and you suddenly fell over. We thought you might be having a stroke."

Don tried to sit up and had to be assisted by Sally. Miss Shirley came and took his blood pressure. It was very high and his heart rate was through the roof. "Do you want me to call an ambulance," Miss Shirley asked concerned.

"No! Not at all. I've just been getting light headed when I try and stand up too fast. It's from being at a very low body fat percentage. I'll be ok in a second."

"What about your vitals—those are concerning," Sally said worried that Don might die before she got a chance to have fun with him.

"Its all from contest prep. Just a few more days and it will all be over and I'll return to normal," Don said trying to reassure them. The ladies were chattering among themselves and thankful that they had not been the one that ended up on the floor. Don stood up very slowly with the help of Sally who gave Don an astonished look when she felt his upper arm.

"Your muscles are as hard as a rock." Sally said and Don thought she accented the word "hard".

"Would you like a glass of water," Miss Shirley said hurrying to the kitchen.

"Yes please." Don looked around and felt like a prizefighter who had beaten the bell and won his bout. He stood on his own with unsteady legs and all the ladies clapped and cheered.

Don told Miss Shirley he would call when he got back from his contest and set a date for him to return. Sally walked him out.

"I hope you feel better and get through this contest without dying," Sally said while holding his arm on the way out. "And I hope when you get back we can see each other outside this building."

Don simply smiled and said "let me get through this contest first." *Why didn't you tell her you had a girlfriend? Are you trying to give her hope? This is how you end up with two girlfriends at once and end up hurting everyone. You've been down this path. Remember the whole change mantra—be intentional. You're intentionally sabotaging everything. You just can't live without the drama of women falling all over you. Well?*

Sally kissed him on the cheek and went back into the house leaving him alone with his thoughts. He wished more than ever that he had a real relationship with Alless. He needed some assurance that it was going to turn into something more than a see you occasionally at night type of romance. He would be honored to parade her around and call her his girlfriend. But he just wasn't sure if that was what she was. It was all so confusing, so uncertain, so weird. He finally found true love and it was something out of a Strange Tales comic book.

He sat in his car and was thankful to have his last visit until after the contest behind him. He had a lot of paperwork to do and proposals to write, but no more visits. He wanted to pat himself on the back for scheduling the days leading up to the contest like he had. He was exhausted and the visits were mentally and physically draining. He had barely made it through the last one.

Don still felt the wetness and heat of Sally's kiss on his cheek. He checked in the rear view mirror to make sure he didn't have lipstick on him. He loved how assertive Sally had been and wondered if it constituted cheating just thinking about her. *You should have told her you have a girlfriend! You haven't changed and you never will.*

Twenty-Seven

August 24, 7 Days Out, 168 pounds

One week to go, Don thought, and for the first time felt as if he was going to make it. He wasn't going to end up in the hospital. He wasn't going to end up in the morgue. He wasn't going to end up chained to post in the basement of an abandoned house. No. He was going to go on stage in the best condition he had ever been in and be happy with that. If he won and got his pro card that would be awesome. If he didn't, he knew he had done everything possible to try and get it. He had no regrets.

He had done a fast, light bicep and forearm workout in the gym all alone. He and Jack still hadn't talked. He figured Jack was giving him space and after the contest, they would reconcile and get back to their hardcore training. Everyone in the gym was giving him space. They wished him good luck and said he looked great, but the normal back and forth was missing. Even JT was keeping it in check.

He still thought about Alless all the time, but he had come to terms with her absence. Maybe she was like Carla in the movie "Vision Quest" and was giving him space to achieve his goal without messing it up. He loved her and wanted to be with her, but his prep brain allowed him to be emotionally detached. He was just going through the motions on autopilot. Put everything in its neat little box and keep churning forward.

He had never been more exhausted, but in an odd way that motivated him. So instead of sitting down and reading or sitting down and watching Chopped he decided to get a little extra walk in. He went out the door in shorts and no shirt. He didn't want to get any semblance of a farmer's tan this close to show day by wearing a t-shirt or tank top. The spray tan would probably hide it, but why take any chances. Besides, it was hot as fuck outside.

The places he normally walked every morning looked vastly different in the daytime. The darkness hid a lot of the blight. Houses he had not paid attention to while driving by or walking by in the dark now sought out his attention. There were more abandoned houses than he had thought. There was a lot more graffiti on houses and empty businesses than he had previously paid attention to.

Don walked up to Broome Park and for the first time saw it full of life. There was a baseball game in progress and two other teams warming up on the soccer fields waiting for their turn to play. The bleachers were filled with overzealous parents and coaches ranted up and down the dugouts as if their very life were on the line. There was the kid in right field day dreaming about being at home in front of his television playing a game on his next generation console. On the mound was the tall, high-strung pitcher who knew if he didn't perform well there would be a beating waiting for him at home. Each kid had a story to tell that would likely go unheard until they sat in a therapist office thirty years later. A dog barked, a baby cried and Don thought how wonderful it all was.

Don was on the upswing of the ebbs and flows of contest prep. He felt good about where he was. He felt good about his life. When he felt like this, he could power through the exhaustion. He could also mute the negativity of the inner voice when he was riding the crest of an emotional high. It was all going to work out for the best. He and Alless were building a unique story that would someday be laughed about around a campfire.

Don walked beyond the baseball field and came across a couple of gentlemen sitting in lawn chairs drinking a beer. Their model airplanes were grounded and they were simply enjoying retirement on a hot summer day. They commented that Don looked like he could use the calories from a beer and offered him one. He declined and explained he was doing a contest. They wished him well and he walked deeper into the park. He came to the bridge where he once thought of broken hearts causing people to hang themselves off the rusted crosswalk. He skirted the tree line and felt a brief sadness at all the empty alcohol bottles along the way.

He came to the back end of a subdivision and had to slide through a hole in the fence to get on the road. He was worried he might cut himself on the fence and then worried that the plant that brushed his leg was Poison Ivy. This was probably a dumb idea he thought and something Jack would have asked if he was crazy for doing.

In the subdivision was a house completely decorated in Detroit Lions paraphernalia. The owner even had a lightweight motorcycle with the gas tank painted like a Lion's helmet. The door to the house was wide open and someone was shouting inside. Don thought if you're that big of a Lion's fan you have every reason to be frustrated.

A few doors down was a church that claimed "The Holy Spirit is not a Cheap Trick: Surrender". Don smiled and wondered if the person in the church who was in charge of the sign was clever or just resourceful. The church offered Sunday School at ten a.m. and Sunday Morning Worship at eleven a.m. Don entertained the thought that he might stop in some Sunday morning. He hadn't been to church in some time. He had read the Bible several times: once as literature, once as theology and once spiritually. It was an incredibly vast collection of stories that flowed into one another. He didn't buy into it as a historically factual book, but found the stories truthful nonetheless.

He came upon a small park that had a bench and two tennis courts. There was no nets and the courts were cracked and had weeds growing up through the cracks. He saw someone lying in the grass at the back of the park where the river was. He wanted to make sure it was someone taking a nap and not someone lying there dead. When he got close the figure sat up.

It was a woman and she looked like she had lived a very difficult life. Her blonde hair was stringy and tangled. Her leathery skin was speckled with open sores and she was missing most of her teeth. She was the antithesis of Alless. She looked around quickly to make sure her belongings were still with her. They consisted of a gray backpack and a Kroger bag filled with miscellaneous items. She stared at Don and then said, "Come sit a spell."

"I'm kind of in a hurry," he said and gestured to the road in front of him. She got to her feet and went to the bench and sat down. Don stood his ground and looked her over. She was what you expected a homeless person to look like. They weren't supposed to be beautiful like Alless. They were supposed to be grimy not gorgeous, stinky not sexy, awful not alluring.

"I want to tell you about something," she said and patted the bench beside her. She sounded drunk.

Don moved over to the bench and put his foot up on it and rested his elbow on his knee. He could smell her body odor and wished he had just kept walking.

"I'm dying of AIDS," she whispered as if there were all kinds of people around who could hear her, "and I need to tell someone about this before I die. But, let me warn you that you can't tell anyone. Legend has it, and I've seen it with my own eyes, if you speak of it you will end up dead or missing sooner than later. It doesn't matter to me because I'm dying anyway and I would just as soon get it over with." She coughed, choked and coughed some more.

Don was freaked out. She was coughing and spraying spittle everywhere. He couldn't remember if HIV was spread through the air in salvia. He was almost certain it was not but he really didn't want to take any chances. He also didn't want to move away and hurt the dying girl's feelings.

"How did you get AIDs," Don asked.

"Don't worry you won't catch it. I had to share needles several times, lots of unprotected sex and even played the role of a vampire to some perverted freak before I finally tested positive. Now, listen closely because I won't be repeating this. It will take all my air to tell you and I'll probably cough a lot throughout. When I'm finished I'll likely need a nap."

Don nodded his head in understanding. And she began a tale interrupted with lots of coughing but nothing else.

"The thing is there is in Flint heroes and heroines. There is also villains and super villains of different sexes. What I am about to tell you consists of a group of super villains. They are an evil bunch, likely demon possessed. I can't imagine a group of humans being so evil if they weren't possessed by an evil spirit. I've heard they are afraid of holy water and crosses, but sometimes when people speak of these things they get confused and can't differentiate…is that the right word…differentiate between what they've heard and what they've seen on television or read in a book. You're so skinny you look like you could have AIDs. The thing is it isn't just that they're evil, they are downright horrifying.

"I had a friend who had an encounter with them and her hair turned white as the blinding snow. Then she turned up missing. Likely dead somewhere. She was a good friend and I miss her. I've lost a lot of friends on these streets so many that when I die I don't think there will be anyone left to grieve me. Unless you could do me that honor. I won't know of course because I'll be dead—unplugged like an old television set.

"The thing is this group isn't anything like you would expect. They're not vampires. They don't steal from you. They're not zombies or ghosts. They don't inhabit your bodies—they're like nothing we know of. They're mysterious and I think that makes them more frightening. Imagine the scariest thing you can think of and these people are worse.

"I'm sorry this is such a long tale, I'd tell it faster if I knew how. You see it is hard to explain something that is outside the normal realm of things. It's like trying to describe the color red to someone who was born without eyes. Everything you try and use to describe it gets lost because they have no experience with such things. I could draw you a picture but the thing is they aren't necessarily scary looking although I hear their queen can be. They just have a scary aura and you end up dead.

"And it's the manner of death that can be really frightening. One old gal was found with her skeletal system gone. She was just a pile of flesh, but get this—she was still alive. How is that possible and how awful that must have been. Another was found just skin and bones. Someone had kept him alive for months in a bedridden state where he didn't even have the muscle to move.

"I hope I'm not scaring you too much. I'm thankful for you being so patient and listening to me despite my fits of coughing. The thing is I haven't even scratched the surface on what I've seen and heard whispered in back alleys and crack houses. It don't matter if you're male or female, adult, child or baby—they don't care. When they come calling you might just as well make your funeral plans.

"I know I haven't really told you anything and I will shortly, but I need you to know just how bad they are. They aren't just bad people, they're possessed and filled with the supernatural. They're human, but not, if that makes any sense to you. I can tell you're educated and I hope you understand despite my foibles. I too was once educated but that first taste of heroin did a number on me. I went from an elementary teacher to a crack whore with one push of a plunger. I couldn't even tell you if I have any family the drugs have so messed up my thinking.

"I'm getting tired. I need to finish this up. I've already taken up too much of your time, but I'm thankful you lent me an ear. Watch out for the Yellow Cart."

Don's interest went from waning to attentive in the span of two shorts words.

"That must mean something to you. That's what they're called. The Yellow Cart. They travel around the streets at night with their yellow carts looking for victims and supplies. They kill people who no one will miss. They torture people who talk about them. The very sight of a yellow cart should instill you with fear. They aren't vampires but they are creatures of the night. You won't see them during the day. During the day you are safe."

"You mentioned they have a queen," Don interrupted.

"Yes, a vile woman."

"What does she look like?"

"No one knows. No one has lived to tell. But many have seen her from a great distance and the legend has it that they would prefer to look on Medusa rather than The Yellow Cart Queen."

"Is there anything descriptive about her?"

"I'm sorry I have heard that she is short and also that she is like an Amazon woman. I have heard that she is bald while another talked of her flowing long hair. The stories are ambiguous but all say they are afraid of her. And if you do see her you will know it. I'm sorry my lips grow weary. I must go back to napping."

"Just one more question please?"

"Just one more."

"Where do they hide out?"

"No one knows for sure. But legend has it they inhabit abandoned buildings and move about so no one knows exactly where they are at. The houses they stay at are often thought to be haunted. Now leave me. Be careful and don't speak of The Yellow Cart again."

She coughed for a good minute and then laid down on the bench using her backpack as a pillow.

Don left her alone and walked back to his house. His mind was racing. Did Alless have something to do with the Yellow Cart? She was pushing a yellow cart and was with a group of strange individuals when they first met. Could she possibly be the Queen. She was beautiful. She couldn't be the horrible Medusa looking type that the lady was describing. Their hideout was said to be haunted. That was making a case for the burned out house, not to mention it often had a yellow cart out front.

He wanted to run right over there, but thought he should think it through and sleep on it. It could all just be a legend. Homeless people had lots of legends. Carnivorous Humanoid Underground Dwellers was a legend born from the homeless population. Although, Don wondered, if some of the myths weren't as scary as the real life situations that homeless people found themselves in daily.

He showered when he got home just in case the lady had something that might have touched him. He took double his normal sleep aides to shut up the inner voice that was having a field day proclaiming Alless was part of this homeless cult. She has a key to my house. If she wanted me dead, she could have done it numerous times over. Just because you heard some farfetched tale doesn't mean it's now going to happen. Go to sleep. You need your rest. Time is short.

The drugs raged a war with his stimulated brain. One tried to pull him into dreamland, the other couldn't stop speculating about the Yellow Cart and Alless' involvement with them. He turned on the television to distract his mind. He watched thirteen minutes of The Toxic Avenger before his mind relaxed and let the drugs do their thing. He would have no memory of dreams that night. Just blackness.

Twenty-eight

August 25, 6 Days Out, 164 pounds

Don woke up determined. He gave himself his last round of shots. No more pincushion. No more shots until he started TRT back up at some point after the contest. The shots hurt like hell, but knowing they were the last ones made them oddly enjoyable. He pumped his fist after pulling the last syringe out of his thigh. He was ready to go.

He looked in the mirror and was stunned by how vascular he was right out of bed. He reached around and felt the cords of his lower back—there was no fat there. He flexed his glutes and although the glute-hamstring tie-in didn't pop as much as he would like, he did like the look of his striated glutes. He noticed a couple of more skin breakdowns and thought he would be glad to see them end. All the food was just around the corner.

He drank his shake and enjoyed the creamy richness of it. Don threw on some sweats and a hoodie. He remembered his keys for once and grabbed the sheathed dagger off the counter. He tucked it into the front pocket of the hoodie and made sure it wasn't visible. He was going to the house and he was determined to get to the bottom of it all.

Yes, he was scared. Yes, he had told Alless he would stay away. *You already broke that promise.* Yes, it was a very stupid thing to do so close to the contest date. But he was determined. He was determined to go to Pittsburgh for the contest with his questions answered. He was tired of being in the dark. It was a beautiful morning with a cool breeze in the air. The full moon gave the night sky a silver hue. It was a picturesque night to explore a haunted house.

Don walked right to the house. The Buick welcomed him and seemed to say "good luck" when he walked by it with his head held high. The smell was bad, but he would not be deterred. The house looked like it was auditioning for the next haunted house movie. He stood on the sidewalk in front of the house and the first thing he saw was the yellow cart next to the porch.

She is here, he thought, even though he wasn't sure who she was. It could be Alless, it could be the Queen of the Yellow Cart, they could be one and the same. He hadn't given much thought to how he would respond to Alless if she was there. Somehow he just expected his questions to be answered by getting into the house. He took a deep breath through his mouth. He was doing his best to keep the stench out of his nose. The knife felt heavy in his pocket. He wasn't sure what good it would do, yet, he somehow felt comforted by knowing it was there.

He took a step up the sidewalk towards the porch. His feet felt heavy. *What the fuck are you doing*, the frightened inner voice asked. *You've done a lot of dumb things but this takes the cake. What are you trying to prove. What answer do you hope to find that will benefit your placing in the contest. You're risking fifteen weeks of agonizingly hard work over the ramblings of an admitted crack whore. Come to your senses! Turn around and go home. Alless will be waiting for you when you get back. Hell, her and Omega might even have moved in by the time you get back. This isn't helping anything. This is ludicrous! Just stop and go home.*

"I'm not afraid," Don grunted and took another step. His feet didn't just feel heavy, they felt tied together. He had to shuffle. He imagined he was the valiant knight entering the castle to rescue the princess. He had read many books with that plot, but in this moment he couldn't think of any of their names. He shuffled again and moved a few more inches. The smell started ratcheting up. Burned oil. Burned rubber. Burned antifreeze. Burned emergency brakes. Burned flesh. Don felt he was pushing into a literal wall of horrific smells that wanted to keep him out. He didn't want to gag because he felt like once he started he wouldn't be able to stop. And he was afraid the smoke monster would come and suffocate him. *Just turn around and go home!*

"I'm not afraid," his voice trembled. The drawbridge was up. The castle was locked tight. The battle wasn't supposed to start until he got inside. He feared he might not make it that far. He shuffled forward again. The old Buick called out to him from down the street, "You got this". Another agonizingly small shuffle step. His stomach churned. The smell was of the type that you didn't get used to; the smell just got worse and worse. It left a sour and metallic taste in his mouth.

Remember how good Alless smelled, he thought. She couldn't possibly have anything to do with this place unless she was being held captive. "I have to save her." He tried to shuffle, but his foot didn't move. He looked down and saw that he had sank into the concrete sidewalk up to his ankles. The oozing gray, wet concrete had a death grip on his lower leg. "It isn't real," he thought aloud and used every ounce of his muscular leg strength to pull out of the concrete and shuffle a couple of steps. He was sweating profusely. It rolled down his backside and gave him a chill. Don had put on deodorant, but he smelled his own body odor and it smelled worse than the elementary teacher turned crack whore who had warned him about the Yellow Cart. He thought he could smell his own fear in a tangible sense. It smelled rancid. *What a horrible decision this was.* And finally Don agreed with the voice.

He looked around hoping to be rescued by the raven. "Come on, bird!" The sky was motionless except for a few clouds drifting across the full moon casting eerie shadows in every direction. He looked out over the field hoping to see Omega come running up and dragging him to safety by his pant leg. No dog. No bird. No rescue. Don tried to shuffle forward again and fell to his hands and knees making a wet plop in the cement. He was going to have to crawl the rest of the way

The cement looked visually hard but was soft under his hands and sucked them in. He pulled each one out and they came free with a sucking sound. He crawled forward. The porch was almost within reach. "If I can just get to the cart, everything will be fine." He moved a few more inches and a whistle rang loudly in his ears. It seemed to paralyze him.

"I'm almost there," he said and fought through the paralysis. He reached up to grab the yellow cart and it was no longer there. "Fuck," he groaned. "None of this is real. Just stand up!" He managed to get his hands free and in a kneeling position saw that his hands looked charred and burned. They didn't hurt. He thought he must be in shock and vomited. Snot ran from his nose and his eyes watered. "It's not going to win," he screamed and lunged forward on his knees reaching the porch.

Don wanted to just lay down and die. He didn't feel like he could fight anymore. He imagined being a boneless mass unable to move or talk. He thought about Alless' perfect lips and the way she kissed him and the way she made him hard almost instantly. He didn't want Sally, he wanted Alless. He wondered if he would ever see her again. And when he determined he wouldn't his body did an adrenalin dump that allowed him to find his feet once more. He stumbled through the doorway knowing that if he fell the mousetrap glue would capture him and he would indeed die a horrible death.

He swayed and heaved, but did not throw up this time. Two minor victories, he was on a roll. He looked for the smoke monster and saw his Fitbit on the blackened wooden floor. He thought I have been here before, it's not all a dream. Don managed a few more steps and saw the staircase leading upward. He heard the crack whore's voice in his head: "Your answers are up those stairs. I didn't think it was possible but you can beat the Yellow Cart if you make it up those stairs. You will be the savior for homeless people present and future." Don's Superman complex ramped up and he took several staggered steps towards the stairs at the back of the house. He was gulping in lungs full of air and fighting the desire to vomit every second.

He noticed that the further back in the house he went the less fire damage there was. He didn't think that lined up with the police report he had read, although, he couldn't remember exactly what it said. His mind was like the great American novel that was written with an ink that was susceptible to water. It was raining all over it and the words were disappearing at an alarming rate. His once great recall ability was gone. Forming a coherent sentence seemed a monumental task as he let his weight go back and forth from one foot to the other. Gibberish was all he could get to come out of his mouth. He wondered if most dementia patients had that moment when they were aware of becoming horribly forgetful. Were they aware what was happening to them as they absent-mindedly trudged toward their death?

Don noticed the smoke monster slithering down the steps like a giant cloud of black smoke. It darted forward at his mouth and he stumbled backward trying to avoid it. He lost his balance and felt himself falling backwards. He hit the floor with a loud crack and then he had that feeling one gets when they are sleeping and jerk awake as they fall into their bed. It was a long fall and not the quick sensation of falling. It seemed his fall through the floor and into the basement was in slow motion. He wanted to fight it and reach for something that might save him; instead, he helplessly collided with the basement floor.

The impact knocked the breath out of him and if the smoke monster got there quickly he would not be able to draw a breath before it closed up his throat. Don thought he heard a crack and tried to move his fingers. They didn't cooperate. He tried to move his legs. Nothing. He feared he was paralyzed and like the original owner of the house would lay in the basement and die of dehydration, if that was indeed how he had died. Maybe the house killed him off. It had enough of him after fifty years.

The smoke monster didn't come and Don laid there in the dark. *Not a whole lot of bodybuilding contest for paraplegics. This was a really well thought out idea. Fifteen weeks of preparation and planning versus a few hours of fly by the seat of your pants, wreck your life decision making. Who is going to take care of you? Alless? You think she will after you completely disregarded her pleas to stay away from this house? I think not. You have officially lost it all. No contest. No Alless. No movement from the neck down. No life. Well down skippy!*

Don's eyelids were heavy and he could feel his body trying to sleep. It would definitely be that sleep you didn't ever wake up from. He resisted. He wanted to pinch himself to see if this was all some horrible nightmare. He felt as if it were a dream and any minute he would wake up. It also felt all too real. He had spent his life making horrible rash decisions that had huge impacts on his life. He tried to recall a Viktot Rote quote that had something to do with not being concerned about making decisions because every decision he made was going to be the wrong one. That quote, like so many others recently, would not come to the surface.

He tried to roll and his muscles just would not cooperate. The brain was firing off all the correct signals and his muscles either weren't getting them or just simply ignoring them. He thought it stupid that he couldn't do the simple task of just rolling over. He was thinking how dumb it was when he saw the shadowy figure in the corner. He went to grab his knife and of course he didn't even flinch.

The dark shadowy human-like mass moved slowly towards him. He could not discern any legs and the figure glided just above the ground. It was moving slower than he had when he was shuffling up the sidewalk. It reached him and hoovered over him still appearing to be just a shadowy mass. A lightning flash through the basement windows revealed there was no figure. It had just been his imagination. A torrent rain pelted the house. Don wasn't expecting any rain. It hadn't looked like any chance of rain when he entered the house. But honestly who knew how long he had been inside. Time seemed to be meaningless inside the house.

He listened as water poured through cracks in the basement wall. Don found it strange that he could feel the cold-water beginning to pool around his body. If he was paralyzed, he shouldn't have been able to feel any sensation. He tried to move again. Nothing. The shadowy apparition was back in the corner. The water was coming in faster and wasn't just pooling around him, it was flooding the basement. It was two to three inches deep when he realized he might end up drowning.

"Please God! I'll start going to church. I'll help out in Sunday school. I will be your servant if you just help me get out of this mess," Don prayed and tried again to move. Nothing. "God, if for some reason you chose not to help me then I want you to know that I am so sorry for all my sins. Please forgive me and receive me to eternal life in heaven." *You hypocrite. There are no non-believers in a foxhole or in a submerged basement. You're a disgrace.*

Don felt the water near his ears. It would not be long before it covered his mouth and nose and he drowned. He saw the shadowy figure glide towards him again. It's not real, he thought as it hovered over him. It grew longer and thinner. Don realized it was the smoke monster and jealousy would not allow it to let Don drown. It dove down into his mouth suffocating him. He couldn't cough. What an agonizing feeling having something in your throat and not being able to cough it up. He was ready to succumb to the house and die. He let his eyelids close and didn't think he would open them again.

Don's body heaved; he coughed, and spit up. He was sitting in the water gagging and coughing. He could move and the smoke monster seemed to have disappeared. He got to his feet and although very weak he managed to take small, slow steps towards the stairs. There was another huge flash and the whole house shook. Then the rain stopped. Don clamored up the stairs on all fours. Fear and adrenalin fueled him. He got to the top and someone grabbed him and threw him across the room. That same someone walked over and punched him repeatedly in the face until the room turned dark. As he slid into unconsciousness, he thought how big and heavy his assailant's fist were.

Don woke up lying on the sidewalk in front of the house. It was still dark. Alless was standing between him and the house with her hands on her hips. If he had hoped to see her lips upturned into a smile he was sorely mistaken. She was clearly angry and upset.

"Don you promised me you wouldn't go near this house again. Why are you here?"

He sat up and his body felt like it had been hit by a truck. His lips felt swollen and his nose stuffed. "I needed answers. I needed to know you will be waiting for me when I get back from Pittsburgh. I didn't want to go to the contest unsure of everything." Don's jaw hurt when he talked. He rubbed his chin and it felt swollen as well. He wondered how much of a mess his face was.

"You thought you could find answers in there? I told you that house is dangerous. There are no answers in there. I wish you had listened to me."

"What about the Yellow Cart?"

"I don't know what you are talking about. I needed you to do one thing for me and you couldn't do it. One damn thing! This hurts my heart."

"I'm sorry. I just had to know."

"Know what, Don? That I wasn't lying when I said the house was dangerous. You had to go inside and take a beating to know that the love of your life wasn't hiding something? I need to be able to trust you." Alless yelled and Don didn't think her voice was so angelic.

"I need to be able to trust you as well," Don said weakly.

"I'm not the one breaking promises!"

"Why are you here? Did you just happen to be walking by and saw me on the sidewalk?"

"As matter of fact I was walking by when I saw two guys throw you out of the house and onto the sidewalk. I thought you were dead. Finally someone I love, who loves me, and he doesn't listen to me and goes and gets himself killed! That's what I thought. Do you even love me, Don?"

"Of course I do!"

"Then why! Why didn't you listen to me?" Alless said and started to cry. Don struggled to his feet and went to hug her. She pulled away and continued, "I don't want anything from you Don other than your loyalty and love. You don't have to buy me expensive gifts or take me on outrageous dates. I just want you not to lie to me. Is that really too much to ask?"

Don felt the justification machine churning in his mind. He had always tried to justify his poor decisions, his lies and his cheating in relationships past. It was a natural response for him. Be different. Be intentional. Make this work. Turn the machine off and own up to your piss poor decision making. "I'm so sorry. It won't ever happen again."

"How do I know? We should still be in the honeymoon phase of our relationship when the thought of lying to one another is completely absurd. Instead you nearly got killed doing the one thing I asked you not to do!"

Really did I lie? Did I cheat on you? I went to an abandoned house and checked it out because I was curious. You're making a mountain out of a mole hill. You're homeless and I have no clue where you are the majority of the time and you're going to bust my chops because I was curious about an abandoned house. Unreal! And if you think I'm buying that load of bull about you just had been walking by, you're crazy! "I'm sorry," Don whispered and felt horrible. He was well aware of his inclination to take his faults and turn them around on the person he was in a relationship with. He refused to do so with Alless. "I hope you can forgive me and if you can't I understand."

"I don't want to worry about whether I can forgive you or not. I want our love to rule each and every day. I just want to be happy and to be loved." The tears were rolling down her cheeks as hard as the water rolled down the walls in the basement.

Don wanted to make her happy just as much as he too wanted to be happy. She lunged forward and embraced him. The both held each other tightly and sobbed. He cried, "I'm sorry". She responded with, "I'm sorry I'm not enough to keep you from having to do what I asked. It's my fault." They cried harder.

She gently pushed him back. "You're less than a week out. I don't want to mess your contest up and I don't want you to mess it up because of me. Let's not see each other until then. Let's focus on you coming back and us being together and living happily ever after. We will have a real life fairy tale."

Don wanted to see her again before he left but he reluctantly agreed. "I love you," he said and meant it from the depths of his heart.

"Please, don't come back to this house."

247

It cut him deeply that instead of saying she loved him, she led him back to the site of his betrayal. "I won't," he said. "I have a ton of stuff to do before I leave in a few days."

They hugged again and kissed. The kiss was different. It was like his coming to the house had created a barrier between them that was cold and icy. The passion was not there. Don hoped after the contest everything would return to normal. He was worried that he had screwed up the greatest relationship he had ever had. He would be lost without the hope she provided. He wouldn't want to go on living without her.

He started to walk away. She didn't even offer to walk him home. His heart hurt.

"Don," she said and waited for him to look back. "Go, win this contest!" He smiled a halfhearted smile and said he planned on it. "I want to make love to a pro bodybuilder when you get back," and her familiar sly smile gave him goose bumps. He thought maybe things will be ok and back to normal when he got back. He needed them to be.

Twenty-Nine

August 27, 4 Days Out, 162 pounds

Don woke up feeling like death. He was still sore, physically and mentally, from the beating he took at the house, but he had also been without carbs for 48 hours. He was right in the middle of what was called Peak Week or more affectionately so Hell Week. It was a time full of myths, bro science, extremes and panic. It was the time many thought they could make their physique better and many ended up making them worse. It was when coaches were expected to earn their keep with their wizardry.

There would be carb manipulation. There would be sodium manipulation. There would be water manipulation and there would be potassium manipulation. If you played this dangerous game you could maybe make your physique five percent better. However, by manipulating these levels you could make your body look twenty percent worse. It was a very thin line between looking full while retaining the shredded look and looking flat and soft.

Don usually kept the status quo. He thought if he looked good a week out then he would look good the day of the show without risking spilling over or flattening out. He kept his diet and training pretty much the same through Peak Week. However, this time around he felt he looked too small and had convinced himself to try to carb load so that he looked bigger and fuller. He had gone without carbs for two days and had already done two full body workouts aimed at depleting his glycogen stores. He would do another one this afternoon. The idea was to completely exhaust the glycogen stores so you could go into a state of supercompensation. Supercompensation suggested that in this state your body could hold more glycogen than normal so when you carbed up you would look bigger and fuller while staying shredded and dry.

The problem Don had with most supercompensation strategies was that they also cut out water while they were trying to carb load. Based on Don's research this was impossible because you needed water to push the carbs into the muscle. It was therefore a recipe for disaster.

A lot of bodybuilders also pounded diuretics the day before the show hoping to accomplish that grainy dry look made popular by Dorian Yates. The problem was the diuretics couldn't differentiate subcutaneous water between the skin and muscle and intermuscular water that gave the muscle fullness. Therefore when they took diuretics they often looked flat and couldn't get a pump before going on stage.

Don wanted to avoid these issues as much as possible and that is the reason he normally just went with the status quo. He might not get that little extra boost, but he wasn't going to destroy weeks worth of hard work and discipline. His carb loading protocol was mild by most standards and he was fine with that.

His work was largely done. He looked great even though he felt he was the smallest he had been since his teens. He still couldn't explain the rapid weight loss near the end of the prep. Normally he lost a lot at the beginning and it leveled off through the weeks. This time he got near the end of the prep and watched the number on the scale plummet past his target weight. It was very strange and he had no explanation for it.

He went out the door for his last walk. Tomorrow he would wake up, get in his car and make the trek across Ohio to Pittsburgh. It was a boring drive filled with lots of tolls and flat landscapes. It would provide him ample time to go over his posing in his head. It would also provide ample time to think about Alless.

He had fallen asleep the night before praying that he had not messed it up beyond repair. He had taken everything that was warm and fuzzy about their relationship and stomped it into oblivion. And for what? To cultivate some morbid curiosity planted in him by a delusional dying crack whore with AIDs. Did he really just completely ruin a relationship over the rantings of some crazy lady who had admitted to him that she was sick and dying—and told him some bizarre twisted tale of make believe. He wished he could take it all back. He imagined himself with a crown on his head and being anointed the King of Relationship Killers.

His inner voice, who he had started to refer to as his inner demon, reminded him that things were not all bad. *Did you really think things were going to work out between the two of you? Let me remind you that your life is not some feel good Hallmark made for television movie. You're not a hero and she certainly was not a princess. You almost let her completely derail your contest prep. Now, how long has it been that you dreamed of earning your pro card in bodybuilding? A long fucking time. How long have you known this homeless girl? A few months? You've worked so hard to obtain your tangible goals and she picks through the trash. In what world did you think that might be a relationship that would work? You would always be suspicious that she was using you. You would always wonder when you came home if her and her homeless friends had picked you clean. I'm well aware there is a hopeless romantic inside you that lives for the fairy tale romance. But guess what? There is a reason it's called a fairy tale. It doesn't happen in the real world.*

251

Trust me you are better off without her and can once again focus on your life long goal of getting your pro card.

Don focused on the street ahead of him trying to block out the voice. It might be making some sense, but it wasn't the final say and had absolutely no regard for feelings and emotion. He kicked an empty aluminum can and watched it go rolling on ahead. He recognized the green can and white lettering but couldn't remember what the brand was called. His memory was falling as fast as his weight.

Don hoped it was just the long process of being in a calorie deficit that was making him forgetful of things. It wasn't just a problem of leaving things like his keys behind. It was not being able to recall quotes. It was not being able to put a name to things that he was sure he knew the name of. It was momentary confusion about what he was doing or where he was going. He hoped it was because of his low body fat, the amount of drugs he was taking and the amount of calories he was burning. However, he had seen many dementia patients lately and he knew the signs and symptoms. He could lie to himself about prep brain fog, but it wouldn't stop early onset dementia from rolling over him.

His body felt like an old broken furnace. It was burning fuel at an alarming rate, it was overheating and all the energy stores had to be used for the tasks at hand. It was the old broken furnace that you knew was going bad, but you hoped and prayed it would just make it through one more winter. One more contest prep--just a few more days. He stumbled over a crack in a sidewalk and rejoiced that he still had enough faculties about him not to fall down. I might be forgetful, but I still have my balance her rejoiced.

Someone was walking towards him on the same sidewalk. He thought the figure looked large and menacing. He worried it was one of Alless' homeless friends coming to finish the job they had started on his face. He had been thankful he escaped a broken jaw or any broken bones for that matter. She had denied she knew the man at all, but did he believe her. Did he really believe anything she said? *Classic Don! You proved to be untrustworthy so you pin your transgressions on her.*

Don looked up as the man approached. They were within twenty feet. He thought about striking first. He would lower his shoulder and charge into the man's midsection knocking him backwards to the ground. Then he would get on top of him and beat him senseless until he told him the truth about Alless.

"Good morning," Don said to the tall hooded figure. The man simply nodded his head and walked by Don without a sound. Don was sure the man had stopped, turned around and was about to ambush him from behind. The hairs on the back of his neck bristled and he felt every nerve on high alert. He could no longer take it and spun around. The man was a long ways down the street and unless he was some fast moving vampire he wasn't about to turn around and attack Don.

He wished he was walking hand in hand with Alless. Their hands fit perfectly together and swung at a natural arc while they walked. He felt a gnawing in his stomach that craved her touch and longed for her lips on his. It then struck him that the man was probably circling back and was hiding behind a car ready to jump out and attack him. *Come on, man, get a grip. No one is going to attack you. You've been walking these streets at this time of the morning for months and you had one confrontation. Just because it happened recently doesn't mean it's going to happen again. You need to calm down and relax before you get that cortisol weight gain. No one is going to jump out from behind a car and hurt you.*

Don agreed but steered clear of walking too close to any cars parked along the street. He started thinking of all the carbs he was going to get this afternoon when he began to carb up. He felt horrible from the lack of carbs, he wasn't feeling great before he stopped ingesting carbs. But it had steadily gotten worse. He wasn't sure if there was a part of his body that didn't ache and his level of tiredness was at an all-time low. Just the idea of throwing one foot out in front of the other during the process of walking was tiresome. And even low impact steady state walking made him sweat. He felt his body was a highly efficient fat burning furnace. He was, however, worried he had burned too much muscle in coming in this lean.

The judges were so fickle and it seemed to change from contest to contest on what they were looking for. Don had found over the years that conditioning was almost always awarded. It didn't matter that your upper body dwarfed your legs—lots of people took home first place with almost no calf development and very little leg development. Big arms were celebrated regardless whether or not you had wide lats. A full chest was praised even if it said atop a bubble gut. Judges were humans and judges were biased—bodybuilding standards be damned.

The little raccoon wandered out in front of him. And frightened him. He thought it was the man from a couple of days ago ready to finish the beating he had started. When the creature proved much too small he imagined it to be a skunk ready to defile his contest prep and his enjoyment of carb loading that evening. When he came to his senses and realized it was a raccoon he felt a feeling of accomplishment. He remembered the raccoon he had encountered on his first walk all those weeks ago. Now almost fifty pounds lighter he wondered even if it was the same raccoon would it recognize him. Did raccoons have the capable memory to recognize people they hadn't seen in months? When he had first saw a raccoon almost four months ago this day seemed so far away. Soon the prep would be over and all has hard work would be put on stage to be judged.

He came to a stop and let the little raccoon saunter on past. It made him smile. Nature always gave him a sense of joy. He loved watching animals at play. He loved staring up at the night sky. He took immense pleasure in overlooking a valley as he stood high on a ridge or mountain top. He liked exploring places off the beaten path. He had a wild sense of adventure that seemed counter to his regimented bodybuilding life. However, his sense of adventure was propitiated by the wonder of how certain diet, drugs and training methods would affect his body. He felt like both an artist and a scientist.

He looked at his Fitbit and gauged it was time to start heading back. He had grown over the last fifteen weeks to know these streets like the back of his hand. Yet he was still shocked when he stumbled upon the street the house was located on. Thankfully, there was the old Buick on one end and the far end of the soccer fields on the other end. If not for those two landmarks, he was certain he would have walked toward the house much more frequently. It had a pull to it that was inexplicable to him. He wished he had never seen it. He wished he could go back to the first time and instead of exploring he wished he had simply walked on by.

And he contemplated did he wish the same about Alless. He did feel that he had experienced real love with her. She had opened up his heart in a way he couldn't recall it every being opened in that fashion—vulnerable and beyond his control. She had also put his final contest prep in jeopardy. *Did she really? She didn't make you do anything. You did all this batshit crazy stuff on your own. As matter of fact, she warned you to stay away from the house where you took a beat down at. How can you blame her for any of it? You need to take some responsibility here. You always blame everyone else for your problems, especially your relationship problems. And to make matters worse you have this annoying little word play that you do where you say you're taking responsibility but in your acceptance of responsibility you manage to backdoor the blame on someone else. Someday maybe you will realize all the opportunities you've thrown away.*

Don could feel the tears roll down his cheeks. He was aware, he was more than aware. And he hated himself because he had made his life so hard when it could have been so very easy. He could have done so much with his life, but his poor decision making left him basically a friendless recluse.

He walked to his door and couldn't break a smile even though the cardio portion of his prep was essentially done. He was too hurt and too exhausted to smile. Maybe after his last workout and the beginning of his carb load would he be able to muster a smile, but he doubted it. He walked into his house alone. The house that he lived in alone. The house he would leave tomorrow for a trip to Pittsburgh alone. He would go and stand on stage alone and walk off the stage to celebrate all by himself. He would take whatever medal he won and sit in his hotel room alone. His decisions, even though he was an introvert, had made him the loneliest person he knew.

Thirty

August 28, 3 Days Out, Weight unknown

Don dreamt of many things that night. He dreamt of winning the contest. He held the trophy up above his head and the giant pro card leaned against his thighs. Camera flashes popped throughout the audience like random fireworks. His wide smile did not portray his thoughts. He was sad he had no one to celebrate with and couldn't wait to get back so he could tell Alless about it. He decided not to stay another night and headed home. He woke up just before the oncoming semi-truck smashed headfirst into his car. His tiny bladder woke him up and saved him from experiencing a horrific crash in his dream.

He dreamt Alless was living with him. They had bought a house on the lake in Fenton and were sitting in front of the fireplace just enjoying each other's company and watching a comedy on the television. She kissed him and he smiled. Then the smoke monster came from the fireplace and found its home in his throat. It made it impossible for him to breath. Alless just ignored it and didn't seem aware that he was dying. He felt angry with her. She laughed at the show on the television as the life was being suffocated out of him. A sore shoulder woke him up and saved him from going to the very edge of death.

He dreamt Alless was putting him in a yellow shopping cart and pushing him down the road. She went to the burned-out house. He wondered where the old Buick was. He begged her to stop on the sidewalk and let him out. She ignored his pleas and just went right in with him. He looked for the giant furnace. It wasn't there. He was powerless to get away and she took him to some sort of laboratory upstairs. She put him on a steel table and restrained his arms, legs and torso.

Don woke up and his first thought was that he overslept and was going to have to hurry to get to Pittsburgh in time to weigh-in. Thank god he was already below weight and didn't have to worry about visiting a sauna before weighing in. His second thought was where in the hell am I? He wasn't in his bed. He was on a hard surface and he couldn't move his arms or legs. He looked around and the room was dark, and the walls were covered in plastic sheeting. He fought against the restraints that were securely holding him down. He was too weak and tired to put any sort of real effort into freeing himself. He was at his captive's mercy.

Alless walked into the room. She was wearing the grungy cargo pants and Detroit Lion's hoodie. Don thought she looked as gorgeous as she had the very first time he saw her. He was thankful she had arrived to get him off this table and save him. He thought how nice it was to not play the role of Superman and let someone save him for once. Then a thunderbolt of anxiety slammed into him as he realized what was happening. She wasn't there to free him; she had been the one who had taken him. She was the Yellow Cart Queen and now she was going to surgically remove his bones and leave him in a flesh pile still alive. The anxiety shook his very core and he couldn't remember any of the tips and tricks to help alleviate its onset. Don reached deep into his memory stores and mumbled:

"Often, every daybreak, alone I must

bewail my cares. There's now no one living

to whom I dare mumble my mind's understanding.

I know as truth that it's seen suitable

for anyone to bind fast their spirit's closet,

hold onto the hoards, think whatever

Can a weary mind weather the shitstorm?

I think not"

Whatever it was supposed to accomplish it didn't help. The anxiety caused his body to tremble, and he bucked against the restraints. He strained and groaned. What an awful feeling fight or flight was when you could do neither. Bile rose up in the back of his throat leaving behind an acidy taste when it descended back down into his stomach.

"Calm down, Don," Alless said noticing the wild look in his eyes. "I'm going to answer all of your questions just like I said I would." She pushed the hair away from his forehead and he found her touch calming. It was calming in the sense that it brought comfort; it was not calming in the sense that he thought she was going to save him. She clearly had no intention of saving him and appeared to be the very one ready to administer his demise.

"I thought you loved me," Don said more aware of his broken heart than the idea that his heart would not be beating much longer.

"I do love you. You are providing me what I need. I have waited so long for this day and it is finally here because of you. So, don't think I don't love you." She said pulling her hair back in a ponytail. In the moment and restrained to a steel table he still found her features to be stunning and exotic even with her hair pulled back like that. "You have a short time before we begin the procedure for you to ask me any questions. I will answer them to the best of my ability. I think I at least owe you that."

There was a coldness about her that chilled Don to the bone. She might not be the Yellow Cart Queen, but she was becoming the Ice Queen. It was almost as if she was trying too hard to be unemotional. She had been so warm and passionate and now he guessed he would never feel that from her again. "What procedure?" was the first question that popped into his head. He was altogether certain he didn't really want to know the answer. He guessed it was much more than a simple procedure that you went home from the hospital on the same day.

"Let me explain the entire procedure and why I am doing it. I will also tell you why I am doing it on you specifically and not some random person off the street. I think it will answer a lot of your questions so please don't interrupt me until I am finished with my explanation. Can you at least do that, Don?"

He became a little pissed off at her because he felt like she was taking another shot at him for going to the house. And how dare she when she was up to something far more nefarious. "I will try, but forgive me if in my anxiousness I blurt out something." It was his turn to be cold.

"I have been giving you 2,4-dinitrophenol for several weeks now. That is why your weight has been plummeting and why your temperature may feel slightly elevated."

"What! When and how," Don interrupted ignoring her plea that he wait for her to finish.

"I've been coming over while you've slept and injecting you with it while taking tissue samples. You left your keys in the door one night and I made a clone. But then you gave me a key anyway so getting in was not a problem. "

"Jesus Christ. Why didn't I wake up?"

"You were slightly awake just not conscious. I used a small spray of ether in your nose to make sure you didn't physically stir. It relaxed you enough so you didn't remember it but didn't go so far as knocking you completely out."

"You've been fucking drugging me all along," Don said more as a statement than a question.

Alless looked down at him sadly. "Please just let me explain everything and then I hope you will understand. It isn't as bad as it seems."

"Who the fuck are you?" Don demanded and pushed against his restraints again to no avail.

"My name is Alless, just as I told you."

"Are you the Queen of the Yellow Cart?" he screamed.

"I don't recognize that title nor do I consider us to be the Yellow Cart. I am aware that some refer to us as such," she said growing impatient with Don's continued interruptions. "Now please let me explain everything and if you still have questions when I am done I will take the time to answer your questions."

"Fine," Don said and felt a tear of betrayal roll out of the corner of his eye. His heart was broke and it was a feeling he had never felt before and one he hoped he never had to experience again. She had been lying to him all along and had never loved him. She had played him like a fool. More tears. His heart ached in a way that a hundred hammer strikes to his limbs never could.

"I am a traveler and researcher from a planet far away. We have been visiting your planet for many years searching for an energy source to replenish our dwindling supply. Our first travelers sacrificed greatly and came on a ship. It was a slow tedious journey and they were nearly dead of old age when they got here. They brought with them the necessary equipment to set up pod jumping stations. That way we could pod jump back and forth between planets without the long tedious journey across space. A large number of us pod jumped here a very long time ago. Unfortunately, we didn't have enough of an energy source to pod jump back. Myself and a few other travelers have been doing experiments and looking for a way to charge the pods with enough energy so we could get back home.

"We found that adenosine triphosphate when hit with a massive electrostatic discharge provides the energy needed to power the pods. The problem was we needed a great quantity of ATP—more than we could safely harvest from animals and humans. We had very poor results harvesting ATP from animals, but did find greater success with humans. However even with the greater success we still could not efficiently harvest the ATP. We lost so much in the harvesting process that it would have taken years to get enough ATP which didn't remain viable for years. It was a conundrum.

"Then you came along and wandered to the house where we were conducting our experiemnts. We found out that because of your larger muscle cells we could harvest ATP with over a thousand times better success rate than we could someone with smaller muscles. We also discovered that when the mitochondria was exposed to 2,4-Dinitrophenol that, although it decreased the formation of high-energy phosphate bonds, the uncoupling of oxidative phosphorylation allowed for an even higher percentage of viable ATP in the extraction process. We calculated that today your body would be perfectly primed for maximum harvest.

"Don, I want you to know I thought of every conceivable way to gather enough ATP to accomplish the mission without causing your death. But, I'm sorry to say, that to get enough ATP this procedure will cause your heart to stop beating."

"Well, just fucking great! You know what? I love you so much that if I can't be with you I don't want to live anyway. You're doing me a favor! And fuck you for your condescending bullshit about me ignoring my promise to you about the house when you were playing me as a Guinea pig all along!" Don yelled as loud as his weakened and strained voice would allow.

"If you hadn't interrupted my experiments the other morning I might have been able to figure out how to keep you alive," Alless shot back without a hint of her angelic voice.

"No, no, no," Don responded, "you don't get to turn it around on me. I've been on the other side of that game way too many times to not recognize what you're doing. You used me! That's all there is to it. You can't justify in any other way. You. Used. Me. And I loved you. I am curious. You said you have been here for years how have you gone undetected for so long?"

"We have been detected. Many people over the years have called us witches. It is because of us that you have your term and attributes of a witch. Omega and Alpha, the raven, are my pets. They do my bidding and while they have some autonomy, they are largely controlled by me. I believe you refer to them as familiars. All of us travelers have an animal or two that we can control and are our friends. Even your concept of a witch riding a broom developed from our early travelers who had small antigravity rods that resembled what you call a broom. We had no means to charge them when they ran out of energy and they ended up in trash collections."

"What about other aliens or so called travelers? Are you aware of them? Is there beings from other planets visiting us?" Don wanted to ask who really killed JFK and where was Jimmy Hoffa's body but he thought he should keep his questions about her or she might expedite the procedure.

"Of course! The universe is a big place, my love."

"Don't fucking call me that," Don said and hated that when she said it he could feel his heart melt. He could forgive her for everything if she just let him go and ran away with him.

"Don, you once said you would do anything to make me happy. Is that no longer true? Nothing will make me happier than going back home and it is only going to happen because of you. You are sacrificing your life for me. It is no different than stepping in front of a gunman's bullet for me."

"It is a lot different. I would be voluntarily taking a bullet for you. This is like you pushing me in front of the bullet." Don hated the ache he felt in his heart. He had an extremely high pain tolerance, but he did not have the tolerance for this kind of pain. This was a crushing feeling from the inside out. It felt like his soul was being squeezed. How could she have been so convincing in her love? How could she be so passionate and loving when her intentions were cold and scientific?

"Do you have any more questions or should we get started?" Alless said matter-of-factly like she was simply about to perform a root canal.

"Yes, I have a lot more questions." Don said and thought he was about to do his best impression of a filibuster. "How do you know this is going to work? How do you know when you get back that your world won't be a desolate wasteland? Maybe it has been invaded by another world and you will go back and be stranded. Instead, you could just stay here with me and live happily ever after."

"I have done a complete stimulation. The pod works. And if something has befallen my world then I will still get to die at home. It will be worth it to me no matter what."

"Alless, what about the house? Why did it seem haunted to me and why was I drawn to it?"

"Don, we are in the upstairs of the house right now. It has been converted into a lab. Over the course of many years we have had several different places where we stayed. The old television antenna bolted to this house has acted like a lightning rod for us and we have been able to collect the electrostatic discharge to couple with your ATP to make a successful Pod jump. We created a barrier around the house with a chemical that acts like a hallucinogen and disrupts your motor skills. It works as a deterrent to keep people away so we could conduct our experiments undetected. It worked for the most part. You were the only one that tried to battle through the metaphorical fence. There was no reason for you to be drawn to the house unless perhaps you became addicted to the chemical. I don't know how that could possibly happen. However, more than likely it was just your own curiosity and pigheadedness that drew you to the house and made you keep coming back."

"Well fuck me sideways, I guess curiosity really did kill the cat!"

"I need to tell you something else, Don." She looked at him sadly.

"Go ahead. Don't be afraid of hurting my feelings now!" Don felt a fresh wave of tears filling his eyes.

"If we weren't doing this procedure, you would be looking at a prolonged death from losing your mind. You have early onset Alzheimer's disease. Your brain has already begun to deteriorate at any alarming rate." Alless put her hand on his.

"Do you want me to thank you? Because I won't. Alless, you are killing me. How could you make love to me all the while plotting to kill me? I opened up to you and I loved you. And you didn't give one iota about me. I trusted you with my heart and you cut it apart as a science experiment. I get you're not human and are trying to get back home—wait! Is this really what you look like? Am I seeing the real you or is this some kind of image you're projecting for me to see. Of course! No wonder I thought you were perfect for me. You read my mind and created this image to be perfect for me. Son of a bitch! Is none of this real?"

"Don, this is me. Our species is very similar to yours and that was why we came here in the first place."

"So what is the end game? What's next?"

"I will wave a wand across your skin that will collect your muscle cells.."

"No, I mean what is your planet's next step when you get back with the information you have? What will you do?"

"Don, I can't speak for my leader. I imagine that our best scientist will take my research and refine it. Eventually, I believe, we will invade your planet and enslave you like cattle and harvest your ATP."

Don jerked against his restraints again. "You can't do this to me! I love you!"

"I love you for giving me what I need to get back home,"Alless said and squeezed his hand.

"Do you have a husband waiting for you back home on your planet?"

"Although we have a lot in common anatomically, our social constructs are vastly different."

"Honestly, I don't believe anything you're telling me. You've done nothing but lie to me. I bet you actually look like a lizard and have scales. Or you're a hairless being with great big eyes and tiny mouths. Let's just get started," Don said exasperated.

"Ok. Now this…"

"Wait. Can you do me one more favor?"

"I can't let you go, Don."

"No, I know. But can you kiss me good-bye."

Alless leaned over and pushed her perfect lips against Don's dry and cracked lips. He imagined his body flooding with adrenalin and made a herculean effort to break his bonds and choke out Alless. His muscles tensed. His neuro pathways fired and with every ounce of strength he tried to pull free of his bonds and kill her. The restraints seemed to be stretching. *Break them and get that bitch in a choke hold and don't let go. Come on!* Alas, he realized the restraints were not going to break. It was useless and he collapsed into the bed resigned to his fate.

Neither said a word as she grabbed a tool that looked like a vacuum hose attached to a small handle. Alless turned a knob on the handle and the flat part of the head glowed orange. Through his own tears he saw that she too was crying. She waved it across the skin of his thigh. Don screamed out. It felt like he was being fileted alive.

You have really fucked us now. I guess this is a fair punishment for all the women whose lives you have destroyed. Too bad they can't see you laying here with a broken heart and dying a horrible torturous death. Or maybe they would wish you had to live with a broken heart like they did. I wish you had listened to me. We would be on our way to Pittsburgh to win a body building championship. But you knew better. You had all the answers. Nope, she wasn't a crack whore, but I bet you're wishing she was now.

Don took a deep breath, despite the agonizing pain, and screamed, "Fuck you" at the inner voice one last time. Then his broken heart beat once more and quit.

Epilogue

September 19

Jack stood by the closed casket and JT came up next to him and put his huge arm around him. They were both wearing Powerhouse t-shirts—it is what Don would have wanted. "Did they ever determine what happened?" JT asked.

"His body was pretty decomposed when they found it in the abandoned house. Their best guess was it was heart failure due to extremely low body fat and dehydration. I just feel there was more to it. He had been acting really strange the last few weeks we had talked and I know he pushed even harder after we had our disagreement in the gym. I talked to a policeman and he said there isn't much of a case. He explained to me there was no evidence at all of foul play."

"Dude, he was really looking shredded. It was like thin skin shrink wrapped over muscle. Just sick."

"It's a shame. I know he was seeing a shrink and I just wish he had listened to her more. He had a lot of issues there at the end. And not just mentally. He was really feeling the wear and tear of the cut on his body physically. He had the mindset that he was going to get his pro card or die trying. I feel bad because I knew the extremes he was going to and I never once told him he needed to dial it back."

"Come on, Jack, don't beat yourself up. That freight train was going to crash whether you stood in front of it or not."

"Did he ever mention anything about a girlfriend to you?"

"No. We didn't talk about too many things outside of gym related stuff," JT said and wished he had gotten to know Don better.

"He had mentioned in passing that he was having sex with this amazing woman, but he didn't want to talk about it. It makes me wonder if he was having a break with reality. He didn't do much other than go to work and go to the gym. Where could he have met a girl? If it was at the gym we would have known. He said it was some girl from the neighborhood. I mean the whole thing seemed kind of made up."

"It's crazy, man."